FLAMES OF WILBARGER COUNTY

BOOK THREE OF THE WILBARGER COUNTY
SERIES

DIANNE SMITHWICK-BRADEN

DSB
Mysteries

Paperback ISBN: 978-0-9992240-6-9

ebook ISBN: 978-0-9992240-7-6

Published By DSB Mysteries
www.diannesmithwick-braden.com

Cover design by Dave King   kingsize95@gmail.com

Printed in the United States of America
Suggested retail price $13.95

This book is dedicated to my parents, my brother, and my paternal grandparents. We enjoyed many fishing trips on the Clear Fork of the Brazos together along with other family members.

FLAMES OF WILBARGER COUNTY

CHAPTER ONE

A LONE FIGURE dressed in jeans and a black hooded sweatshirt sat on a bench under the gazebo of Orbison Park in Vernon, Texas. He held a worn red composition notebook in his hands. It was his old journal. He had found it among his mother's belongings. The first entry was dated October 24, 2004.

I still remember the first time. Mother and I had gone to my grandparents' house for Thanksgiving. I may have been four or five. I know I hadn't started school yet.

I took a box of matches from the kitchen and hurried to the bedroom that I shared with my mother when we visited. I hid in the corner of the closet and tried to light one of the matches. The stick broke. I tried another and another. I kept trying to light the matches as I had seen Grampa do so many times. Most of the match sticks lay broken on the closet floor.

Finally, one ignited. The flames danced as I giggled with delight. I was fascinated and held the match until the fire burned my fingers. The match fell to the floor and soon ignited the pile of broken matches that I had carelessly dropped.

It was beautiful, but the heat was too much for me. I opened the door and crawled out of the closet. I stood and watched as the clothes and boxes of Mimi's shoes fed the fire. I laughed as the flames grew larger and licked the ceiling.

I woke up in the hospital later that day. I was being treated for smoke inhalation and minor burns. The damage to the house was limited to a single room. Grampa and Mimi never left matches within my reach again.

I was in elementary school when I took one of my mother's candles and carried it to an abandoned house. No more matches in closets. I had learned my lesson. I didn't want anyone to see me while I practiced with the lighter that I had found. I was fascinated by the way the fire danced in the dark.

I was amazed when even the slightest breeze altered the dance of the candle flame. It wasn't long until I tried to create my own dance. Somehow I managed to knock the candle over while I fanned the flames. The fire spread quickly. I ran from the house and hid across the street to watch.

The flames reached higher. I was mesmerized as the house became engulfed. Firemen came and fought the blaze. I wanted to scream at them to stop, but I stayed in my hiding place. I watched until the last ember died. I went home angry and disappointed.

The house was a total loss, and the fire was ruled as accidental. Authorities believed someone had been taking shelter in the abandoned house and had been trying to stay warm.

By the time I was a teenager, a number of fires had been set with varying degrees of damage. All were determined to be arson. The authorities hadn't connected the fires to one another or to me.

I became an artist with fire. Painters signed their work. Why couldn't I? I wanted to be recognized for my artistry.

What name should I use? It couldn't be a common everyday name like my own. It had to be one of distinction. One who ignites such magnificent creations should have a name to match. I researched until I found a name that I felt was suitable. The Roman god of fire was called Vulcan. Vulcan had a son, a fire-breathing giant named Cacus.

That's it! It's powerful! It's fearsome! I am Cacus!

He took a pen from his pocket and made a new entry in his journal.

April 15, 2015

Mother told me she had destroyed all of my old journals. I found this one among her belongings while cleaning out her room. I wonder why she chose to keep my first one but not the others.

I miss her. I believe she was afraid of me at times. She was afraid something would bring the giant back to life. She didn't understand that it had never died. It was only sleeping.

I know she feared for my safety. She was afraid that I'd go to jail. Maybe, it would have been better if I had. It might have killed the giant instead of temporarily subduing it.

I promised Mother I would stop. I managed to keep that promise for ten years with her help. Without her and the medication, I would not have been able to keep the giant under control. Mother is gone now, and so is the medication.

The giant wants out to play. It's been resting long enough. It must create again. It is time!

Cacus closed the journal, picked up a nearby backpack, and walked away.

* * *

Lizzie Fletcher hung up the phone and absent-mindedly drummed her fingers on the desk. It was the third time in a week that she had to turn away potential customers. It wasn't really a bad problem to have, but it was still a problem.

The Paradise Creek Inn was located on the Fletcher family farm in Wilbarger County, Texas. The house had been built by Lizzie's great-great-grandfather. It had been her grandmother's suggestion to renovate the old house into an inn.

The Fletcher family owned and operated the Paradise Creek Inn. Lizzie saw to the day-to-day tasks as the managing partner and lived at the inn. Her parents and grandmother helped as they were needed.

It was mid-April, and the inn was booked to capacity for the foreseeable future. All four guest rooms were booked every weekend through the summer and into the fall. Parties and events were scheduled almost every week. Business was booming and outgrowing the capacity of the inn.

This was the kind of problem that Lizzie had dreamed about having when the inn opened a little over four years ago. Very few potential guests called or booked rooms at that time. Business began to pick up after the bodies were found on the property and had remained relatively steady since then.

Lizzie feared that with every guest they had to turn away, future business would be lost. Owning an inn had been her dream. That dream had finally been realized, and she didn't want to lose it.

"Earth to Lizzie," Ellen Fletcher said as she entered the office and looked at her daughter.

"Hi, Mama."

"You seem to be deep in thought," Ellen observed.

"I just had to decline a wedding party. I hate doing that! It wasn't that long ago that we were practically begging for business," Lizzie replied.

"I know. We need to come up with a solution soon. We don't want people to stop calling. Your daddy had an idea last night, but we need to sit down and discuss it together," Ellen offered.

"Where is Daddy? Maybe we can talk about it over lunch."

"He's in town. He went to meet with Andrew Clifton at the bank to see what options are available to us," Ellen informed Lizzie. "Your granny has a few ideas, too."

The phone on the desk rang. "It sounds like y'all are a step ahead of me," Lizzie said as she reached for the phone.

Ellen left the room and went to the kitchen while Lizzie spoke with the customer. She wandered around the room, looking at everything.

"Now you're deep in thought," Lizzie said, startling her mother as she came into the room.

Ellen laughed, "I was wondering what we could do to create more usable space."

"I think there's only one way to do that," Lois Fletcher said as she joined them.

"What's that, Granny?"

"We need to build an addition to the house," Lois said decisively.

"Do you really want to do that? This is where you grew up. You and Grampa raised Daddy and Aunt Grace here."

"This world is always changing. The only way to avoid it is to die. I'll still have my memories of this old house, no matter how it looks at any given moment. We need this business to continue. It won't bother me to make changes to keep the inn running."

"Well, I guess that's settled then," Ellen added. "James should be back soon with news from the bank. We can talk about it in more detail once we know our options."

The phone rang again, and Lizzie rushed to answer. She returned a few minutes later.

"That was Jessica Taylor. She's on her way out here with her fiancé to discuss the arrangements for their rehearsal dinner and wedding."

"That's only two weeks away, isn't it? Aren't they cutting things a bit close?" Lois asked.

"I think it's just pre-wedding jitters. She was out here last week with her mother. They don't always see eye to eye about the plans."

"Well, I guess we'll have to wait until you've taken care of the future bride and groom before we can talk about the inn," Lois said. "James may not be back before then anyway."

The three Fletcher women busied themselves with chores around the inn while they waited for the young couple to arrive. Ellen and Lois cleaned the guest rooms until they were spotless in preparation for their guests, while Lizzie planned the weekend menu.

It was going to be a busy weekend. Her family would be there to help, but she wanted to make it as easy for everyone as possible. She was making her shopping list when Jessica and Kanden arrived.

"I'm so sorry to bother you again," Jessica said in a rush.

"It's no bother at all," Lizzie assured her as she led them to her office.

Kanden Kyzer was a good-looking young man. He stood just under six feet tall with dark hair and brown eyes. He was lean and muscular. He was a firefighter with the Vernon Fire Department.

His fiancée Jessica Taylor was a pretty petite blonde with blue eyes. Her dimpled smile made her all the more attractive. She was a nurse at the local hospital. They complemented each other perfectly.

"We've run into a bit of a problem," Kanden said.

"Well, maybe we can find a solution," she said. "What can we do to help?"

"Will it be a big issue to change our wedding colors?" Jessica asked nervously.

"That depends on how much of a change you want to make," Lizzie calmly said to the couple.

"It isn't a huge change," Kanden assured her. "My groomsmen are friends from the fire department. We went to be fitted for our tuxes last week. One of them is a really big guy. His tux had to be specially ordered. I got word today that it won't be here in time for the wedding."

"We thought that the guys could wear their dress blue uniforms instead of black tuxes," Jessica added. "But they won't go with the red, black, and white colors."

Lizzie smiled at the young couple and asked, "What change would you like to make?"

Jessica looked nervously at Kanden before answering, "Would it be possible to use navy blue instead of black? Everything else would stay the same."

"That won't be a problem at all," Lizzie assured them. "I can easily replace the black table cloths with navy blue. You had planned for all of the flowers to be red and white. I can use navy blue accents instead of black."

"I like that idea," Kanden said. "We wanted the guys to be in uniform, to begin with, but Mrs. Taylor didn't think red, white, and blue would be appropriate for a wedding."

"That's a small change that's easily made. The biggest issue will be your cake. Have you talked to your baker?"

"The cake is going to be white with red roses. The change won't affect that at all," Jessica said.

"Are we going to tell your mother about the change? Don't you think she'll notice we aren't wearing tuxes?" Kanden asked his fiancé nervously.

"Why should I be the one to tell her? I'm not going to tell her," Jessica said defiantly.

Kanden grinned and said, "If anyone is going to tell her, it should be you. I'm certainly not going to."

"She'll find out on the day of the wedding along with everyone else," Jessica said.

Lizzie grinned at the pair and asked, "Is there anything else you'd like to discuss?"

"No, that's all," Jessica said. "If mother says anything about the color change, I'll set her straight then. I don't want you to have to deal with her temper."

"I appreciate your concern," Lizzie said. "It's been my experience that on the day of the wedding, the mothers are so busy doting on their daughters that they barely notice anything else."

"I hope you're right," Kanden said. "Mrs. Taylor is a nice woman most of the time, but this wedding seems to have brought out her mama bear instinct."

"I'm sure everything will be just fine," Lizzie said as she escorted the couple to the front door.

"Thank you, Lizzie," Kanden said.

Jessica suddenly stopped and asked, "What about the rehearsal dinner? Mother is sure to notice the different color at dinner."

"We plan to use candles and indirect lighting. Black and navy blue are hard to distinguish in low lighting. I doubt she'll notice," Lizzie assured her.

"You're right, of course. I don't know why I didn't think of that," Jessica said. "I guess I'm more nervous than I thought. Thank you, Lizzie. I don't know what we'd do without you."

"It's my pleasure. I'll see you May first."

The young couple waved as they drove away. Lizzie waved before she closed the door.

"Did you get everything settled?" Ellen asked as she and Lois walked down the stairs.

"Yes, they needed to make a color change. Thankfully, it's a small, easily made change," Lizzie answered and explained the situation to her mother and grandmother.

"Her mother isn't going to like that at all," Lois said. "She'll probably be out here as soon as they tell her."

"They aren't planning to tell her," Lizzie said with a grin.

The three women were laughing when James Fletcher came in the door. "What's so funny?"

"A bride and groom are keeping secrets from her mother," Ellen replied.

"What did you find out in town?" Lois asked.

"Let's talk about it over lunch," James said as he rubbed his growling stomach. "I'm starved."

Lizzie and Ellen made a quick lunch while Lois and James set the table.

"James," Lois said to her son as they sat down to eat. "Don't keep us in suspense."

James smiled at his mother affectionately and said, "Drew and I went over our finances. We're in pretty good shape, but he didn't think it would be wise to sink all of our liquid assets into renovations. He's willing to loan us what we need."

"What did he suggest we do?" Ellen asked.

"He said that we should draft a plan and then get estimates from three or four local builders. I think we all have some ideas, but we need to come to a consensus before we try to draw the plans."

The Fletcher family discussed their ideas for expansion. They talked about the pros and cons of each idea as they walked through and around the inn. Finally, they came to an agreement about what they needed.

It was agreed that the addition would be made to the south side of the house. That would ensure that the day-to-day operations of the inn would remain isolated from the guest area. It would also keep the patio and pool area intact while allowing room for future patio expansion.

The addition would consist of a large room at ground level. The space would be equipped with moveable walls so that it could be used for a variety of events. A hallway would surround the large room allowing for more privacy for the planned additional guest rooms. There would be two new rooms on the east, south, and west sides of the addition. That would give the inn a total of ten spacious guest rooms as well as more event space. It would also entail creating doors or an open floor plan to allow access from the existing house.

Lizzie made the drawings as her family made suggestions. Soon they agreed to a preliminary plan. Lizzie and her family were excited about the future and looked forward to having more room to accommodate their guests. James made appointments with contractors for estimates, as Drew had suggested.

CHAPTER TWO

DRAKE WAGNER LEANED his muscular six-foot frame against the railing of the fire lookout tower as his green eyes surveyed the landscape. He had been working with the National Park Service in Colorado since he left Texas. This had always been his dream. He had loved the mountains and the forest since his family had visited when he was a child. He spent hours and hours learning everything he could as he grew into a man. It was no surprise to anyone when he chose forestry as his major in college.

He sighed as he moved away from the rail and into the one-room cabin of the tower. He poured himself a cup of coffee and looked around the small room. There were windows on all sides which afforded a three-hundred-sixty-degree view of the surrounding park.

There were only a few old furnishings in the cabin. The sleeping area consisted of two twin-sized beds with a dresser between them on the south end of the room. The kitchen area was opposite the sleeping area. It contained a small sink, oven, stove, and refrigerator. A heater stood in the center of the room near a dining table and two rickety chairs.

There was no electricity or running water in the tower cabin. A large propane tank situated below the tower supplied power. The heater and lights were necessary at night and in the colder months. During the warm summer days, the sun provided enough heat and natural lighting. Drinking water, food, and bedding had to be packed in and packed out.

Drake would be on duty at the watch tower for twenty-four hours. Normally there were two rangers on duty, but his partner's wife had gone into labor during the night. They would soon welcome their first child. He would be alone and isolated until his relief came the next morning.

Drake finished his coffee and stretched before unpacking his gear. He had been looking forward to some time alone. He wanted peace and quiet. His apartment building was near a freeway, and his downstairs neighbors frequently had loud arguments. No peace and quiet there. He had jumped at the chance to take this shift when it was offered.

He thought about his job as he again surveyed the area around the tower. He would soon be receiving his ten-year service pin. It didn't seem possible that it had been that long, but then again, he felt like he had been here forever. This job that he had dreamed about for so long was becoming a dull routine.

His personal life had also become unexciting. He had dated several women since he had moved to Colorado. All but one of those relationships had been short-lived. The longest one had ended three months ago. Shelley Graf had long blonde hair and pale blue eyes. Her smile was infectious. After two years in an on-again, off-again romance, Shelley had given him an ultimatum. She wanted to be a wife and mother. He wasn't ready for marriage.

All of his siblings were married. Faith was the only one without a child. Eli and Jan had the newest addition to the family. Little Darcie Wagner would soon be sixteen-months-old. Drake had yet to meet her.

He smiled as he thought about his nieces and nephews growing up near family and friends as he had. He liked his life in Colorado, but he missed his family. He missed being around for all of the family events and milestones. He had no family in Colorado and few friends.

Reminiscing about home always led to thoughts of Lizzie Fletcher. He ran his hands through his dark hair and began to pace. He tried to busy himself with work. Unfortunately, there wasn't much he could do at the moment that would take his mind off of the past. He surveyed the landscape on all sides of the tower and tried to push thoughts of Lizzie out of his mind.

Drake managed to keep himself busy until sunset. He turned on the propane and lit the heater. He lit one lamp before settling on his bunk to read. His thoughts turned again to home and Lizzie rather than to his book. This time he didn't try to push those memories away.

Lizzie had been Faith's college roommate. He thought she was the most amazing woman he'd ever known from the moment they met. Her vivid blue eyes had him mesmerized from the start. He had always heard that a woman with red hair would have a fiery temper. Lizzie was an exception to that rule. They dated for four years and had talked about marriage. He had saved enough money to buy her a ring and had made plans to propose after her graduation.

Then, the nightmare that destroyed everything began. Three months after a drunken bachelor party, Megan Ford was pregnant. She claimed that he was the father of her child. He had no memory of sleeping with her. It broke Lizzie's heart.

Drake relived the pain as he remembered their last conversation as a couple. He suspected that he wasn't the baby's father, but Megan refused to have a paternity test. He thought that if he proposed, she might agree to the test. If not, he planned a long engagement and to have the baby tested after it was born. The pain on Lizzie's face still haunted him.

"Am I supposed to wait around until the baby is born while you're engaged to marry someone else? What am I supposed to do if you find out that you slept with her after all? I love you, Drake, but I can't stay here and watch you with someone else."

Lizzie took a few deep breaths before she said, "I have a job interview in Chicago next week. If I'm offered the job, I'm going to take it."

He proposed to Megan the day after Lizzie moved to Chicago. A few months later, Megan had a miscarriage. A paternity test revealed that Drake was not the father of her child. Drake broke off the engagement and moved to Colorado. He hadn't tried to contact Lizzie. He knew the damage had been done.

He didn't see Lizzie again until his brother's wedding five years later. He was the best man, and she was the maid of honor. She was more beautiful than he had remembered. They exchanged pleasantries and a dance or two. He had been pleased to discover that she didn't hate him after all.

The next time he saw her was at his parents' anniversary party at the inn. He was impressed with the inn and with Lizzie. She had everything running like clockwork. Even a thunderstorm and an unexpected temper tantrum from Megan didn't shake her.

They spent a little time together while he was home. He had hoped that seeing her again would be like old times, but it wasn't. They didn't argue about or discuss the past. Lizzie was friendly and seemed to enjoy seeing him, but it wasn't the same. He felt as if there was a huge wall between them. He had told her that he wanted to rekindle their romance. She seemed reluctant but didn't say no.

He wondered now why he had never called her. He returned to Colorado and resumed life as usual. He hadn't given Lizzie another thought until the baby shower for Jan and Eli.

Drake smiled as he remembered the ice storm and being stranded at the inn. Lizzie had fallen asleep on his shoulder as they sat on the sofa that night. They had worked together alongside her family to keep everyone warm and safe. He recalled the conversation they'd had on Christmas Eve.

"I'd like to try again, Lizzie. I know it's been a long time. I know that I hurt you. Can't we put that all behind us and start over?"

"Drake, I don't know what to say. I don't think I'm ready for another relationship right now. I'm still getting over the last one."

"I see," Drake said, clearly disappointed.

"I'm sorry, but that's how I feel. You were my first love. I care about you; I always will. I'm just not ready for what you're offering."

"I'm hearing: 'not now but maybe later,' " Drake teased.

Again, he had resumed life as usual when he returned to Colorado. He hadn't called her. He hadn't thought of it again until now. He shook his head, disgusted with himself. She might have changed her mind if he had made an effort.

Am I still in love with Lizzie, or is she just part of my memories of home? he asked himself. *Maybe I do still love her, and that's why I haven't had a successful relationship since I've been here. But why haven't I made an effort to win her back?*

Having Lizzie in his life again was a dream, a dream he had not pursued. Maybe, it was time to chase that dream. It might be more difficult now that Lizzie was seeing Wade Adams again, but he knew Lizzie. He knew how to reach her heart. If she wasn't totally in love with Wade, he might have a chance. Unfortunately, he'd have to move back home if he wanted her in his life.

Did he really want to leave his life in Colorado? There certainly weren't any forests back home. Copper Breaks State Park was near Quanah, but it wouldn't be the same. He'd need a more reliable source of income than farming. He supposed he could work at the state hospital in Vernon if necessary, but he knew he'd hate that sort of work.

He was torn. He liked his life here, but he missed his family. He decided to look into options back home before he made a decision.

Drake's homesickness and plans to win Lizzie's heart evaporated with the rising sun. His mind was filled with his weekend plans and his next assignment. When his relief arrived, he packed his gear quickly and drove back to his apartment. Thoughts of moving home were a distant memory as he went about his daily routine.

A few days later, Drake was working in the office at the main gate to the park. He could get used to working in an air-conditioned building. He sighed with satisfaction and leaned back in his chair with his feet up on the desk. He was satisfied with the turn his life was taking.

Life was good. He had heard through the grapevine that he was being considered for a promotion. He was looking forward to the regular schedule and increase in pay that would come with the advancement.

Drake's reverie was interrupted by the ringing of his cell phone. He looked at the caller id before answering.

"Hello, Eli," he answered with a smile.

"Drake, do you have time to talk?"

"I'm on my lunch break. What's up?"

"It's Dad."

"What's wrong with Dad?" Drake asked as he sat up in his chair.

"We aren't sure. Mom found him in the field unconscious. Faith and I are with her at the hospital. He's probably going to be sent to Wichita Falls."

"Do you know what happened?"

"He was supposed to go into town with Mom this morning. He was late getting back to the house. Mom got in the car and drove to the field when he didn't answer his cell phone. She found him lying on the ground beside the tractor. She doesn't know if he fell and hit his head or if something else is wrong. She said the tractor wasn't running, and it hadn't been moved."

"What does Doctor Hughes say?"

"He's still examining Dad. I probably should have waited to call you, but I thought you'd want to know," Eli said.

"I'm glad you called. How is Mom holding up?"

"She's worried but trying to be strong. You know Mom."

Drake smiled and said, "Yep."

"I'll let you get back to work. I'll call you when we know more."

"Thanks for letting me know."

Drake sat staring at his cell phone, deep in thought. He wondered what could possibly be wrong with his dad. He had always been so strong. He was seldom sick. Maybe, he'd been working too hard.

He resumed his work day but checked his phone every few minutes. After what seemed like an eternity, he received a text saying that Ben was being taken to a Wichita Falls hospital for more tests. Drake worried even more.

The call finally came two hours later. Drake answered immediately.

"How is he?" Drake asked without saying hello.

"The doctor thinks he's had a stroke," Eli informed him.

"Is he awake?"

"He's awake, but he isn't able to talk. He's lost all function on the left side of his body."

"Does he know what's happening or where he is?" Drake asked, desperate for information.

"We don't know. He'll open his eyes and look at us when we talk to him. We can't tell if he understands what we're saying," Eli said sadly.

"How long will it be before we know for sure?"

"It will probably be sometime tomorrow before they finish running tests. I'll call you as soon as we know anything," Eli assured him.

"I have some vacation time coming. I'll see if I can arrange to be there by tomorrow. I'll let you know. Call me if anything changes or if you have an update from the doctor."

Eli promised he would, and the brothers ended their conversation. Drake immediately started making phone calls. He needed to be there with his family. He needed to see his dad.

Drake arranged for the time off and rushed home. He canceled all of his plans for the near future and began looking at his travel options. After checking airline flights, he decided that his best option was to drive. He would be able to leave right away, and he wouldn't have to rent a car.

He packed as quickly as he could and practically ran out the door. He made a stop for gas and a bite to eat before he was on the road. He called Eli and told him that he was on his way.

"There's been no change since we last talked," Eli told him.

"It's a ten to eleven hour drive depending on traffic, and you're an hour ahead there. I should be there between six-thirty and seven in the morning."

"Don't you need to get some sleep?" Eli asked, concerned.

"I'll sleep after I see Dad."

"Be careful," Eli said before he hung up.

Drake pointed his truck toward Texas and drove through the night. He stopped only when he needed gas. He bought coffee and snacks each time to make sure that he stayed awake. He didn't really need it, but it gave him something else to think about as he drove.

He arrived at the hospital at six-forty a.m. and rushed to his dad's room. His mother, Carol, was asleep in the recliner next to her husband's bed. His father, Ben, was sleeping peacefully. He didn't want to wake them. He quietly pulled a rolling chair near the right side of the hospital bed and sat down. He watched his parents as they slept.

Drake put his head down on the edge of his dad's bed to pray and fell asleep. He woke with a jerk. Ben was reaching for his oldest son's arm.

"Hi, Dad," Drake said as he smiled at his father. "I got here as soon as I could."

Tears shimmered in Ben's eyes. He couldn't speak, but he patted Drake's arm and sighed deeply before closing his eyes again.

"Drake, when did you get here?" Carol asked as she got up from her chair.

"Less than thirty minutes ago," he replied as he hugged his mother.

"I'm so glad you came. How long can you stay?"

"I have two weeks of vacation and some sick leave that I can use."

"Don't jeopardize your job over this. Your dad wouldn't want you to do that."

"I won't, Mom. What happened? Do the doctors know anything more?"

"We're waiting on test results now. Hopefully, we'll find out something definite this morning."

The nurses arrived to care for the Wagner family patriarch. Drake and his mother moved to the waiting area as Eli and Hart stepped off the elevator. They were soon joined by Gage and Faith. They discussed Ben's circumstances and waited for news.

"Drake, we have a spare bedroom if you'd like to stay close to the hospital," Gage offered. He lived in Wichita Falls. Eli and Faith both lived in Vernon, while Hart lived in Bowie.

"I can get a hotel room. Mom should use your spare room."

"I'm not leaving this hospital," Carol replied forcefully. "You can stay with Gage. You need to get some sleep soon. Your brother's house would be the best place for you to rest."

"Yes, ma'am," Drake replied with a grin. "What about the rest of you? Where are you staying?"

"We're all close enough that we can drive back and forth," Eli replied. "You and Mom should stay with Gage."

"I told you. I'm not leaving this hospital," Carol said stubbornly.

"Mom, you're going to need some rest at some point," Faith said.

"I'll get some rest when I find out that my husband is going to be okay."

A nurse entered the waiting area and said, "Mrs. Wagner, Dr. Brownlow would like to visit with you and your family."

The Wagner clan followed the nurse to Ben's room. Dr. Brownlow closed the chart he was holding and looked at the group.

"Good morning," Dr. Brownlow greeted them. "I've been over the test results. Mr. Wagner has had a stroke. It appears that he has had a head injury as well. The stroke probably caused him to fall. He most likely hit his head on something as he fell."

"Will he recover?" Carol asked.

"Mr. Wagner is relatively healthy. It will take time, but he should recover most, if not all, of his motor functions. It will be a slow process. I'd like to start his rehabilitation as soon as possible. He'll remain here for a few days, and then, I recommend an inpatient rehab facility for a period of time."

When he had answered all of the family's questions, Dr. Brownlow went on his way. The Wagner children decided to sit with their loved ones in shifts. Among the five of them, someone would be with their parents at all times.

It was agreed that Eli, Faith, Gage, and Hart would take turns staying at the hospital during the day. The arrangement would cause less disruption to their work and home lives. Drake would stay at night. If he needed a break, one of the others would stay.

Drake stretched out on the bed in Gage's spare room. It would probably take months for his dad to recover. His mother would need help taking care of him and the farm. His siblings lived closer than he did, but they had families. He had no other responsibilities. It would mean giving up his dream job and the upcoming promotion. He'd also have to find work at some point. The farm income probably wouldn't be enough to support the three of them and pay for his dad's needs.

Drake's mind was practically made up. He needed more information from the doctor about his father's prognosis. He would make his final decision then. He made a phone call to his boss to let him know what was happening before drifting off to sleep.

CHAPTER THREE

EVERYTHING WAS ready for the rehearsal dinner. Lizzie scanned the room, looking for anything that needed an extra touch.

Three long tables had been set up in the dining room and arranged in a horse shoe shape. Each had a navy blue table cloth with a red table runner down the center. White taper candles inside hurricane globes were placed on the table runners. Each globe was surrounded by miniature red and white silk roses. Fresh white rose petals were scattered between the globes. White linen napkins folded in the shape of a rose marked each place setting.

The bride and groom would be sitting at the head table, which had been strategically placed in front of the fireplace. A silk garland of red and white roses wound together with greenery, a braided cord of navy blue, and twinkle lights adorned the mantle and draped down each side of the fireplace.

The staircase banisters were adorned identically to the fireplace. Near the bottom of the stairs stood a screen decorated with silk roses and engagement photos of the bride and groom. All they needed now were the happy couple and their guests.

Lizzie was lighting the candles when an energetic young man

with dark hair and a winning smile strolled into the dining room. He was wearing a pair of faded jeans and a red t-shirt with "I Heart My Church" emblazoned across the front.

"Hello," Lizzie greeted him. "Are you with the wedding party?"

"Yes, ma'am. My name is Dave," he said as he extended his hand with a big grin. "Most people just call me Preacher Dave."

"I'm Lizzie Fletcher; it's nice to meet you," Lizzie said as she smiled and shook his hand.

"It's good to meet you, too. I've never been out here. This is a really nice place," he said, looking around the room.

"Thank you. Did you have any trouble finding us?"

"No, but I left early just in case. It looks like I'm the first one here."

"I'm expecting Kanden and Jessica any minute. Make yourself comfortable."

"Do you mind if I look around?"

"Not at all," answered Lizzie.

She finished lighting the candles and dimmed the lights while Preacher Dave explored the inn.

"Do you stay pretty busy out here?" asked the preacher when he returned to the dining room.

"We weren't at first, but lately, we've been turning business away," Lizzie told him.

"Maybe you need a bigger place," Dave suggested.

"As a matter of fact, we're expanding. Construction begins the first week of June."

"Are you going to stay open during construction?"

"We plan to stay open unless it becomes an issue. The builder has agreed to disrupt our routine as little as possible."

"That's great! My wife would love this place. I think I'll bring her out here sometime."

"You're welcome any time," Lizzie began. "You'll probably want to call a month or two in advance if you plan to stay for a weekend."

The pair turned as the bride and groom greeted them.

"Hi, Dave!" Jessica said as she and Kanden entered the room. "Lizzie, this looks amazing!"

"I'm glad you like it. Do you want to have dinner before or after the wedding rehearsal?" asked Lizzie.

"How is it usually done?" Kanden asked.

"It can be done either way. May I suggest rehearsing first? If there is a problem with the lighting, we can solve that problem tonight rather than right before the ceremony."

"That's an excellent idea," said Mrs. Taylor as she joined the group. "It's better to find issues sooner rather than later. I want everything to be total perfection tomorrow. Lizzie, this looks absolutely beautiful. I don't know how you do it."

"Thank you, Mrs. Taylor."

The young couple looked at Lizzie and tried not to smile. Lizzie quickly looked away when Kanden gave her a conspiratorial wink. Preacher Dave grinned and otherwise pretended not to notice.

When everyone arrived, Lizzie directed them outside. The wedding ceremony was to take place on the grounds beneath a large tree. The evening sun would be below the roofline of the inn, creating just the right amount of light for the wedding party and shade for the guests. A white arch had been placed beneath the tree, and chairs had been placed strategically to create a center aisle.

Preacher Dave took his place beneath the arch, "Isn't this awesome? This is a great place for a wedding. We're standing out here in the middle of God's creation, and the two of you are about to make a lifelong commitment to each other before Him."

The wedding party walked through the ceremony several times. They decided it was time for dinner when Mrs. Taylor felt they had everything worked out to her satisfaction.

The guests were quiet while they ate dinner. They had all been ready to eat at least an hour earlier. As dessert was being served, stories about the bride and groom began. Most of them were sweet or funny. Some were mildly embarrassing. Lizzie thought she would have to intervene before one long, winded tale finally came to an end.

All in all, she felt that the evening was a success. The guests continually complimented the inn and the dinner. Some wanted to talk with her about booking a weekend stay, and some wanted to talk about booking their own weddings or other events. Lizzie gave them each her card and suggested they call her the following week.

As the guests were leaving for the evening, Jessica whispered to Lizzie. "Mom hasn't said anything. I don't think she noticed the color change at all."

"She probably won't," Lizzie assured her. "Don't worry; just enjoy your big day."

The following afternoon, Lizzie and her family were busy adding the final touches for the wedding and reception. It was the largest wedding that the inn had hosted to date. Every available space of the inn was to be used for the event. Extra chairs had been rented to accommodate all of the guests. Lizzie had hired extra wait staff.

Parking was an issue for such a large crowd. It was decided that the guests' vehicles would be parked in the east pasture. Parking valets were hired and supervised by James and the Fletchers' friend and full-time employee, Dan Hayes.

All of the guest rooms had been booked for the weekend. The bride and groom would be staying the night at the inn before leaving for their honeymoon the following day. The remaining three rooms had been booked for use by the wedding party.

Lois strategically placed vases of silk roses and scented candles throughout the inn. She hung a swag of roses and greenery on the front door while James and Dan lined the porch rails with garland and twinkle lights.

Lizzie and Ellen decorated the white arch with a garland of red and white silk roses intertwined with navy blue cord, greenery, and twinkle lights. The chairs were covered with white fabric accented with a red sash. Those at the ends of each row were decorated to match the arch.

The reception was to be held on the patio with extra seating in the dining room. A number of round tables had been set up in both spaces. They were alternately covered with red or navy blue tablecloths and accented with smaller squares of red or navy blue. Small white candles were nestled in arrangements of red and white silk roses. Rose-shaped napkins again marked each place setting.

The bride and groom's table was decorated as it had been the night before but had been moved to the larger patio area. Lanterns surrounded the patio, and twinkle lights were strung overhead to light the area and create a romantic glow.

The wedding was scheduled to begin at seven p.m. Preacher Dave arrived at six-thirty dressed in a dark suit, white shirt, and red tie. He grinned at Lizzie and said, "Mrs. Taylor wanted me to be color coordinated, too."

Lizzie laughed as she led him upstairs to the guest room occupied by the groom and his groomsmen. Kanden answered when she tapped on the door.

"I bring you the preacher," Lizzie said with a smile. "Is there anything you need?"

"I think we've got everything. When do we need to start downstairs?" Kanden asked nervously.

"You should go down in about twenty minutes so that you'll be able to avoid seeing the bride before its time."

"Thanks, Lizzie."

Lizzie had already moved down the hall when Kanden closed the door. She tapped on the bride's door. Mrs. Taylor answered.

"Oh, hello, Lizzie. Come in."

"Hi, Mrs. Taylor. Is there anything you need?"

"I don't think so. Jessica, can you think of anything we need?" asked Jessica's mother.

"No, I'm just ready to get this party started."

Lizzie smiled and said, "Y'all look beautiful. Mrs. Taylor and

Mrs. Kyzer will start downstairs in about fifteen minutes. The men will go down after that. I'll come and get you when it's time for you to start."

"Thank you, Lizzie!"

It seemed as though Mrs. Taylor's dream of a perfect wedding was about to come true. Kanden was smiling nervously as he waited beside Preacher Dave for his bride. He and his groomsmen looked very handsome in their dress uniforms. The white roses on their lapels added the perfect touch.

Jessica's bridesmaids were lovely dressed in their off-the-shoulder, red satin gowns. They carried small bouquets of white roses. The bridesmaids were followed down the aisle by the flower girl in her red satin dress and the ring bearer in his black tux. The wedding guests smiled in delight as they walked hand in hand.

Lizzie waited until the children were halfway down the aisle before stepping inside to talk with Jessica. She was stunning in her strapless white mermaid-styled wedding gown with a chapel-length train and perfectly placed beads, sequins, and lace appliqués. She carried a bouquet of red and white roses trimmed with navy blue accents.

"Are you ready?" Lizzie asked with a smile.

"May we have a moment, please?" asked Mr. Taylor nervously.

"Certainly, just tap on the door when you're ready," answered Lizzie with a reassuring smile. *Apparently, Mr. Taylor didn't get the word about the men wearing their uniforms instead of tuxes,* Lizzie thought to herself. He looked quite handsome in his black tux, red vest, and tie.

She glanced in the window to see Jessica's father whisper in his daughter's ear and give her a tremendous hug. He broke the hug and tapped on the door to indicate that they were ready.

Lizzie cued the wedding march. Dave asked the wedding guests to stand as the door opened, and Jessica started down the aisle on her father's arm. Kanden beamed as he watched his bride walk toward him. Mr. Taylor's voice broke as he gave the bride away.

All hopes for the perfect wedding were deflated after the rings had been exchanged. At that point, the ring bearer decided that his job was done. The three-year-old was hot and tired of standing still. He plopped down on the ground and proceeded to take off his shoes and socks.

Guests sitting several rows back could hear the much more mature and ladylike four-year-old flower girl whispering to him to put his shoes back on and get up. His only response was to stick his tongue out before ignoring her completely. She tried to get his attention by waving her flower basket in his general direction. She finally tossed the entire basket at him and crossed her arms over her chest in frustration.

Preacher Dave continued the ceremony with a bigger smile on his face as the only indication he'd seen anything amiss. The audience members who were able to see the children tried to hide their laughter. Other audience members wondered what they had missed that was so funny. Mrs. Taylor was not amused and scowled indignantly at the children through the remainder of the ceremony.

Ellen and Lois had the wait staff in motion as soon as Preacher Dave said, "Ladies and gentlemen, I present to you, Mr. and Mrs. Kyzer."

The guests mingled as the photographer positioned the wedding party for photographs. James and Dan moved the arch and positioned it behind the head table while the Fletcher women and wait staff, moved chairs to the patio. It wasn't until the family photos were being taken that Mrs. Taylor noticed something wasn't quite right.

"Kanden, what are you doing in your uniform? Where's your tux?"

"Well, about that..." Kanden began.

"Mom, I'll explain later," Jessica assured her. "Right now, just smile for the camera."

Mrs. Taylor gave her daughter a sideways glance but said no

more. The reception was in full swing when Mrs. Taylor found Lizzie.

"Lizzie, I couldn't be happier. The wedding was beautiful and the reception fabulous. Thank you for all of your hard work. Is your family here? I'd like to thank them, too."

"It was our pleasure, Mrs. Taylor. My folks are here working in the kitchen and dining room," said Lizzie.

"I'm going to tell all my friends about this. You'll probably have more wedding business than you can handle," said Mrs. Taylor. "Incidentally, you were right about the navy blue," she added with a smile and went in search of the rest of the Fletcher family.

After the garter was thrown, the best man disappeared for a few minutes. Chris Quintero returned as Jessica was throwing the bouquet. He parked a red 1955 Cadillac El Dorado convertible with red and white interior at the end of the front walkway.

The guests lined the sidewalk armed with little bottles of bubbles and prepared to say bon voyage to the bride and groom. Kanden and Jessica walked hand in hand through the gauntlet of loved ones and well-wishers before climbing into the back seat of the vintage car. They turned and waved as Chris chauffeured them temporarily away from the inn.

Lizzie and her family quickly cleared away the remnants of the dinner and the cake, leaving the décor in place until the following morning. They would tactfully retire for the evening so that the newlyweds could have some privacy.

"Good night, Lizzie," said Ellen as she hugged her daughter. "We'll be here early in the morning to help finish cleaning up."

"Good night," Lizzie replied. She hugged her father and grand-mother before saying, "Thank you for your help. I'll see you tomorrow."

CHAPTER FOUR

A MAN WEARING jeans and a black hooded sweatshirt stood in the shadows across the street from the Vernon Daily Record. It was late, and there were few cars on the streets. He waited until he was sure that he wouldn't be seen before he crossed the street and bought a newspaper from the kiosk in front of the building. He tucked it under his arm and hurried back into the shadows.

Cacus quietly entered his apartment. He could hear his next-door neighbor's television as he closed the door. He sat down at the kitchen table and scanned the newspaper. He was disappointed that there was only a short article about the recent grassfires saying that the cause was undetermined but believed to be accidental.

Cacus took his journal out and began to write.

May 14, 2015

The grass fires have been fun. The Odell fire was my favorite so far. I loved how the wind took the flames across the pasture. I wish that the farmer hadn't been smart enough to plow a fire break beside the fence line before the fire department got there. I'd liked to have seen how the fire took the barn.

There still hasn't been any mention of my artistry in the papers. The fire chief probably believes all of those fires were accidental. I think it's time that I made it obvious that I am an artist creating masterpieces. I'm sure my darling will enjoy my work, but she must be made aware that it's mine. I'll have to find a different type of canvas and create a more notice-able signature.

I need to make plans and buy supplies, but I can't keep them here. I'll have to be careful. I need to find a different place, a place that no one would suspect.

Cacus closed his journal and settled down for the night, but he didn't sleep. His mind raced as he made his plans.

* * *

Wade Adams was sitting at his desk. There had been at least two grass fires a week since mid-April. He knew that his team could handle anything that came up, but he wasn't sure that leaving for the weekend was wise. Still, it had been pretty quiet in Wilbarger County, and there hadn't been any fires this week. It was quiet enough that he could look over the applications for Deputy Sheriff without interruption.

He finally had some good applicants. His first priority was to hire a woman so that Deputy Maddie Clifton would have some back up when it came to female inmates. He would like to hire two women, but there was one male applicant that had outstanding credentials. He didn't know if there was enough money in the budget to hire three new deputies. He'd have to meet with the county commissioners to see if there were funds available.

If they were in desperate need, he could call Lizzie for help. She wasn't on the payroll at the moment but was still listed as an interim deputy. He was sure she'd be willing to help, depending on what was happening at the inn.

Wade didn't want to ask for Lizzie's help. She'd been really busy lately. He didn't want to interfere with her family business. There was another reason for his reluctance. He didn't want to put their relationship on hold again. They were apart for six long months during the Rayland murder cases.

He smiled as he thought about the day they met. It was April 1, 2012, when Wade and Dr. Hughes came to Lizzie's rescue after a storm had practically dropped an injured man on her door step. He was at the inn daily after the bodies were discovered. He had asked her to have dinner with him after the cases were closed. Had it really been more than three years ago?

He wouldn't ask for her help unless he had no other choice. As Wade pondered the applications, Deputies Brandon Lodge and Calvin Baker tapped on his door.

"Come in," Wade answered.

"We're going to take my jeep rock climbing at the old copper mines in Oklahoma this weekend. Want to come along?" Lodge asked.

"I didn't know there were copper mines in Oklahoma. Where are they?" Wade asked.

"They're about twelve miles from Olustee. It takes about an hour to get there," Baker answered.

"I'd like to see those sometime, but not this weekend. Lizzie and I have plans. Maybe we can go with you next time."

"Fletcher can come, too," Lodge said with a grin.

"I'm sure she'd enjoy it, but we're going out of town."

"Okay, we'll see you Tuesday," Baker replied.

Wade's thoughts turned to his own weekend plans as he watched the two deputies leave the office. He had invited Lizzie to his family reunion. His family gathered every year on Memorial Day weekend. It was a reunion, camping trip, and fishing trip all rolled into one.

Wade had been so busy since the last reunion that he hadn't been able to visit his family as much as he would have liked. He was looking forward to seeing them all again and introducing them to Lizzie. She had already met his parents, but this would be the first opportunity for the rest of his family to meet her.

He thought about the reunions of the past and smiled to himself. These gatherings were always fun. He knew that Lizzie would fit right in and that his family would love her.

He should have taken her to meet them before now, but he had hesitated. Each time he thought about it, memories of the past made him reconsider. The last woman he had taken to the family get-together had left him broken-hearted.

Wade had been born and raised in Abilene, Texas. He graduated from Abilene High School in 1997. He had always dreamed of being a police officer. He studied criminal law and received his associate's degree from Cisco College. From there, he went to the Abilene Police Academy. He became an official member of the Abilene Police Department six months later.

Two weeks after he finished his field training period, he met Tiffany Douglas. She had been carjacked one hot, humid night in July. Wade just happened to be one of the lucky officers who answered the call. He still remembered how beautiful she was in spite of the tears and makeup streaming down her face. He asked her to have dinner with him the following evening.

They had been together for two years when he proposed. They made the announcement at the family reunion. Wade's family welcomed her with open arms.

They planned to be married the first weekend of 2003. She moved in with him when the lease was up on her own apartment. Together they made wedding plans and began looking for a house. Life couldn't have been more perfect. That all changed when Wade was wounded while on duty.

He and his partner had responded to a domestic dispute call. The woman at the home was carelessly waving a gun in the direction of her boyfriend. She tossed the gun aside when Wade's partner ordered her to put the gun down. The gun went off as it hit the floor. The bullet grazed Wade's calf. He was taken to the hospital, where he was treated and released.

Tiffany was inconsolable. She had nightmares about Wade being killed. She worried and nagged. She called him multiple times throughout the day to make sure he was safe. They argued constantly when he was home.

Two months before the wedding, Wade came home to an empty apartment. He found an envelope on his pillow containing a tear-stained letter and his ring.

My darling Wade,

I'm sorry that I'm not there to talk to you in person. I know we've always talked things out, but you know how hard it is for me to talk when I'm emotional. This is the only way that I can say what I need to say.

I know you love your work and that it's what you've always dreamed of doing. I know that you wouldn't be happy doing anything else. I wouldn't dream of asking you to give it up.

It's been so hard since you were wounded - for both of us. We can't seem to get along anymore. You've been trying to keep things together. I'm sorry that I haven't made it any easier.

I'm terrified that you'll be seriously hurt or killed. My fear is making me crazy. I'm making you unhappy, and I worry that it will affect your work. That scares me and makes me crazier.

I can't live this way. I don't want to live the rest of my life not knowing from one minute to the next if you're safe. I can't stand the thought of telling our future children that Daddy won't ever come home.

Wade, I'm sorry, but I can't marry you. I never meant to hurt you, but I'd rather say goodbye now than some terrible day in the future.

Love always,

Tiffany

Wade's injuries had been relatively minor. He didn't understand Tiffany's reaction and hadn't known how to handle it. He was about to suggest they postpone the wedding and attend counseling together. He had hoped they could still work out their problems. Her letter took away all hope. He neither saw nor heard from Tiffany again.

Wade went through the motions of his daily life. He got up. He went to work. He ate. He slept. The next day he'd do it all again.

His family and friends worried about him while he lived his life on autopilot.

He was beginning to break through the fog several weeks later when he happened to notice an advertisement. The Sheriff's department in Wilbarger County was looking for qualified candidates for the position of deputy sheriff.

A change might be just what I need. Everything here reminds me of Tiffany, he thought. He discussed the new job opportunity with his family. They didn't want him to leave, but they thought the change might be good for him. It wasn't as if he'd be moving across the country; Vernon was less than three hours away. He talked with his former training officer and his partner before making his final decision.

Once his decision was made, he never looked back. He would be starting a new chapter in his life with the New Year. It wasn't what he had been planning, but he was optimistic about the move and life in a new town.

Wade made a name for himself as an investigator while working as a deputy sheriff. He was friendly and outgoing yet completely professional when the job dictated.

Sheriff Rusty Morton made the decision to retire before his term ended when his wife was diagnosed with cancer. Wade and Deputy Kyle Jensen both wanted the job and were equally qualified. The county commissioners decided to hold a special election to choose the interim sheriff. Wade won easily because he was well-liked and respected. He took office in January 2007. Jensen later resigned and took a position with the Texas Highway Patrol.

It was hard to believe that May of 2015 was almost over. He'd have to make a decision in the next few weeks about running for re-election. He and Lizzie had been together for a long time, with the exception of those six months apart. He wanted to discuss it with her before he put his name on the ballot again.

Wade looked down and realized he was still holding the

applications. He put them in his desk drawer before standing and stretching.

Craig Dodson stepped through the doorway. "Are you out of here?"

"It's all yours. I'll be at my aunt and uncle's place for the weekend. I won't have any cell reception while I'm there. Call the number on the notepad by my phone if something comes up," Wade replied.

"Have a safe trip and a good time. We'll handle things here."

"Thanks, I'll see you Tuesday," Wade said as he put on his hat and strolled out of the office.

Inside the Paradise Creek Inn, Lizzie paced. She was both excited and nervous about her weekend with Wade. She had packed and repacked her bag twice. She had brushed her shoulder-length red hair back from her face three times. She had applied a little more mascara to enhance her vivid blue eyes. She needed to find something to occupy her mind and dispel the nervous energy. She decided to focus on business until Wade arrived.

Lizzie went to the office and looked over the calendar for the coming week. All of the guest rooms were booked for the weekend. The menus had already been planned, and the food purchased. Everything was in order. There was nothing else she could do to occupy her time. Her thoughts returned to her own weekend plans.

She had met Wade's parents shortly after they began dating. They came to visit periodically. She liked them both and believed that they liked her. The thought of meeting the rest of his family all at once was unnerving. She preferred meeting new people one or two at a time.

She went to the kitchen, emptied the dishwasher, and put the dishes away. She checked to make sure her cell phone was charged and fidgeted with the cord. She double-checked her bag to make sure she had everything she might need.

"Are you ready?"

Lizzie jumped. She turned to see her grandmother grinning at her.

"Oh! Granny, you scared me! I didn't hear you come in."

"I realized that when I saw how you jumped," Lois Fletcher said with a chuckle. "I didn't mean to scare you, but it was pretty entertaining."

Lizzie smiled at her grandmother and said, "I'm glad you enjoyed it."

"When is Wade going to be here?"

"He's on his way. We have one guest coming tonight. The others have already arrived. I left their names and room numbers on the desk in the office. Thanks for covering the inn this weekend, Granny," Lizzie said as she hugged her grandmother.

"You're welcome, dear. It gives me something to do."

"I'd like to have one of those," Wade said with a twinkle in his eye.

"Well, come over here, and I'll give you a hug, too," Lois said playfully.

Wade grinned as he hugged Lizzie's grandmother. Lizzie smiled as she watched. He was at least six feet of lean muscle. She loved to play with the little curls of dark blonde hair around his ears and his shirt collar. His green eyes and warm, friendly smile always stirred her soul.

"Are you ready, Lizzie?"

"Yes, I think so. Are you sure I don't need to bring anything nice to wear?"

"You can take whatever you want, but chances are it will be torn, stained, or both."

"All right, I'll take your word for it. I just hate the thought of meeting your family looking grubby."

"You look beautiful no matter what you wear. They'll love you at first sight."

Lizzie blushed and smiled gratefully at him. "I guess I'm ready then."

"Good, I'd like to get there before dark. I want to get the tent set up while there's enough light."

Lizzie said goodbye to her grandmother while Wade loaded her belongings in the truck. Soon they were on their way to meet Wade's family.

"Take a nap if you want. We'll probably be up most of the night. There's nothing much to see on the way there," Wade suggested.

"I'm too nervous to sleep now. I'd offer to drive so that you can sleep if I knew where we're going."

"I'd tell you there's nothing to be nervous about if I thought it would do any good. I can understand meeting a lot of new people can be scary. I promise you they won't bite. I know they'll love you as much as I do. Well, they'll love you, but probably not as much as I do," he said with a sideways grin.

Lizzie smiled and said, "I love you, too."

CHAPTER FIVE

HAWLEY, Texas, is a small town located approximately fifteen miles north of Abilene. Wade's Aunt Nannette and Uncle Donald lived outside the city limits. Their house was less than a quarter mile from the Clear Fork of the Brazos River. Wade stopped at the house before driving the short distance to the river. His uncle was sitting on the front porch watching for new arrivals.

"Hello, Uncle Don," Wade said as he got out of his truck.

"Boy, you're a sight for sore eyes," Uncle Don said. "Who's that pretty little gal you have with you?"

"This is Lizzie Fletcher. Lizzie, this is my uncle. Donald Edwards."

"It's nice to meet you," Lizzie said as they shook hands.

"It's nice to finally meet you, Lizzie. We've heard a lot about you. I'm real glad you're here. Y'all, come on in. Nannette's inside. I know she'll shoot me if she doesn't get to see you before you go down to the river."

Wade and Lizzie followed Uncle Don into the house. He was a brawny man of five feet eleven inches. He farmed and raised horses for a living. He had a full head of gray hair and kind brown eyes. Lizzie liked him right away.

"Nan! Look who's here," Don called to his wife.

"Wade! Oh my goodness, it's good to see you," Aunt Nan said as she hugged her nephew. "You must be Lizzie. It's nice to finally meet you. Sean and Gloria have nothing but good things to say about you," she said as she hugged Lizzie.

Nannette Edwards was about two inches shorter than her husband. She had the same dark blonde hair as Wade and his father, Sean. She was slender with twinkling blue eyes. She was a part-time nurse and helped on the farm.

Lizzie was beginning to relax. If the rest of Wade's family were this nice and welcoming, she'd have a great weekend.

Wade and Lizzie visited with the older couple for a bit before Wade said, "We'd better get down to the river. I need to set up our tent before it gets dark."

"I'd help you, but we're still waiting for most of the family to arrive. Your folks and grandparents went down about an hour ago. We'll be down there by supper time," Uncle Don said with a wink.

"You know your Uncle Don isn't about to miss a meal if he can help it," Aunt Nan joked.

Wade and Lizzie waved as they climbed into the truck. They bounced the short distance to a barbed wire fence and through the gate. When they reached the campsite, Wade backed into a small clearing beside a tree and turned off the engine. As the couple got out of the truck, they were joined by Wade's parents.

"I'm so glad you could come this year," Wade's mother said as she hugged him. "I'm glad you were able to come with him," she said as she moved to hug Lizzie.

"I'm glad too, Gloria," Lizzie replied.

Wade's mother was a little taller than Lizzie. She had short brown hair that had been slightly frosted with gray. Her brown eyes were warm and friendly.

Wade's father, Sean, was an older version of Wade. They were the same height and build. Sean's eyes were blue like his sister Nan's. Sean offered Lizzie his arm and led her over to meet his parents.

"Lizzie, I'd like you to meet Gene and Peggy Adams."

"It's nice to meet you," Lizzie replied.

"Glad to meet you," the couple replied in unison.

"Sit down here and tell us all about yourself," Wade's grandfather said.

Lizzie enjoyed getting acquainted with the older couple. She could see the family resemblance passed down from parents to son in both generations. Gene was bald except for a rim of white hair around his head. His brown eyes danced with mischief. Peggy had short white hair and a round face. It was obvious that her son and daughter had inherited her blue eyes.

"Have you ever fished with bank poles?" Gene asked Lizzie.

"No sir, I haven't."

"Well, it's about time you did."

Gene Adams explained fishing with bank poles as he cut a length of twine and tied a fish hook to one end. Lizzie watched and listened while he worked.

"We'll cut some green tree limbs to use for poles; then, we'll tie these hooks to them," Gene told her.

Wade unloaded the truck while Lizzie visited with his family. He walked over to the group with a look of frustration on his face.

"What's wrong? Did you forget something?" Peggy asked.

"I don't have our tent," Wade said, obviously upset with himself. "I bought it yesterday, and I took it into the office. I must have forgotten to take it back to the truck. I'm sorry, Lizzie."

"Do we really need a tent?"

"We can manage without it, but I wanted you to have some privacy since it's your first time here."

"That's okay, Wade," Lizzie assured him. "What else can we do about sleeping arrangements?"

"We could sleep inside the truck or in the truck bed. It'll be cramped inside, but there'd be fewer mosquitoes. We can use the air mattress if we decide to sleep in the back of the truck," Wade said.

"You'd probably be more comfortable in the bed of the truck. I brought a big can of insect repellent to deal with the mosquitoes," Lizzie said.

Wade smiled at her affectionately. "It sounds like we have a plan then. I'll start airing up the mattress."

"Do you need my help?" Lizzie asked.

"You can help me with the air mattress."

While Gene and Sean went in search of green limbs for fishing poles, Wade and Lizzie worked together to get their sleeping quarters in order. Gloria and Peggy talked as they watched the pair.

"They're good together," observed Peggy.

"Yes, they are," Gloria replied.

Gene and Sean returned with their arms full of green tree limbs that were two-and-a- half to three-feet long. Each limb was approximately three-quarters of an inch in diameter, allowing the limbs to bend without easily breaking. Wade joined them as they worked to trim the poles. One end of each limb was sharpened to a point.

"All we need now is bait," Sean said. "I'll get the minnow buckets and the seine."

"What's a seine?" Lizzie asked.

"It's a net for catching fish. We'll use it to catch minnows for bait," Wade replied. "The catfish in this river like those better than worms."

They like grasshoppers, too," Gene added.

"Is there anything I can do?" Lizzie asked.

"Sean and Wade can seine for minnows. You can come over here, and I'll show you how to tie the hooks onto these poles," Gene said with a grin.

Other family members soon began to arrive. Wade's brother, Wyatt, and his wife, Becky, drove in with their children, Gavin and

Bailee. Gavin was eight, and Bailee was five. Fifteen minutes later, Wade's cousins arrived. Stephen Edwards and his nine-year-old son Kaden were setting up their sleeping area when his sister Julie Mayfield arrived with her husband Skye and their kids - Xavier, a nine-year-old boy, and Avery and Karsyn, six-year-old twin daughters.

Wade and Sean returned to the camp with two full buckets of bait. The youngsters were disappointed that they hadn't been there in time to help. Sean told them that they could help catch grasshoppers if needed.

"We're going to catch so many fish that we'll need all the bait we can get," he told them.

The children set off to explore while Lizzie was introduced to the new arrivals. Stephen resembled their mother, Nannette, while his sister Julie had more of their father's features.

"When are Nan and Don coming down?" Gene asked Julie.

"They're waiting for Uncle Bud and Aunt Daisy," Julie replied.

"Have you already set out the poles?" Skye asked as he shook Wade's hand.

"Not yet. We just got back with the bait," Wade replied.

"Good. I didn't want to miss that again this year."

"You boys can start setting them if you want," Gene said. "I believe I'll stay here and play with the kids."

"Lizzie, would you like to go?" Wade asked hopefully.

"Yes, I want to see how this works."

"Grandpa's watching the kids. I'll go and keep you company," Julie volunteered. "Becky, are you coming?"

"Nope. I'll stay here and help Grandpa,"

"You go on with the others. I can handle this," Gene protested.

"If you go now, you won't have to run them tonight," Wyatt offered.

"Sold!" Becky replied emphatically. "I'd rather find a snake in the daylight than in the dark."

"Since there are eight of us, let's split up and get it done faster,"

Sean suggested. "Wade, Lizzie, Julie, and Skye can go down river. Wyatt, Becky, Stephen, and I will go up river."

Each group took a bucket of minnows and half the fishing poles. It was hot and humid on the river bank. Lizzie's group decided to cool off by wading in the cool water while setting the poles. Wade explained that the best place to set the poles would be near a tree or thick brush. The fish tended to stay in those areas to avoid predators.

He demonstrated setting the pole by jabbing the sharpened end deep into the mud of the bank so that the hook dangled just under the water. He baited the hook and made sure that the minnow was deep enough to swim but shallow enough to see from above. When he was satisfied, he moved away and looked for a place to set the next pole.

Skye and Julie were wading slightly ahead of Wade and Lizzie. The two men alternated, setting and baiting the poles. The four-some talked and joked as they made their way down river.

"Let's set the last pole here and walk back on dry ground," Wade suggested.

"That sounds like a good idea," replied Skye.

Skye and Julie crawled out of the river with Wade and Lizzie close behind. They struggled up the steep bank as briars and thorns tore at their jeans and scratched their arms and faces.

"That's a tough climb," Wade commented.

"It'll be worse in the dark. We'll need to bring a machete and cut some of those briars back," said Skye.

The group soon arrived back at the campsite. Aunt Daisy Holland and Uncle Bud Adams had arrived while they were away. Wade's grandfather introduced Lizzie to his siblings. Bud was the oldest of the three. Daisy was the middle sibling. They were both widowed, and their children lived out of state. They found it conve-nient and economical to share an apartment in Abilene.

Donald and Nannette arrived as the evening meal was being prepared. The first meal always consisted of sandwiches and chips.

The youngsters usually ate first. They played together while the adults ate and visited.

The group built a campfire as darkness approached. The campfire was multifunctional. A grate was placed over the coals to serve as a support for the cast iron skillets and the coffee pot. Breakfast consisted of bacon and scrambled eggs. Lunch and dinner would be fried catfish and fried potatoes, along with a can of beans.

They brewed campfire coffee in an old-fashioned coffee pot and kept it on the grate all night. Coffee grounds were never dumped out; they just added more coffee when water was added. The brew got stronger as the night wore on.

Although the days were warm, the nights were often chilly. The fire would provide heat and enough light to keep the nocturnal animals away. Julie told Lizzie that raccoons were the worst problem. Even with the fire, it was wise to put all of the food away before going to sleep. Lizzie listened as she watched an armadillo skirt the edge of the camp.

Most of the youngsters were tucked safely in their sleeping bags when Gene decided it was time to check the bank poles. Avery and Karsyn refused to go to sleep unless their mother stayed with them. Because Julie was busy with her girls, Gene decided to join Wade's group for the trek.

"Grab a tow sack and a flash light, Lizzie," he said, indicating a burlap bag. "We'll hold the lights and the fish while these boys get down in the water."

They made their way through the vegetation to the river bank. Lizzie understood why Wade had told her to bring old jeans. Briars and thorns were everywhere along the bank. She was thankful for the protection the jeans gave her legs.

Wade and Skye shined their lights on the first pole. It was bent low in the water. They climbed down the bank and lifted the line to see what they had caught. Wade carefully removed a catfish from the hook. His grandfather dunked the sack in the water before Wade placed the fish inside.

"We need to keep them wet so they'll stay alive. The freshest catfish are the best. We don't have a way to refrigerate them down here, so we keep them alive until we're ready to eat them. We'll tie the bag up and leave it in the water when we get back to camp," he told Lizzie.

They returned to camp with eight catfish. It was estimated that they weighed between two and three pounds each. The other group returned with similar results.

The ritual was repeated several times throughout the night. Each time they crossed the river, the water seemed colder. When they returned, they would huddle around the fire to get warm before going to bed for an hour or two of sleep.

Lizzie hung her wet jeans on the side of the truck before crawling into her sleeping bag. She was glad Wade had forgotten the tent. She could see stars winking at her through the canopy made by the trees. She drifted off to sleep listening to the breeze softly rustling the leaves.

Lizzie woke to the smell of bacon frying. Wade's mother and grandmother had started breakfast. Wade and the other men were nowhere in sight. She climbed out of her sleeping bag and put on her jeans. They were still damp and extremely cold. She shivered as she put on her shoes. They were as cold as her jeans. She went through her morning routine as quickly as she could and went to help the busy cooks.

"It looks like we'll be having fresh fish for lunch and probably supper tonight," Gloria told her. "Sean said they were really biting last night. They've gone to check the poles before breakfast."

"We'd better have plenty of fish," Peggy joked. "There will be more relatives coming to visit, and they all love catfish."

"May I help with something?" Lizzie offered.

"You can add some wood to the fire. Those boys will be ready for breakfast when they get back," answered Peggy.

By lunchtime, Lizzie had learned to clean and filet catfish

perfectly for frying. She had to agree with Wade's grandfather. Fresh catfish tasted better than any she had ever eaten.

The remainder of the day was similar to the previous afternoon. They'd cool off in the river when it was hot. The kids played while the adults visited and checked the bank poles periodically. They ate and then ate some more.

Wade and Lizzie went to check the poles late that afternoon, with the boys tagging along. Most of the lines still had bait. The only thing they caught was a turtle. The boys wanted to take it back to camp to show everyone. They took turns carrying the turtle and pretending to be pirates. They had found long sticks to use as swords. Lizzie followed behind the boys as Wade led the group back to the camp site.

They were about to cross the river again. It was Kaden's turn to carry the turtle. He handed the imaginary sword to his cousin and proudly carried their prize. Gavin and Xavier were fighting imaginary foes when they accidentally bumped into a wasp nest hanging from a limb above their heads. The boys were unaware of what had happened. They continued to play as they ran ahead. The angry wasps went after the nearest victim.

Lizzie screamed in pain as the wasps stung her face, neck, and arms. Wade ran toward her and tried to swat them away. He took off his shirt and covered her as best he could before leading her across the river to the camp. He was stung himself a few times in the process.

"What happened?" Gloria asked with concern.

"Wasps," Wade replied as he guided Lizzie to a chair.

Peggy and Gloria rushed to her side.

"Wade, get some mud from the river," Peggy ordered. "It will soothe the stings. Do we have any onion to spare?"

"I'll look," Gloria replied.

"Are you allergic to insect stings, Lizzie?" Peggy asked.

"I haven't been in the past," Lizzie replied weakly.

Wade returned with a plastic cup filled with cool river mud. "What else can I do?" he asked with worry.

"Look in my bag in the trunk of the car. There should be some acetaminophen tablets and antihistamine capsules in there. Bring two of each and something to wash it down," said Peggy. "Get some for yourself, too."

Wade went on his errand, as Gloria arrived with a bowl of water and onion slices. She gently bathed Lizzie's stings. The cool water eased the pain a little bit. Wade returned with the medicine and gave it to her. After taking the pills, Gloria and Peggy tended to her injuries.

"The onions and the mud will ease the pain and reduce the swelling. We'll use the mud on your face and the onion on your neck and arms. I wouldn't want the onion to get in your eyes," Peggy explained as she applied the home remedies.

"Maybe you should lie down until you feel better. We'll see what Nannette can do for you when she gets off work. I'm sure she'll have something better than mud and onion," Gloria said with a sympathetic smile.

"Thank you. I'm sure I'll be fine in a little while," Lizzie said bravely.

After his own stings had been tended to, Wade asked Lizzie what happened. She could see the anger on his face as she told him.

"It was an accident, Wade. It could have happened to anybody. I'm glad the boys weren't stung. I'll be fine as soon as the medicine starts to work."

Two hours later, Lizzie woke to the sound of voices she didn't recognize. She climbed out of the truck and joined the others.

More relatives had arrived, and Lizzie was introduced. They looked at her curiously until Wade explained that she had been the target of angry wasps.

"We were about to check the lines again. Do you feel like coming?" Wade asked.

"Yes, I'd like to go."

They made their way to the river bank. Lizzie and Julie held the flashlights and tow sacks while Wade and Skye tended to the hooks. Eventually, they reached the last pole where the bank was so steep. Lizzie noticed that most of the briars and thorns had been trimmed away.

"We'll need some help getting back up here. It's slippery, and there's nothing to hold onto now," Wade told Lizzie.

Wade and Skye slid down the bank to the river's edge. There was a nice-sized fish on the line. Lizzie tossed her tow sack to Wade. Skye removed the fish from the hook and placed it in the burlap bag.

"Julie, shine that light on the hook so that I can see to bait it," requested Skye.

The light revealed something moving in the water toward the two men.

"Snake!" both men shouted at the same moment.

They needed no help getting up the steep bank after all. They scrambled up the bank as quickly as they could. Skye had ripped the pole from the bank and made the climb, unaware that it was still in his hand. Wade stomped the tow sack and the unfortunate fish inside as he clawed for higher ground.

Lizzie and Julie laughed until tears ran down their faces. The two men just shook their heads and grinned.

"You should have seen your faces," Julie said as she wiped her eyes.

"I wish we could have gotten that on video," Lizzie joked as she tried to contain herself.

"Did you stomp that fish to death?" Julie asked with a smirk.

Wade seemed to realize that he was holding the sack for the first time. He opened the bag to examine the unfortunate creature and decided that it wasn't damaged.

Wade looked at Skye and asked, "Do you want to put that pole back in the water?"

Skye looked at the pole and back at Wade. "No! Do you?"

"Let's just leave it here by the tree. We'll put it back out on the next run," Wade suggested.

"Do you think that water moccasin will be gone by then?"

"We'll just skip this spot if it isn't."

The women continued to tease the men about the snake as they followed them through the tall vegetation back to camp.

"I think we'll hold the flashlights and let the girls check the hooks next time," Skye suggested.

"I like that plan. With any luck, we'll see how they like being surprised by a snake," Wade added.

They crossed the river and walked into the camp. Suddenly, the others stopped and stared. Lizzie wondered what was going on as she stopped beside them. Walking toward the group was a tall, slender brunette. She looked as if she had just stepped out of fashion magazine. Her eyes were locked on Wade.

"Hi, Wade," she said with a beautiful smile.

"Tiffany?" Wade replied, obviously surprised, and said nothing more.

Lizzie couldn't believe her ears. *Tiffany? Wade's ex-fiancé? That Tiffany?* She looked at Wade. The look on his face confirmed her suspicion.

Lizzie stood in silence as Skye and Julie coolly said hello. She wanted to crawl under a rock. Meeting Wade's ex was the last thing she wanted to do, especially at this moment. She had one badly swollen eye and mud all over her face. She smelled of fish, sweat, and onions.

Wade turned and reached for her, but she took a step back and shook her head. The couple moved away from the group toward Wade's truck.

"Are you okay?" he whispered with worry on his face.

"Um, I'm not sure," she replied. "Is that who I think it is?"

"That's Tiffany. I don't know why she's here, and I don't care."

"Wade, I know it's rude, but I really don't want to meet her right now."

"I know it's a shock. I'm just as surprised as you."

"It's not just the surprise! Look at me! I look like a character from *The Walking Dead*, and I smell like yesterday's garbage!"

Wade fought the urge to laugh as he said, "Sweetheart, you don't look that bad, and you don't smell any worse than the rest of us."

"Do you mind if I interrupt you two?" Nannette asked as she approached. "I understand Lizzie could use some help."

"Boy, could I!" Lizzie replied with tears in her eyes.

"Let's go to the house. The light is better, and I'll be able to see the stings better after you've showered that mud off."

"I'll tag along if that's okay," Wade said.

"Of course, it's okay; it seems to be a bit crowded down here right now anyway," Aunt Nan said, indicating the latest arrival.

Wade grabbed Lizzie's bag, and the three drove the short distance to the house. Lizzie fought back tears when she looked in the mirror. She knew that crying wouldn't help anything and willed her eyes to stay dry. She tried not to think about her appearance as she showered and put on clean clothes. After Aunt Nan tended to her stings, she attempted to hide her wounds with makeup. Tiffany had gone when they returned to the campsite.

Some of the cousins began playing their guitars, and the family joined in for a sing-along. The air was filled with music and laughter. The new arrivals made camp for the night and helped run the fishing lines.

Lizzie chose to stay at camp for the rest of the evening. She was clean, and she wanted to stay that way in case Tiffany came back. Thoughts of Tiffany ran through her mind. *Why was she here? What did she want?* She tossed and turned throughout the night.

CHAPTER SIX

"GOOD MORNING," Lizzie said as she joined the Adams women preparing breakfast.

"Good morning, Lizzie. How are you feeling?" Gloria asked.

"Much better; thank you for taking care of me," she said with a smile.

"You look a lot better this morning," said Peggy.

"That's a relief," Lizzie joked. "Is there something I can do to help?"

"Not at the moment. Just sit down and relax," Gloria said with a smile.

"Good morning," Julie said as she joined the women. "Lizzie, I owe you an apology."

Lizzie looked at her in surprise, "Why would you owe me an apology?"

"It's my fault that Tiffany showed up last night."

"What?" Peggy asked as she looked at her granddaughter angrily.

"I didn't invite her Grandma. I saw her in town a few weeks

ago. She mentioned how she used to enjoy the family reunion and asked if it was still on Memorial Day weekend. It never crossed my mind that she'd show up."

Peggy's glare changed to a look of understanding, "I wouldn't have thought so either."

"I'm so sorry, Lizzie," Julie apologized.

"It's not your fault. How could you have known?"

Julie's worried look faded, and she hugged Lizzie tightly. "Thank you for understanding."

"Does anyone know why she came?" Peggy asked.

"It doesn't matter," replied Gloria. "I'm just glad she's gone."

"I think she was expecting a warmer welcome than we gave her," Becky said as she joined the group. "No one had much to say."

"Skye said he heard Wyatt ask her to leave," Julie added.

"He did," Becky replied.

"What did she say?" Gloria asked.

"She said she was sorry to intrude. She just wanted to stop by and say hello, for old times' sake. Wyatt told her that we had all moved on and that Wade was happy. He also told her that if she hadn't moved on, it was time she did."

"Good for Wyatt!" Peggy retorted.

"I thought y'all liked her," Lizzie said in confusion.

"We did like her, but she hurt Wade badly. He wasn't himself for a long time. We don't want to see him go through the pain she caused again," Gloria answered.

"Tiffany and I were friends while she was with Wade," Julie said. "We used to see them often. I can honestly say that the two of you are more suited to each other."

Before Lizzie could reply, Peggy said, "The men are coming back. Let's not talk about this in front of Wade unless he brings it up."

The men returned with big smiles on their faces. They couldn't wait to show the ladies what they had caught. They placed twenty catfish side by side on the wet burlap bags. Each fish weighed at least two pounds.

"Those are the perfect eatin' size," Gene said proudly.

"Looks like you've got a lot of fish to clean after breakfast," Peggy teased.

"If they keep biting, we'll have a lot more to clean before the weekend is over," said Sean.

Wade sat down beside Lizzie while they ate their breakfast. "You look like you feel better," he whispered. "Are you having a good time?"

"I am," she replied with a smile.

Wade's aunt and uncle arrived in time for the noon meal. Donald nodded at Wade and indicated that he'd like a word in private. Wade joined his uncle away from the camp.

"There was a call on the answering machine when I got back to the house. The man said his name was Greg or Craig or something like that," Don said. "I figured it was someone from your office."

"Craig Dodson is one of my deputies. What did he say?" Wade asked.

"He didn't give any details. He just asked that you call him as soon as you can. I thought it might be important. I'm sorry I didn't get the message sooner. I was out taking care of the horses," Don said apologetically.

"That's all right, Uncle Don. Would you mind giving me a ride to your house? I can't get a signal on my cell phone down here."

"You can use our land line. Cell reception isn't all that great at the house either."

Lizzie could see the concern on Wade's face as he followed Don. "What's wrong, Wade?"

"Dodson left a message for me. He wouldn't have called unless something really serious came up. I need to find out what's going on. I'll be back soon," Wade said as he got into his uncle's truck.

Dodson picked up the office phone on the first ring, "Wade, I'm sorry to bother you at your family reunion."

"That's no problem. What's going on?"

"Lodge and Baker are both in a hospital in Altus, Oklahoma."

Wade groaned. "What happened?"

"Details are still sketchy. They were rock climbing in Brandon's jeep at the copper mines. No one seems to know exactly what caused it. The jeep rolled over some jagged rocks. They had their seatbelts on, but they had taken the doors and the top off. Some other rock climbers found them. They were taken to the hospital in Altus. They're alive but pretty banged up. I was planning on driving over to check on them when I get off duty," Dodson said.

"If you wait until I get there, I'll go with you," Wade offered.

"I'll wait. Wade, there's something else you need to know," Dodson said.

"What is it, Craig?"

"There was another wildfire this weekend. Someone set fire to a wheat field ready for harvest. The harvesters were on their way to thrash it and saw the smoke. They didn't realize it was the field they were supposed to be working until they got there. They called the fire department and did what they could to help. The farmer lost most of his crop.

"When did it start?"

"The call went out at nine this morning."

"Was anyone hurt or any buildings damaged?"

"No, only the field was burned. The fire chief wants to meet with you as soon as possible."

"It'll be a few hours before we can get back to town. I can meet with him first thing in the morning," Wade told his deputy with a sigh.

"I'll let him know."

"Is there anything else?"

"Well, I wasn't going to mention this until later, but since you asked, Megan Ford was brought in by Trooper Jensen last night.

Wade rolled his eyes and sighed. "What was the charge?

"She was stopped for speeding. Trooper Jensen smelled alcohol and asked her to step out of the car for a sobriety test."

"I'll bet she didn't like that," said Wade.

"Not in the least. She attacked Kyle. The report is on your desk."

"Is she still in lock-up?"

"She made bail this morning."

"I'll let you know when I get back to town," Wade said before disconnecting the call.

Wade returned to the campsite and explained what had happened and that he needed to leave.

"That's terrible, Wade. Do you think Brandon and Calvin will be okay?" his mother asked.

"I hope so," Wade answered distractedly.

Wade and Lizzie quickly loaded the truck and said goodbye to his family. Soon they had merged onto the highway and were driving back to Vernon.

Wade said, "Lizzie if you don't mind, I'll take you home first so that Craig and I can leave as soon as I get cleaned up."

"I don't mind. Will you let me know how they are after you've seen them?"

"I'll call you as soon as I get home," Wade said. He told her about the fire and Megan's arrest. A few seconds later, he began to laugh.

"What are you laughing about?" Lizzie asked.

"I'm picturing little bitty Megan attacking gigantic Kyle Jensen. It must have looked like a Chihuahua attacking a Great Dane. I can't wait to read that report."

"I don't think I know Kyle," Lizzie said with a grin.

"He's a big man, six foot six, and at least two hundred pounds of pure muscle. Most people are afraid of him because of his size, but he's one of the nicest guys you'll ever meet."

The couple talked about their friends and the weekend. They talked about everything except Tiffany's inexplicable visit. Wade glanced at Lizzie just as she tried to cover a yawn.

"Why don't you take a nap? We still have an hour before we get to your place. I know you haven't had much sleep this weekend."

Lizzie smiled at him gratefully. "I think I will. I can't seem to keep my eyes open."

"Sweet dreams," Wade said as he brushed a lock of hair from her cheek.

Lizzie closed her eyes and quickly drifted off to sleep. Wade was lost in his own thoughts for the remainder of the drive.

Wade called Dodson as soon as he walked through his front door. The news Dodson had given him kept replaying in his mind as he quickly showered and dressed. *Why would someone burn a wheat field just before harvest? Lodge and Baker have been rock climbing for years. Did they make a mistake? Was it a freak accident?* He was abruptly brought back to the present when Dodson rang the doorbell.

The two men chose to take Dodson's vehicle because Wade's had not been unloaded. They arrived at the hospital an hour later to find the attending physician in Baker's room. They waited in the hallway to talk with him.

Dr. Parr was five foot ten inches tall with tired gray eyes hidden behind thick glasses. His brown hair looked as if he was in the habit of running both hands through it. Wade was reminded of photos he'd seen of Albert Einstein. Wade and Dodson introduced themselves and asked about their friends.

"Mr. Baker regained consciousness about an hour ago. He has a concussion, some broken ribs, and his right leg is broken. He also has some cuts and contusions. He must have been in the passenger seat. His more serious injuries were on his right side," the doctor told them. "Mr. Lodge was not as seriously injured. He has a concussion and a broken collar bone. He has several cuts and contusions as well. His ribs are bruised, and his ankle is sprained. He regained consciousness shortly after he arrived here."

"May we see them?" Wade asked.

"Yes, of course. You might want to start with Mr. Lodge. He's more coherent than Mr. Baker is at the moment," Dr. Parr said as he led them to Brandon's room. "Mr. Lodge, you have visitors."

Brandon Lodge had a large purple lump on the left side of his head. He had cuts on his face and hands. He looked at Wade and Dodson sadly. He tried to sit up but gasped in pain and fell back onto his pillow.

"I guess it's a good thing you didn't come with us, Wade," he said and winced when he spoke.

"I guess so," Wade said with a smile.

"Do you know what happened?" Dodson asked.

"Not really. We'd been climbing for a few hours. We decided we were hungry and started toward town. I was driving on the mining road, and all of a sudden, it felt like the road just crumbled. The jeep started rolling, and all we could do was hold on," Brandon told them. "I don't remember much after that. The next thing I knew, I was being examined by the doctor."

Dr. Parr took the opportunity to explain the injuries to his patient, "I'd like to keep you under observation for a day or two because of your head injury. Your other injuries will take some time to heal, but you should make a full recovery."

"How's Calvin?" Brandon asked with concern.

"Mr. Baker's injuries are more serious than yours, but he should make a full recovery as well. It will just take a little longer. You should rest now. I'll come back in the morning."

Wade and Dodson shook Lodge's hand. They told him to call if he needed anything before they left the room.

"I've already talked with Mr. Baker about his injuries. I'll leave you to visit with him while I make my rounds," the doctor said as he waved goodbye.

Wade tapped on the door to Baker's room. Calvin turned his head slowly and smiled weakly when he saw his colleagues.

"Come in and join the party," he joked.

"How are you feeling?" asked Wade.

"I've been better," Calvin replied. "I could be worse."

"Do you know what happened?" Dodson asked.

Calvin's story was almost identical to Brandon's. He mentioned seeing a cloud of dust shortly before the road began to crumble.

"Is Brandon okay?" Calvin asked worriedly.

"The doctor said you both will make a full recovery. It will just take time," Wade assured him.

"That's good," Calvin said weakly as he fought to stay awake. "I think the pain medicine is putting me to sleep," he said with a yawn.

"We'll go and let you rest. Call us if you need anything," Wade said.

Baker nodded slightly before he drifted off to sleep. Wade and Dodson quietly left his room. Neither man spoke until they reached the car.

"Shall we visit the Jackson County Sheriff's office?" Dodson asked, already knowing the answer.

"That's a good place to start," Wade replied. "If it's not too dark, we'll check out those copper mines before going home."

After visiting with the Jackson County Sheriff, Wade knew little more than he had learned already. There were no witnesses to the incident. Based on the evidence at the scene, it was believed to have been a freak accident. The ground had been very dry. The winds had been high and eroded the loose soil in the area. As a result, rock slides had been more frequent. It appeared that Brandon had driven too close to the edge of the road. It either triggered the rock slide, or they began to slide at that very moment. The two men thanked the sheriff and stood to leave.

"Do you mind if we have a look at the scene?" asked Wade.

"Those boys don't remember much about the accident. I'd like to see it for myself."

"Be my guest. Just watch out for loose rocks."

Wade and Dodson found the accident site using the map that the Sheriff had given them. The road was roped off to prevent other accidents. They left the car and walked to the scene. It looked as if something huge had taken a bite out of the road.

The sheriff and his deputy stood away from the edge for safety but close enough that they could see the rocks below. Both men were amazed that their colleagues hadn't been killed. They could see nothing that indicated foul play.

Dodson took out his smart phone and began to take photos. He hoped the pictures would jog the memories of the injured men. He also hoped they would see something in the photos that they were unable to see in person. The two men discussed their friends as they drove back to Vernon.

Wade called Lizzie immediately after he returned to his house. She was relieved to hear that Baker and Lodge would make a full recovery. After they said goodnight, Wade unloaded his truck and relaxed in front of the television for a little while.

He had enjoyed the weekend, but he was tired. He hadn't had a lot of sleep the past two nights. He smiled as he remembered how his family had accepted Lizzie. He hoped she would be a part of the family reunions for years to come.

His thoughts turned to Tiffany. Why had she been there? What could she have possibly wanted? Lizzie was obviously upset about it. Wade was surprised that she hadn't brought up the subject on the ride home. He wasn't sure if she was more upset about Tiffany's presence or the fact that she wasn't looking her best. He decided it was probably a bit of both.

He could understand how she felt. He wasn't happy when Drake made an appearance. He had said nothing about it either time because they weren't dating. The first time that Drake turned up, he and Lizzie had just met. The second time was during the Rayland case, and they had technically broken up.

Wade knew that Drake would be back. The Wagners and Fletchers were connected. Lizzie's cousin Jan was married to Drake's brother Eli. Faith Foreman was Lizzie's closest friend and Drake's sister.

He decided he'd deal with the issue if and when it was necessary. Tomorrow would be a long day, and he needed his sleep.

CHAPTER SEVEN

WADE WAS at the office early. He had a full day ahead, and now that he was short two more deputies, he needed to get started as soon as possible. He took the deputy sheriff applications from his desk drawer and looked over them once more.

Dashleigh Reynolds, Marina Gonzalez, and Clint Odom were highly qualified applicants. He felt sure that all would be an excellent fit for his department. He wanted to hire all three candidates. Unfortunately, the county commissioners had only approved the budget for two new deputies.

The clock on the office wall said seven-thirty. His meeting with the fire chief was scheduled for eight. He picked up the phone and dialed.

"Hello," Wilbarger County Commissioner, Wendell Johnson, answered his phone promptly.

"Mr. Johnson, this is Sheriff Adams. I'm sorry to be calling so early. I hope I didn't wake you."

"No, no; we're about to go to the lake for the day. What can I do for you, Sheriff?"

"I have a problem, and I hope you can help," Wade told him.

"I'll do my best. What's the problem?"

"Deputies Baker and Lodge were injured in an accident this weekend. Both are in the hospital in Altus," Wade began.

"How seriously are they hurt?" Johnson asked.

"They both have concussions, broken bones, cuts, and bruises. The doctor said they will make a full recovery, but it will take time. Baker is more seriously injured than Lodge," Wade informed the commissioner.

"Were they injured on duty?"

"No, sir. They were off duty and rock climbing at the old copper mines. Apparently, the trail gave way, and the jeep rolled several times."

"That's going to make you extremely shorthanded, isn't it?"

"Yes, sir. That's why I've called. The fire chief is due here shortly. He has some suspicions about the recent grass fires in the area. If those fires were deliberately set, I'm going to need all the help I can get. I have three good applicants for deputy sheriff. I'd like to hire them all."

"I see," said Wendell. There was a pause before he continued, "I suggest that you hire your top two choices right away. I'll meet with the others as soon as possible to see if we can find money in the budget for the third. I know two of the commissioners are away for the weekend, and one is away on vacation. It might be our usual meeting time next month before we can manage it."

"I understand. Thank you, sir," Wade said gratefully.

"Keep me posted about those fires and about your injured men," Johnson said.

"I will. Goodbye."

Wade looked at the applications again. He decided to interview them all as soon as possible. He would ask his current deputies to be part of the interviews.

"Good morning, Sheriff," Deputy Gordon Reed said as he peered through Wade's open door. "You're here earlier than usual."

"Good morning," Wade replied. "We're going to be shorthanded until I can hire some help. We'll probably be putting in some overtime for a while."

"That's okay with me. It keeps me out of trouble," Reed joked.

"Chief Gaines is due here shortly. Would you make some phone calls for me?"

"Yes, sir."

"Call these three people to set up interviews," Wade said as he handed the names and phone numbers to his deputy. "The sooner they can come in, the better. Is Maddie coming in today?"

"She'll be in before ten."

"Neither of you was scheduled for today, were you?"

"No sir, but since Baker and Lodge are out of commission, we decided to come in."

"I can't tell you how much I appreciate your willingness to fill in. I hope to get at least two people hired this week. After they're trained, we can get back to having enough people to function. I'd like to have a staff meeting when Dodson and Maddie arrive."

"Yes, sir."

Wade was making copies of the applications. The copier was old and loud. He didn't know anyone was nearby until Reed tapped him on the shoulder.

"Chief Gaines is here to see you," Reed informed him.

Wade had previously met the Vernon Fire Chief on numerous occasions. Leo Gaines was a man of average height and muscular build. He was the first African-American member of the Vernon Fire Department and had worked his way up the ranks. He was an intelligent and personable man. He wasn't the kind of man to jump to conclusions.

"Good morning, Leo. Would you like some coffee?"

"Good morning. Coffee sounds good."

The two men shook hands before Wade led him to his office. Wade handed his guest a cup and walked around the desk to his chair before the conversation began.

"What can I do for you?" Wade asked.

"I have some concerns about the wildfires we've been having. There's no doubt that the last two fires were deliberately set. I'm worried there might be a fatality before we can stop the person responsible."

"What evidence do you have?"

Chief Gaines opened the case he had been carrying. He carefully removed evidence bags and photographs. Wade examined the contents of the evidence bags while he listened to Gaines.

"That was found at the scene near Harrold," Gaines said as he put the first set of evidence bags on Wade's desk. "At first, we suspected the farmer had started that fire as a controlled burn, although he denied it. This was found at the Lockett scene," he said, taking out the second set of evidence bags.

Wade nodded as he compared the evidence from both fires.

"These photos were taken at both scenes," the chief said as he pointed out similarities in the two sets.

"It looks like they were both set by the same perpetrator," Wade said. "Tell me what's on your mind."

"Based on the usual arsonist profile, the perpetrator is probably a male between the ages of fifteen and thirty. He's probably fascinated with the fire department. There may be a history of substance abuse and a criminal record. He most likely works alone. There are a lot of other factors that I won't go into now. He'll be difficult to catch and even more difficult to convict."

Wade nodded and said, "But this one left evidence."

Chief Gaines nodded and continued, "It appears that our arsonist used some sort of flammable liquid. We found those melted objects near the point of ignition."

"Why didn't he just throw a match into the dead vegetation?" Wade asked.

"This is just a guess, but I think that our arsonist has done this many times. I think he may have been responsible for some or all of the recent grass fires. I think he's proud of his work. He's created a signature."

"So our arsonist wants us to know who's responsible."

"That about sums it up."

The two men sat silently while Wade looked at all of the pieces of evidence again. The similarities were undeniable.

"Leo, I think you're right. This arsonist may be setting fires all over the state. Maybe the state fire marshal has information that could help."

Chief Gaines grinned and said, "Our state fire marshal retired. You're looking at the interim state fire marshal for the county. The job is mine until someone else is willing to take it. I'd like for our departments to work these cases together."

"I think that's a good idea. Would you like to have the evidence sent to our lab? My people are quick and thorough," Wade assured him.

"I was hoping you'd say that," Gaines said with a laugh.

Wade reached for the phone on his desk. "Reed, we have some evidence that needs to be taken to the lab. Bring the necessary paperwork, please."

"Yes, sir."

Reed tapped on the door. The men completed the paperwork to transfer the evidence, and Reed rushed it to the lab.

"I'll get a copy of the lab reports to you as soon as we have the results," Wade assured him.

"I'm hoping this won't be a long drawn-out case. Once all of the wheat is harvested and new crops are planted, our firebug won't have much left to burn," Gaines said as he stood.

"I hope you're right. Keep me posted."

"You can count on it," Gaines said as he left the office.

Wade was deep in thought when he heard a light tap on his door.

"Did you want to have a meeting?" Maddie asked.

"Yes. Is Dodson here yet?"

"He came in at the same time I did," Maddie informed him.

"Good. Have him meet us in the conference room," Wade said

as he buzzed Reed's desk. "Reed, lock the door and put the phones on hold, please. We'll meet in the conference room."

"Please, have a seat," Wade said as he handed copies of the applications to his deputies. "We have three qualified applicants for deputy sheriff. Unfortunately, we only have approval to hire two for the time being. I'd like for y'all to be here when they come in for their interviews. I want your input since you'll be working closely with them."

"For the time being?" asked Dodson.

"We may get approval to hire a third after the county commissioners meet," said Wade. He shared the details of his conversation with Commissioner Johnson.

"Do you know when the interviews will be?" Maddie asked as she read through the top page of the stack.

"Reed has been setting those up for me," Wade said as he looked at Reed.

"They're all scheduled for tomorrow afternoon," Reed informed him. "I'll send you the appointment times."

"Will y'all be available?"

Everyone nodded, and Reed asked, "Where do you want to conduct the interviews?"

"Let's meet in here," answered Wade.

Dodson looked at Wade with concern before asking, "What did Chief Gaines have to say?"

The sheriff shared all of the information that he had learned during the meeting with Chief Gaines. Dodson took the opportunity to share the latest information he had about Lodge and Baker.

"I called the hospital this morning and spoke with both Lodge and Baker," he told the others. "Lodge will be released from the hospital this afternoon. The doctor will probably release him to come back to work in a couple of weeks. Baker will be in the hospital at least until tomorrow. The broken leg is going to keep him out of commission for a little longer."

"If Lodge is able to come back in two weeks, he'll be running the office, and the three of you will be training our new hires. Until they're trained, I'm afraid there will be a lot of overtime, especially if the wildfires continue," Wade told the group.

The deputies assured Wade that they would be available as much as possible. With that assurance, Wade adjourned the meeting, and everyone went back to their assigned tasks.

A half-hour later, Dodson knocked on Wade's door, "Did you see the report on Megan Ford's arrest?"

"No, I had forgotten all about it," Wade answered. "Tell me what happened."

"I sent Reed and Maddie home at five that night. I stayed until nine. I asked the dispatcher to contact me at home if we had a call. At eleven fifteen, I was notified that Trooper Jensen was bringing in an assailant. I had no other information and decided not to call in the others. I was unlocking the main door when Jensen arrived. His face was covered in blood. I naturally assumed he had arrested a man near his own size. I couldn't believe it when he pulled Megan Ford out of the back seat. I've never seen her act like that. I would have sworn that she was having a bad drug reaction. I went over to help Jensen get her under control. She bit me before I knew what was happening. She kicked and cursed at the top of her lungs all way into the cell. She may have gotten some bumps and bruises herself as we moved her inside."

"She actually bit you! How bad was it?" Wade asked, amazed.

Dodson rolled up his sleeve, revealing the bite mark. It was a nasty bruise with a perfect impression of Megan's teeth.

"Did you get a photo of that for the file?"

"Yes, Jensen went to the emergency room after he left here. I went before coming in yesterday. The medical reports and photos are in the file."

"All right. What else happened?"

"She refused the sobriety tests, so we had no choice but to book her for driving under the influence, resisting arrest, and assaulting peace officers. After we booked her, she made her one phone call to her mother."

Wade read the report written by Trooper Jensen. He shook his head in disbelief as he learned how the big man had been injured. Megan had opened the car door as requested. When she closed it, she turned and kicked the patrolman in the groin. Naturally, he bent over in pain. She then dug her nails into both sides of his face leaving deep scratches. He caught her foot in midair as she tried to kick him again. She struggled and fought as he cuffed her and led her to the patrol car.

The sheriff looked at his deputy and nodded, "It looks like everything is in order here. Let's get the paperwork done to file charges."

"Yes, sir," replied Dodson.

CHAPTER EIGHT

WADE WAS ABOUT to leave for lunch the next day when Dodson tapped on his door.

"I just had a call from a man claiming to be Megan Ford's attorney," Dodson said. "He wants to talk to you."

Wade sighed, "Now?"

"I told him that you would be busy until late this afternoon. He said he'd call back after lunch."

"Thank you. Do you know what he wants to talk about?"

"Apparently, Miss Ford feels that she was mistreated while staying here Saturday night."

"The lawyer is probably hoping to have her charges dropped or file charges for brutality."

"I wouldn't be surprised," Dodson agreed.

"If he calls again, put him off until we've finished the interviews."

"Yes, sir," said Dodson before he left the room.

The first applicant for deputy sheriff arrived promptly at two o'clock. Clint Odom was shown to the conference room where Wade, Dodson, and Maddie were already seated.

Wade stood and extended his hand. "I'm Sheriff Wade Adams; this is Deputy Craig Dodson and Deputy Maddie Clifton. You met Deputy Gordon Reed when you arrived."

Odom shook hands with Wade and nodded at Dodson and Maddie. "It's nice to meet y'all. Is this the entire department?"

"No, but we're more shorthanded than we were when you applied. Two of our deputies were injured this weekend and will be out for a while," Wade explained as he indicated that Odom should sit down.

"I see," Odom replied as he sat in a vacant chair.

Clint Odom was five feet nine inches tall and weighed in at 190 pounds. His dark brown hair was cut in a military style. The freckles on his cheeks and across his nose made him appear much younger than twenty-seven. His brown eyes looked directly into the eyes of his interviewers.

Wade asked the usual interview questions. He was pleased with the answers he'd been given, but he'd wait to make a decision until he had talked with his current deputies. He gave Dodson and Maddie the opportunity to ask questions.

"Mr. Odom, do you have any questions for us?" Wade asked the prospective deputy.

"Are you often shorthanded here?"

"We've been shorthanded for a while. One of our deputies retired some time ago. This is the first time since then that we've had any qualified applicants. The recent injury of two deputies at the same time has put us in quite a bind," Wade explained.

"Will there be a lot of overtime?" Odom asked.

"That's highly possible until we're fully staffed again. Will that be a problem?" asked Wade.

"No, sir." Odom declared. "Is there a probationary period?"

"Yes, all new hires are on probation for six months. At the end of six months, you'll be evaluated and possibly eligible for a pay raise."

"I can't think of any other questions at the moment," said Odom.

"We have two more applicants coming for interviews. The county commission approved hiring two deputies now and possibly a third at a later date. I recommend that you go ahead and get all of the paperwork and your physical done as soon as possible," said Wade.

"I will, sir, thank you."

"I'll let you know as soon as the other interviews are done and we've made a decision," Wade said as he shook the man's hand again. "Reed, get Mr. Odom started on the necessary paperwork. Give him the number to Dr. Hughes's office and the address, too, please."

"Yes, sir," replied Reed as he escorted the young man out.

The team reconvened in the conference room immediately after Odom left the office.

"What did you think of Clint Odom?" Wade asked his deputies.

"His background checks out," said Dodson. "He's ex-military with a spotless record and multiple commendations."

"He didn't seem to mind overtime. I got the impression that he'd welcome the extra hours," Maddie added.

"Reed, what did you think?" Wade asked.

"He seems like a good choice," Reed answered.

"What time is our next interview?" Maddie asked.

"Thirty minutes," replied Reed.

"Let's meet back here in twenty minutes," suggested Wade.

Wade and his deputies were making their way back to the conference room when the next applicant arrived. Reed knew he wanted to hire her right away.

Dashleigh Reynolds was a pretty young woman who had just graduated from the police academy. She was hoping to find her first job as a peace officer. She was five foot six with strawberry-blonde hair and brown eyes. She enjoyed running in her free time and had entered several marathons.

Reed escorted her to the conference room and motioned behind her that she had his vote. Maddie and Dodson tried not to grin as Wade introduced himself and his deputies.

The team asked Reynolds the same questions and shared the same information they had with Odom. When the interview was over, Reed gave her the necessary paperwork and information. The deputies were asked for their opinions of the applicant.

"I think she would be easy to work with, and she didn't seem to mind working nights," said Maddie.

"I was impressed with her answers, particularly since she has no experience," added Dodson.

"I think we should hire her," Reed said with a twinkle in his eye.

Wade jokingly rolled his eyes at Reed, "I don't know how much work you'll get done if we hire her."

"On second thought, we don't want to hire her," Reed replied.

"Why not?" asked Maddie.

"I can't ask her out if we're working together," answered Reed.

"That's true," Wade said as he remembered how difficult it was for him while Lizzie worked with the department.

The team had a short break before the final candidate arrived for her interview. Marina Gonzalez was a no-nonsense woman with a stern expression and lovely brown eyes. Her long brown hair hung in a braid down her back. She had been a deputy sheriff in Comal County until her husband took a job with the state hospital in Vernon. She had lots of experience and didn't mind working overtime or at night, particularly since her husband would also be working nights.

"What do you think about Marina Gonzalez?" Wade asked.

"I like her. She has the experience to handle just about any situation that comes her way," Maddie said.

Reed and Dodson shook their heads in agreement.

"I liked her, too. I liked them all," Wade said as he scratched his head.

"Which ones do you want to hire now?" asked Dodson.

"I don't know. It's a tough decision," Wade said and stared at the floor. After standing silently for a moment, he said, "You'll be working with them more closely than I will, especially in the beginning. I'd like each of you to list the applicants in order from first choice to last and your reasons for that ranking. I'd like to have those before you leave today. I'll let you know my decision after I've looked over your choices."

"Yes, sir," the deputies replied in unison.

The deputies quickly had the applicants for deputy sheriff ranked as requested and placed the papers on Wade's desk. He would have liked to have had input from Baker and Lodge as well, but he knew that wasn't possible. He ranked the applicants himself before reading his deputies' opinions.

Wade called his deputies into his office to announce his decision. "I've made my own evaluations and looked over yours. We didn't rank everyone in the same order, but it is unanimous that we hire Marina Gonzalez and Clint Odom first. Dashleigh Reynolds ranked third with all of us primarily due to her lack of experience. If the county commissioners approve hiring another deputy, we'll hire Reynolds as well."

"When will they be asked to start?" Maddie asked.

"I hope they can start Monday. It shouldn't take them more than a week to get all of the paperwork and their physicals done. I'll call them and let them know we've made a decision," Wade replied.

Odom and Gonzalez were pleased to be offered the positions and agreed to report to work the following Monday. Wade dreaded making the last phone call, but he knew he had no choice.

"Hello," Dashleigh answered.

"Miss Reynolds, this is Sheriff Wade Adams."

"Oh, hello, Sheriff. How are you?"

"I'm well. I've called to tell you that I have some good news and some bad news."

"Give me the bad news first, please."

"The other two applicants have more experience, so I've decided to hire them first," Wade informed her.

"Do you have any suggestions as to how I can gain experience if no one will hire me because I have no experience?" she asked.

"I understand your frustration," Wade replied. "There is still some good news. If the county commissioners approve hiring another deputy, you'll be hired at that time."

"That's better than thanks, but no thanks," she said. "How long do you keep applications on file?"

"I keep qualified applications indefinitely, and you're qualified," Wade answered. "You wouldn't have gotten an interview otherwise."

"That's good to know. Will I need to withdraw my application if I accept another position?"

"I'd appreciate it if you'd let me know, but you don't have to withdraw your application. I'll keep it on file and make a note if you accept another job."

"I've applied in several places and have had a few interviews. I'll let you know if I take a job, but I would like to keep my name in the hat with your department."

"Consider the job yours if you want it the next time we have an opening," Wade assured her.

"I will. Thank you, Sheriff."

Shortly after the sheriff and his deputies returned to their normal routines, a paunchy man marched into the office. He appeared to be in his mid-forties. His thinning hair was combed over in a failed attempt to hide his balding head. He asked to see Sheriff Adams.

"May I ask what this is in reference to?" Reed asked.

"I'm Graham Shaffer, and I have an appointment."

"Have a seat, Mr. Shaffer; I'll see if he's available," Reed said as he rose from his desk.

The attorney sat down impatiently as Reed walked slowly toward Wade's office. Reed tapped on the door and waited.

"Come in," Wade's voice called from inside.

"Mr. Shaffer is here to see you. Are you ready for him?"

Wade sighed, "As ready as I'll ever be. Show him in."

"Yes, sir."

Wade stood as the attorney approached his door. "Mr. Shaffer, I'm Sheriff Adams. Won't you sit down?"

"Thank you, Sheriff," answered the attorney.

"What did you want to see me about?"

"I represent Miss Megan Ford. She feels that she was gravely mistreated while in custody here."

"I see. Why does Miss Ford feel she was mistreated?"

"Well, Sheriff," the attorney said as he smiled and leaned back in his chair, "she was physically abused while in custody. We should have a report from her physician outlining her injuries by tomorrow morning."

Wade chose to change the subject in an effort to control his temper before answering the attorney's charges. "I'm acquainted with at least the names of most of the attorneys in this area. I don't recall hearing your name before, Mr. Shaffer."

"I'm new in town, Sheriff. I opened my practice here earlier this month."

"Oh? Where are you from?"

"I have offices in the Dallas and Austin areas. I don't really like living in a big city, so I decided to open a branch office in Vernon. I wanted to escape the hustle and bustle," answered Shaffer. "My other offices are in capable hands. I plan to visit them all periodically while I establish myself here."

"Do you have many clients here?" Wade asked.

"As a matter of fact, Miss Ford is my first client. She came to see me this morning, a lovely young woman. She stated that everyone else she had consulted told her that she had no case."

Wade opened the file on his desk and handed a report to the attorney. "This is the arrest report. Tell me if you think Miss Ford has a case after you've read it."

The attorney took the report with a smug look on his face. Wade watched in amusement as the man's expression changed while he read.

"Do you have the medical reports about the injuries the officers sustained?"

Wade passed the reports across the desk without a word. The attorney read the reports and then handed them back to the sheriff and sighed.

"It appears that there is more to Miss Ford than meets the eye. Are you planning to pursue charges against my client?"

"They've already been filed."

"My client might agree to a plea deal."

"You'll have to take that up with the district attorney."

"Thank you for your time, Sheriff Adams."

"Mr. Shaffer, I've known Miss Ford for several years. You'll have your hands full if you plan to continue representing her."

"I expect you're right. Still, it might make my life a bit more exciting. Good afternoon, Sheriff Adams," the attorney said and left the office.

CHAPTER NINE

THE OLD FARM house was abandoned. An empty barn stood forty yards away. There were no neighboring houses in sight.

A battered old truck stopped in front of the house. Cacus got out and looked around cautiously. Carefully, he went to the door and knocked. The door creaked open, and Cacus peered inside.

The house appeared to have been abandoned for a very long time. A thick layer of dust covered the floor. Ragged curtains hung from dirty, broken windows. Cobwebs hung from every corner. On one side of the room were cabinets and a sink. A small table and two chairs sat on the opposite side of the room. An old refrigerator and cook stove stood nearby.

Cacus walked to a door in a corner of the room. The door led to what appeared to be the living area. A dusty old sofa sat near a window. An overturned end table lay between two chairs opposite the couch. There were dusty pictures and assorted knick-knacks around the room.

He crossed the room to yet another door and gently pushed it open. A rat scurried across the floor and under a dresser that stood near an old bed. A rocking chair sat near the only window in the room.

Cacus left the old house and walked to the barn. He opened the doors just enough to allow him to quickly slip inside. There were a few farm implements hanging from the rafters and a plow parked inside. The barn was large enough to park two or three vehicles.

Cacus watched the house for three days before moving in. At night, neighboring lights could be seen from the abandoned house. He'd need to make a few changes, but he didn't want any changes to be noticed from the outside. He didn't want anyone to know that he was there. The owner of the property might still return.

He boarded up all of the windows from the inside. He decided to use the bedroom as his living area. He'd leave the rest of the house as he found it. After putting away his belongings and supplies, he sat down to write in his journal.

May 26, 2015

This is the perfect place for me to stay. My pickup will fit easily inside the barn if I move the plow out of the way. There's plenty of room for my supplies. I'd considered moving in permanently, but that would be risky. Someone might notice frequent activity. Still, it would be worth the risk if the house had power and water.

I've managed to create a number of masterpieces. I enjoyed the way the dry grass and wheat stubble burned. My favorite work so far was the wheat field ready for harvest.

There are a few wheat fields that haven't been harvested, but the giant is bored with those. It's time now to find a new canvas.

Cacus closed his journal and gathered the supplies he needed for his next masterpiece.

* * *

Megan Ford threw her cell phone across the room and screamed. Her mother, Roxanne, hurried out of the kitchen to see what was happening.

"Megan! What on earth?" she asked with concern.

"That was my lawyer. He said that I don't have a case and that I should consider making a plea deal. He's going to try to arrange one," Megan replied angrily.

"Did you tell me the truth about Saturday night?"

"Of course, I did, Mother. You know me."

"Uh huh," Roxanne replied warily. "When will Mr. Shaffer know about a plea deal?"

"He has a meeting with the district attorney tomorrow. He said he'd let me know afterward."

Roxanne Ford was glad to be home the next day after a long shift at work. She was about to pour herself a glass of iced tea when the phone rang. She immediately went upstairs to Megan's room after the phone call ended. She was annoyed to find Megan still in bed.

"Megan, Mr. Shaffer is on his way here to talk to you."

"I don't want to see him."

"Megan Ford, you get out of that bed right now!" Roxanne said sternly as she yanked the covers off the bed.

"Okay, okay; I'm up," Megan said as she sat up in bed and stared at her mother. "I'm not a child anymore, Mother."

"Then you should stop acting like a child," Roxanne replied angrily and left the room.

Roxanne was answering the knock at the front door when Megan strolled down the stairs.

"Come in, Mr. Shaffer."

"Thank you, Mrs. Ford. Good afternoon, Megan."

"I understand you have news for me," Megan replied sharply.

"Yes, I do. I'm quite pleased to have arranged a plea deal that I believe you'll both appreciate."

"Won't you sit down, Mr. Shaffer," Roxanne said.

"Thank you," the attorney replied while staring at Megan.

"Mr. Shaffer, what kind of deal were you able to arrange?" asked Megan.

"Please, call me Graham."

"What did you find out, Graham?" Megan asked with irritation.

Roxanne listened carefully and glared at her daughter as the attorney explained the charges against Megan and her possible sentence. The deal he had managed to make with the district attorney wasn't much more than a slap on the wrist.

"That's wonderful, Mr. Shaffer. I don't know how we'll ever thank you. Isn't that right, Megan," Roxanne said as she looked at her daughter with a raised eyebrow.

"Yes, thank you so much, Graham," Megan said with a forced smile.

"You'll still have to appear before the judge and enter a guilty plea to the lesser charges. That's scheduled for Friday morning at ten. I'll meet you at the courthouse at nine-thirty."

"Why do I have to go to court? I thought everything was arranged," Megan said with a frown.

"It isn't official until you make your plea in court," Graham said. "I must be going now. I'll see you at the courthouse."

"Thank you again, Mr. Shaffer," Roxanne said as she escorted him to the door, and Megan returned to her room.

To Roxanne's relief, Megan was on her best behavior while in court later that week. However, her behavior deteriorated when they returned home. Megan slammed the passenger door of her mother's car and stomped up the steps to the house. She stood by the front door, tapping her foot as Roxanne made her way onto the porch and unlocked the door. Megan stomped into the house and flopped onto the couch.

"Megan, I don't know why you're so upset," Roxanne said.

"It wasn't supposed to happen that way! It was humiliating! I was supposed to get off scot-free! I should have found a better lawyer!" Megan shouted.

Roxanne stared at her youngest daughter. "Mr. Shaffer did an excellent job for you, Megan. He was able to convince the district attorney that you didn't know what you were doing because you were drunk. You were facing felony assault charges in addition to that charge for driving under the influence. Your sentence could have been as much as ten years for assaulting those two officers. I think you got off easy. The fine you've been ordered to pay could have been much more. Doing community service will only cost you a little time."

"I still think a better lawyer would have managed to bring charges against them and gotten me off," Megan insisted.

"Another lawyer wouldn't have represented you free of charge," Roxanne pointed out as she left the room.

Megan continued to pout while her mother made dinner. She reluctantly went to the table when Roxanne sat down to eat.

"Connie and Leah are going to be here later this evening," said Roxanne. "Will you be here to help us sort things out?"

"I guess so. I still don't understand why we have to move."

"I'm not able to take care of this big old house anymore. I need a smaller place with lower expenses. I can save more for retirement if I make the move now."

"What about what I want?" Megan asked angrily.

"Megan, I didn't mind helping after your divorce, but things have changed. You're thirty-two-years-old. You've got a decent job and can afford your own place now."

"You're kicking me out?" Megan shouted.

"You can stay with me as long as you need to, but I can't afford to support you. If you stay with me, you'll have to pay your share."

"But Mom," Megan began.

"No buts. It's time for you to grow up. You have to start taking responsibility for yourself and your own actions."

Megan stared at her mother open-mouthed for a moment before stomping up the stairs. She sulked in her room until her sisters arrived.

Megan's older sisters, Leah and Connie, arrived in time for dinner. They had their father's brown eyes and brown hair, while Megan had her mother's blonde hair and blue eyes. All of the Ford women had hour glass figures that brought them a lot of masculine attention.

"When are you going to put the house on the market?" asked Connie.

"The realtor said that I need to move out as much personal stuff as possible so that potential buyers can picture themselves living here. I'm hoping to get it on the market by the first of July."

"We'd better get started early then," Leah said.

"Where do you want to start, Mom?" asked Connie.

"I thought we could start down here and work our way up to the attic," Roxanne suggested.

The four women set to work early the next morning. After the attic had been emptied and swept out, they decided to relax before dinner. Megan accidentally knocked one of the boxes over as she came down the stairs. The contents spilled across the floor. She began picking up the old photographs and newspaper clippings. She carried the box into the living room and handed a photo to her mother.

"Mom, which one of us is this with Daddy?"

Roxanne took the photo and paled.

"Mom, are you all right?" asked Leah.

Roxanne took a deep breath before saying, "Yes, I'm fine. It's just...I'd forgotten all about this picture."

"What's wrong, Mom?" Connie asked with concern.

Roxanne stared at the photo as Megan placed the box on the floor beside her. The girls sat and looked at their mother with worry.

"I should have told you this a long time ago. I could never seem to find the right time or the right way to bring it up." Roxanne took a deep breath before continuing. "The baby on your father's lap... is his son."

"We have a brother?" Connie asked in astonishment.

"Yes, your father had an affair with this boy's mother."

"What happened to him?" asked Leah.

"I don't know. Your father told me that the woman moved away shortly after this photo was taken. As far as I know, he never heard from her again. I don't even know their names."

"How old would he be now?" asked Megan.

"I'm not sure. If I remember correctly, you were four or five years old at the time he was born," Roxanne said and took another deep breath.

Leah took her mother's hand and said, "That would make him twenty-seven or twenty-eight years old."

"Yes, I suppose it would," replied Roxanne. "There are some old newspaper clippings in that box too. I need to tell you about them."

"Go ahead, Mom," Connie said encouragingly.

Tears ran down Roxanne's cheeks as she began the tale, "I told you when your father died that he had suddenly been very sick and died in the hospital. That isn't what happened." Roxanne stood up and paced back and forth before continuing, "I can't think of an easy way to tell you this, so I'll just say it. Your father died in jail."

"In jail?" Leah asked.

"Why was he in jail?" asked Megan.

"There were a lot of fires here at that time. Even the place where your father worked burned down, and he had to find a new job."

"I think I remember that," said Leah.

"It was during that time that your father began acting strange. He'd leave and be gone for hours with no explanation. I had no idea where he'd been or why he had gone. That went on for two or three months. I thought he was having another affair. You were all at summer camp when I decided to confront him. Before I had the chance, two sheriff's deputies arrived with a warrant for your father's arrest. They believed he had been responsible for setting the latest fire."

"He wasn't, was he?" Megan asked. "He couldn't have been."

"I didn't believe it either. I arranged for an attorney and went to see your father at the jail," Roxanne said with tears streaming down her face. "I never would have believed he could have done such a thing, but he confessed."

"He confessed?" Leah asked in disbelief.

"He was charged with only one count of arson, but he confessed to every one of them," said Roxanne as she wiped the tears from her face.

"How did he die? Was he sick?" asked Connie.

"He hung himself," replied Roxanne.

"Why did he do that?" asked Megan in a whisper.

"I don't know. I've wondered that for years. The last thing he said to me was, 'Tell my girls that I'm sorry.' He died later that night."

"Maybe he did it so we could have his life insurance," suggested Leah.

"There was no life insurance. No retirement. Nothing to help us financially," Roxanne told them.

"Why didn't you sell this place then?" Connie asked.

"I didn't want to tear your world apart any more than it had been already. I did my best to make your lives as normal as possible."

"How have you dealt with this alone all these years?" Leah asked as she hugged her mother.

"I had to be strong for my girls," Roxanne replied quietly,

That evening, while alone in her room, Megan read each of the newspaper clippings carefully. She couldn't believe that the man she remembered could have possibly been responsible for those fires. She was certain he hadn't committed suicide. All she had to do was find a way to prove it.

Megan woke up early the next morning. She got up and dressed quickly to join her mother and sisters downstairs.

"What's the plan for today?" Megan asked.

"Connie and I have to go home this evening," said Leah. "We thought we'd go through all of the forgotten treasures we found and then go out for a nice lunch together."

Roxanne's daughters treated her to lunch at her favorite Mexican food restaurant after they had sorted through all of her unwanted items. Graham Shaffer approached them as they were eating.

"Hello, ladies. How are you this fine afternoon?"

"Quite well, Mr. Shaffer," answered Roxanne. "These are my daughters, Leah and Connie."

Pleasantries were exchanged before Graham asked Megan if he could speak with her privately. Megan followed him outside the restaurant.

"Megan, I'm sorry to interrupt your lunch," Graham stammered. "I suppose I should have phoned you instead, but I saw you as I was leaving..."

"Is there something about my case that we need to talk about?" interrupted Megan impatiently.

"I'm proposing a strictly social appointment. Will you have dinner with me tomorrow evening?" the attorney replied with a blush.

"Oh, I see," Megan said in surprise. "Isn't there a rule about socializing with clients?"

"Your case is closed, and technically I no longer represent you."

Megan stared at him a moment and was about to deliver a scathing retort. She reconsidered when an idea flashed through her mind. Instead, she said, "Yes, I'll have dinner with you."

Graham was delighted, "Wonderful! I'll pick you up at seven tomorrow evening."

"I'll see you then," Megan said and flashed him her best smile before rejoining her family.

"Was that about your case?" Roxanne asked with worry.

"No, it wasn't," Megan answered, obviously pleased with herself. Her plan was already taking shape in her mind. "I have a date."

CHAPTER TEN

NATE AND JOYCE TUCKER had a wonderful trip. They had spent the weekend with their children and grandchildren. It was the celebration of their granddaughter Aaren's high school graduation. Her graduation gift from her parents, Aubrey and Troy Green, was a trip for the entire family to Six Flags over Texas and a Texas Rangers baseball game in Arlington.

"Nate, my phone is dead. I guess I took too many pictures. Is yours charged?" Joyce asked.

"No, you killed my battery texting all those pictures to me," he said jokingly.

"I guess I'll have to wait to call Aaren until we get home."

"Why do you need to call Aaren? We saw her less than three hours ago."

"I know," replied Joyce. "I wanted to congratulate her and tell her how much we love her one more time. We may not see her very much when she starts college in the fall."

Nate reached across the seat of the truck and took his wife's hand. She smiled and squeezed his hand lovingly as she fought back tears.

"Is that smoke?" Nate asked aloud as he stared out the windshield.

"I think so. It looks like it isn't far from our place," Joyce answered with concern.

Nate stepped on the gas and hurried toward their house. He sped through Lockett and turned north onto Farm to Market Road 2073. There was no doubt about it. The fire was on their land. The setting sun made the grayish-white plumes of smoke look particularly ominous. He knew it was just a matter of time until that smoke turned black as it began to burn structures and equipment in addition to the dry grass.

As they drove closer, they were able to see the source of the smoke. A row of round alfalfa bales were stacked at the edge of the pasture. They were all engulfed in flames. The fire had already spread to the grass in the pasture. The west wind fanned the flames and kept the blaze moving quickly.

"Joyce, get in the house and call the fire department. I'll open the gate and try to get the cows out of the pasture before the fire gets to them," Nate directed.

Joyce hurried inside while Nate drove toward the gate. He reached it just as the wind shifted and fanned the smoke and flames toward him. He parked the pickup nearby and hoped that the few cattle in that pasture would run to it as they did at feeding time.

Nate covered his face with one arm to protect himself from the heat and smoke. It was difficult to see and breathe. He struggled to open the gate. The latch was stuck again. He had to use both hands as he tried with all his might to break it free. He coughed and cursed himself for not fixing it when he had the time.

Finally, the latch gave way. The sudden release caused Nate to fall as the gate swung open. Before he could move out of their path, he was trampled by some of the livestock as they ran through the opening.

Nate tried to get to his feet, but he fell immediately back to the ground. He could see the fire roaring only a few yards away. He knew he had to get out of the fire's path. He moved as quickly as he could, but the fire moved faster than he could crawl. He cried out in pain when the flames ignited his jeans. He began to roll on the ground as best he could in an attempt to get away from the flames and put out the fire that seared his legs.

Joyce ran out of the house, prepared to battle the blaze with all the wet towels she could carry. She watched in horror as her husband rolled on the ground. She quickly ran to him and smothered the fire with the towels before trying to help him get up.

"Joyce! Get… out of… here! Leave me! I can't… walk!" Nate said as he gasped for breath.

"I'm not going anywhere without you! Let me help you!"

"I… can't… get…up!"

Without another word, Joyce wrapped her arms around her husband's chest and tried to lift him. He tried to get to his feet, but his injuries were too severe. He screamed in pain and fell back to the ground.

"Go… leave… me!"

"No!" screamed Joyce as tears ran down her face.

She wrapped her arms around his chest again. It took every ounce of strength she had to drag him to safety. There was nothing more she could do. The fire was too big for her to battle alone. She was thankful that her husband and the cattle were out of harm's way for the time being.

Joyce sat on the ground cradling her husband's head in her lap. She sang his favorite hymn as she watched a fiery whirlwind dance toward their home.

"Wait! Who is that?" she asked. "Nate, someone's coming to help!" She began to giggle with relief when she saw their neighbors drive into the yard with a spray rig full of water.

"Joyce, are you all right?" her neighbor D'Anne asked as she ran to her side.

"I'm okay, but Nate's hurt," she replied. "I called the fire department. They should be here soon."

"I'll call them and see if they're close. Jeff is going to use his rig to try to protect the house," she said. She dialed the number on her cell phone and informed the dispatcher that an ambulance would be needed as well. As she ended the call, she said, "Joyce, is someone else here?"

"No one. Why?"

"I thought I saw someone near the house," she said as she looked toward the house again. "I'll wait with you until the ambulance gets here. Do you need anything? What can I do for you?"

"I don't know. I can't seem to think straight right now."

Nate was struggling to breathe and moaning in pain when the fire department and ambulance finally arrived. He was given oxygen immediately and taken directly to the hospital with his wife by his side.

Joyce paced in the waiting area while her husband was being treated. She had already called her son and daughter to tell them what had happened. They joined her at the hospital and watched her pace.

"Mom, please sit down and rest. You must be exhausted," said her daughter, Aubrey.

"I can't sit still," she replied as she made another lap.

"There's Dr. Hughes," said Jason as he stood.

Joyce rushed toward the doctor and asked, "How is he?"

"Both of Mr. Tucker's legs are broken. He has three broken ribs, and there are some serious cuts and bruises," Dr. Hughes informed them. "He has second and third-degree burns on both legs. He could possibly survive those injures, but his lungs are severely damaged, making his condition critical. I've considered sending him to the burn unit in Lubbock, but I don't think he'd survive the trip." Dr. Hughes sighed before continuing, "I'm sorry to have to tell you this, but I recommend that the family be called."

"How long?" asked Joyce.

"I don't think he'll survive the night," Dr. Hughes said sadly.

Joyce took a deep breath and nodded, "Thank you, Doctor. May we see him?"

"Yes, of course. I'll have him moved to a room so that you can have some privacy."

They followed Dr. Hughes to the examination room and prayed for Nate as they stood by his side. The doctor looked at Joyce more closely.

"Are you burned, too?" asked the doctor while pointing at her hands.

Joyce stared at her hands and seemed to realize for the first time that she had also been injured.

"It must have happened while I was trying to help Nate," she said.

"Let's get a better look at you while we wait for your husband to be moved to a room," said Dr. Hughes as he guided her to another exam room.

Joyce's burns were relatively minor. Dr. Hughes treated and bandaged her hands before she returned to Nate's side. He had been moved to a private room where he briefly regained consciousness. He gave his family a feeble smile before going to sleep again.

"Mom, you should stay here with Dad. Aubrey and I will go to the waiting room and call the family," said Jason.

"All right. Call your aunt first. She can help you make some of the calls."

Joyce waited until her children had left the room before she allowed her tears to fall.

* * *

James and Ellen Fletcher had just crawled into bed when the telephone rang.

"Who would be calling at this hour?" Ellen asked.

"It's either a prank call or bad news," answered James as he reached for the phone. "Hello," he answered warily.

"James, this is Jason Tucker. There was a fire at the farm tonight. Dad is in Wilbarger General Hospital. He isn't expected to live through the night."

James hung his head and released a deep sigh before saying, "I'm so sorry to hear that. How is Joyce handling it?"

"She's pretty shaken up. She was burned, too, but didn't realize it until Dr. Hughes noticed. I guess we're all pretty rattled. Aubrey and I didn't notice her burns either."

"Is there anything we can do?" James asked.

"Would you mind coming to sit with us? It will take a while before family members can get here. It would mean a lot to all of us," said Jason.

"Certainly. I was planning to be there anyway," James assured him. "Is there anything else we can do?"

"Mom is covered with ash from the fire. Could you possibly bring her a change of clothes?"

"Of course. We'll be there as soon as possible," said James before ending the call.

"What's wrong?" asked Ellen as she got out of bed.

"Nate Tucker is in the hospital. They've been advised to call in the family," he said before explaining what had happened.

"Should we wake Lois and Lizzie?" Ellen asked.

"I'll tell Mom if you'll call Lizzie. They'll want to know even if they don't go with us."

Lois went to the hospital with James and Ellen. Lizzie stayed behind to care for her guests but sent her love.

The Tuckers were like family to all of them. James and Nate Sr. had been friends in high school. Nate had been at the house so often that Lois treated him as if he were her son as well. Ellen and Joyce befriended each other in elementary school. It seemed only natural that when Nate and Joyce began dating that James and Ellen would, too.

Lizzie and Jason were the same age, while Aubrey was a few years older. They both thought of Lizzie as a sister. Although the younger generation had drifted apart, the two families had been so close that many people thought they were related.

The Fletcher and Tucker families cried and prayed together as they thought about Nate's condition and his prognosis. They laughed together as they reminisced about the trouble they had gotten into when they were younger.

Nate Tucker passed away before dawn with his family and dearest friends close by.

CHAPTER ELEVEN

GRAHAM ARRIVED Monday evening promptly at seven for his date with Megan. She greeted him wearing a dress that was cut low enough to keep the unsuspecting attorney's eyes only on her.

"Oh my, you look lovely, my dear," Graham said as he eyed Megan's cleavage.

"Thank you, Graham. It was so nice of you to ask me to dinner," Megan replied sweetly.

"I thought we'd have dinner at the steakhouse if that's all right with you," he said as he escorted her to his car.

"That's perfect," she said and squeezed his arm.

This is going better than I had hoped, he thought as he closed Megan's door and walked to the driver's side.

Megan endured the expected small talk of a first date until the waitress had taken their order. She decided it was time to get to the matter she most wanted to discuss.

"Graham, may I ask you a question?"

"Certainly. What's on your mind?"

"Would it be possible for someone to read an old criminal case file?" she asked as she leaned toward her date.

"Yes, many court records are available online now. Are you concerned about someone finding your case file?"

"No, it's not that," she said with a pout. "It's about another case."

"You have more than one offense on your record?" Graham asked with surprise.

"No," Megan sighed heavily, threatening even more exposure of her cleavage. "I don't know if I should tell you this."

"You can tell me anything. Your secrets are safe with me," he said as he forced himself to look at Megan's face.

"Mother told us some very upsetting news this weekend. It seems our father was arrested and committed suicide while he was in jail," Megan said sadly.

"Oh, that's terrible."

"I was wondering if it would be possible to see the case files. There might be something there that would explain why."

"We can probably find the case online," Graham said as he patted her hand.

"I'd like to see the actual file. Daddy may have left a suicide note. If he did, I want to see it. I want to hold the note in my hands and see his handwriting. I was only eight when he died. I don't have many memories," Megan said, and to her surprise, real tears began to fall.

"I'm sure we'll be able to arrange to see that file. Where was he arrested?" Graham asked, still patting her hand.

"He was arrested here and died in the County jail," Megan said, wiping her eyes.

"I'll contact the sheriff's office first thing in the morning," Graham said as their food was served.

"Thank you, Graham," Megan sniffed. "I don't know what I would do without you."

Graham beamed at her as he cut into his steak. They were enjoying their meal when Eli and Jan Wagner entered the restaurant. Megan glared at them, but they were unaware of her presence.

"I take it that you don't care for those people," Graham said as he followed her gaze.

"Not particularly," snarled Megan.

"Who are they?" Graham asked.

Megan explained in great detail her version of her relationship with the Wagner family and Lizzie Fletcher. Graham listened and absorbed the entire story, asking pertinent questions at the right moments. Suddenly, she stopped talking. Something or someone had drawn her attention away.

The infatuated attorney turned to see what had attracted his date's attention. He watched as the man seemed to be looking for someone and then joined the very people Megan had been discussing. He turned back to Megan. He was not pleased to see the expression on her face. Megan suddenly realized that she had been staring and immediately began damage control.

"I don't understand why they've all been so mean to me," she sobbed and dabbed at imaginary tears with her napkin. "I'm sorry. I wasn't expecting him to be here. He doesn't live here anymore."

"I assume that is Drake Wagner, the man you were once engaged to marry."

Megan nodded and continued dabbing her eyes.

"Why don't we skip dessert and go for a drive? Maybe some fresh air will put them out of your mind."

"Graham, you're so good to me," she said.

Graham smiled and called for the check. He walked her to the car and opened the door for her. When he started the car, the Sirius XM radio station Prime Country was playing *Old Flame* by Alabama. He turned to look at Megan, who seemed unaffected by the irony.

Megan glanced at her date. Why was he looking at her that way? It made her feel uncomfortable. "Do I have something on my face?" she asked.

"No, I was just admiring your beauty," Graham said as he drove out of the parking lot. "I thought we'd drive around town. You can show me the sights and tell me the history of Vernon."

Megan didn't know much about Vernon's history, but she showed him the schools and the most frequented places in town. They drove into the countryside as it began to get dark. They watched the sunset and looked at the stars. Megan was relieved when Graham started the car and drove back toward Vernon.

Graham parked in her drive and turned off the engine. He looked at her and put his arm on the back of the seat.

"Megan, I've had a wonderful time. I hate to cut our evening short, but I have a meeting with a new client first thing in the morning," he said as he absent-mindedly stroked her hair.

"I've had a lovely evening, too. Thank you."

"Would you like to have dinner again later this week?" he asked hopefully.

"Yes, I'd like that very much," Megan said with a sweet smile.

"Excellent! I'll walk you to your door before saying goodnight."

Megan waited for him to open the passenger door and smiled sweetly as he took her hand. They walked arm in arm to the front door. She took the key from her handbag and purposely dropped it.

"Oh! I'm so clumsy," Megan said.

"That's quite all right," Graham said as he bent to retrieve it.

Megan leaned over as Graham began to stand. He looked up to find her breasts only an inch from his nose.

"Thank you so much, Graham," Megan said as she took the key from him. "You're such a gentleman."

"You're welcome, my dear," he said as he leaned toward her for a goodnight kiss.

Megan wrapped her arms around him and gave him a kiss that would have aroused a dead man. Graham was glassy-eyed and speechless when the kiss ended.

"Goodnight," she said as she stepped inside and closed the door.

Graham stared after her with his mouth hanging open for a full minute before he recovered enough to return to his car. Megan watched from the peephole in the door and fought the urge to giggle at his reaction.

Megan was very pleased with herself when she went to bed that night. She was sure she had the unsuspecting attorney eating from the palm of her hand. He had agreed that she should go with him to see the case files. He'd manage any barriers the sheriff's department might put between her and the information she wanted. She hoped to be able to clear her father's name with Graham Shaffer's help.

Graham was equally pleased. He had fallen hard for Megan Ford. He couldn't have been happier when she asked if she could accompany him to visit Sheriff Adams. It would be a dream come true to spend the rest of his life with his beautiful Megan.

He had not been pleased with her reaction to seeing Drake Wagner. Graham needed to find a way to make her forget about Drake and fall in love with him instead.

True to his word, Graham contacted the sheriff's department as soon as he got to his office the following morning. He explained what he needed and set up an appointment. His next phone call was to Megan.

"Hello," Megan answered sleepily.

"Good morning, my dear. Did I wake you?" he asked cheerfully.

"Who is this?" Megan asked with irritation.

"This is Graham. I wanted to let you know that I've made the appointment with the sheriff's office."

"I'm sorry, Graham. I didn't recognize your voice. I guess I'm not quite awake yet," Megan replied, trying to sound pleasant.

"That's quite all right. I know it's early for you," he said.

"When is the appointment?"

"It's scheduled for Thursday afternoon at four. You won't be at work then, will you?"

"Yes, but I can skip lunch and leave early," Megan said.

"Maybe, we could have dinner and see a movie together afterward," he said.

"That would be wonderful," Megan said sweetly.

"Excellent! I'll pick you up at three-thirty."

"See you then, Graham," she said and blew him a kiss through the phone and ended the call.

Megan considered the benefits of having an attorney in her life. She had always heard that lawyers were wealthy. She wasn't attracted to the odd little man, but it might be worth her time to keep him around. Having a lawyer at her beck and call might be useful, particularly if he had money.

"Mrs. Graham Shaffer. Megan Shaffer. Mrs. Megan Shaffer," she said aloud. "I could get used to that."

She decided to string him along for a while. She looked through her closet. She'd probably need to buy a few new things to keep him interested. Unfortunately, that would take money she didn't have, especially since she'd had to pay that fine.

She needed to find a second job, and the sooner, the better. She decided it would be a good idea to start making some calls and check the classified ads in the newspaper. On second thought, that could wait until later in the week. She didn't want anything to interfere with seeing her father's file and clearing his name.

CHAPTER TWELVE

WADE ARRIVED for his appointment with Joyce Tucker ahead of schedule. He waited in his truck for a few minutes and looked at the devastation caused by the fire. He dreaded this interview. He had met the Tuckers at the Fletcher home shortly after he and Lizzie began dating. They had felt like family right away.

He had put this meeting off until after the funeral, but he couldn't wait any longer. He needed to find Nate's killer as soon as possible. He got out of his truck and walked to the door. He took a deep breath before knocking.

"Hello, Wade. Come in. Mom's in the living room," Jason informed him as he led the way.

Joyce stood and walked toward Wade. She hugged him as she said, "It's good to see you, Wade."

"It's good to see you, too. I just wish it was under better circumstances."

"Please, sit down," Joyce said as she wiped a tear from her cheek. "This is our neighbor, D'Anne Boyd."

"It's nice to meet you," said Wade.

"It's good to meet you, too."

Wade sat down beside Joyce and asked, "Do you feel like answering a few questions?"

"I don't know that I can be of any help, but I'll answer everything I can."

"Can you tell me what you saw when you got home Sunday night?" Wade asked.

Joyce described everything in detail as if she were reliving it. Wade stopped her before she began to talk about Nate.

"Did you see anything unusual or anyone who shouldn't have been here?" he asked.

"No, I didn't notice anything other than the fire," Joyce answered.

"I did," said D'Anne. "I thought I saw someone run behind the house while I was calling for an ambulance."

"Do you know who it was?" asked Wade hopefully.

"No, I couldn't see a face. I think it was a man, but I'm not sure."

"Can you describe what you saw?"

"He was slim and, I'd guess, average height. He was wearing dark pants and a dark hooded shirt. The hood was covering his head and face. I remembered thinking it was unusual to be wearing such warm clothing at this time of year."

"Will you show me where you were standing and where you saw him?"

D'Anne led Wade outside while Joyce and her family followed. She stopped and looked toward the house and then walked a little farther.

"I was standing about here," she said. "I saw him run from the edge of the pasture toward the house and behind it."

"Do you mind if I have a look around?" he asked Joyce.

"Not at all."

"I may have a few more questions after I've finished," Wade said.

"We'll be inside. Just come on in," replied Joyce.

Wade scanned the ground, searching for anything that might give him a clue to the stranger's identity. Finding nothing helpful, he turned to go back toward the house. He didn't notice the hole he stepped into until he was tumbling to the ground.

He lay face down for a moment, recovering his senses and hoping that no one saw him fall. As he got to his feet, he noticed something. A yellow object was partially hidden in the grass near the house. Wade used a pen that he kept in his shirt pocket to pick up the butane lighter. It was one that people commonly used to light candles, fireplaces, and barbeque grills.

"Hello!" Wade called as he entered the house.

"We're in the kitchen," answered Aubrey.

"Do any of you recognize this," Wade asked, holding the lighter for them to see.

"No, we have one, but it's blue," answered Joyce.

Jason and Aubrey didn't recognize the item.

"I don't either," D'Anne answered.

"It may be nothing, but I'll have the lab check it out anyway. I have one more question. I don't want to ask this, but it's necessary. Did Nate have any enemies?"

"No, I don't know of any," replied Joyce. "I don't have any either, to my knowledge."

Aubrey and Jason didn't know of any enemies that their father might have had.

"I want you to know that we'll run a background check on Nate to see if there is someone who might have been angry enough to burn your place."

"Do you really think someone targeted Mom and Dad?" asked Aubrey.

"Honestly, no. I believe it was the arsonist that's been setting grassfires all over the county. We wouldn't be doing our jobs if we didn't investigate every possibility."

"Do what you need to do to catch the person who killed my husband," Joyce said firmly.

Wade said goodbye and walked to his truck. He put the lighter in an evidence bag before driving back to town.

Wade took the lighter he had found immediately to the lab. He gave instructions to send him the results of their tests as soon as they were available. The technician handed him the lab report on the evidence brought in by the fire chief.

Wade sat at his desk reading the lab report and shook his head. They needed rain badly. There were deep crevices and cracks in the parched ground. The normally green vegetation had withered and created an abundance of fuel for wildfires. Accidental fires were always a concern at times like this, but now they had the added worry of arson.

He reached for the phone and dialed the number for Leo Gaines. It rang several times before the fire chief answered.

"Gaines," he said

"Hello, Leo. This is Wade Adams."

"Good morning, Wade. What can I do for you?"

"I have the lab report on those fires at Harrold and Lockett. I thought I'd bring your copy to you and discuss the results."

"Any time you're ready. I'll be here all day unless there's another fire."

"I'm on my way," Wade said, and he hung up.

Chief Gains had the coffee ready when Wade arrived. The two men shook hands and sat down before beginning their discussion.

"Here it is," Wade said as he handed Leo a copy of the report.

After reading it, Leo said, "This guy isn't making it easy for us."

"No, he isn't," Wade replied. "Everything he uses is cheap and easy to get. He could get his supplies anytime, anywhere, and no one would bat an eye. He could be ordering online or buying in person. I had hoped his accelerant would be something that would be easy to trace. Instead, he uses high alcohol content liquor available at any liquor store in a variety of sizes."

Leo looked at the report again. "Polyethylene is in almost every plastic bottle made. What makes your lab people think it's a water bottle?" he asked.

"It's an educated guess, and we could be wrong. One of the pieces of evidence was a piece of blue plastic with a spot of white. One of the techs happened to notice the similarity to the sport top on his water bottle and did a comparison. The plastic pieces found at the fire scenes had the same composition. The sport top has a higher density than the plastic in the bottle. The lower density plastic probably melted completely, leaving only the sport top."

"That's a lucky break," the fire chief said.

"Maybe," said Wade, "but what does it tell us?"

The two men sat processing the information in their own minds for a few minutes before the fire chief spoke.

"This arsonist may have a routine or ritual," Leo began. "He fills the plastic bottles with liquor. He can control the amount of liquid and the direction he wants much easier with the sport top. He doesn't have to carry heavy, breakable glass bottles. The smaller bottles are easier to handle and hide. Anyone who finds them would assume he plans to drink the contents. He finds a place he wants to burn and squeezes the alcohol where he wants it to go, and lights it. Then, he hides somewhere nearby so that he can watch it burn."

"That sounds plausible," Wade said.

"He might also light the stream as he is squeezing the bottle, or he might light it before throwing," added Gaines.

"That would explain finding the melted plastic at some of the scenes," observed Wade.

"Where does he get the supplies? Which stores or which websites?" asked Leo.

"That gives us a place to start looking," said Wade. "Did our firebug set the fire at the Tucker place?"

"The evidence we found looks the same as the others," Gaines answered and reached into his desk. "Your lab can confirm it."

Wade nodded as he took the evidence bag and said, "We may be dealing with murder now. We need to catch this guy before he kills anyone else."

"I know," Leo said sadly. "Nate Tucker was a good man. I can't imagine why anyone would want to kill him."

"Is this guy likely to change things up?" Wade asked.

"He might, but it isn't likely unless he can't get his usual supplies," Leo replied. "My concern is that he'll keep stepping up his game. He may decide to burn something bigger and more hazardous. His choice of places to burn is more likely to change before he changes his use of supplies."

"I'll get my people looking for his supply source as soon as I get back to the office," Wade said as he stood to leave.

Chris Quintero tapped on the frame of the open office door. "Chief, I'm sorry to interrupt. May we speak with you both?"

Chief Gaines nodded and looked at Wade with a raised eyebrow as they followed the firefighter into the next room. Every firefighter on the shift waited.

"What do you want to talk about?" asked Gaines.

Lynn McClain seemed to be the spokesman for the group. He stood and cleared his throat. "Sir, we've been talking about the fires. One thing led to another, and we realized that the fires, with the exception of one or two accidental fires, happened when we were on duty."

"Is that right?" Gaines asked with interest.

"Yes, sir," Quintero added. "Timmons checked the shift calendar against the dates of the fires."

"It's true, sir," said Judd Timmons. "All of the arson fires have happened while this shift was on duty."

"What do you think that means?" asked Wade.

"It could mean that the person responsible works the same type of shift," McClain said.

"Or it could mean that the firebug is one of us," added Tonya Balderas.

Chief Gaines looked at the faces of the firefighters. "I can see that y'all think that's the case."

"Yes, sir," Rashad Weaver said. "There aren't many jobs that have the same shifts as we do."

"Well, Sheriff. There's another point to investigate."

"I'd better get back to the office and get started," Wade said.

Chief Gaines followed Wade to his truck and said, "I'll fax a complete roster to you as soon as possible. It could be one of us. It may even be one of the people sitting in that room."

"I understand. We'll get started on it right away. I'll keep you posted," said Wade as he started his truck.

CHAPTER THIRTEEN

WADE'S STOMACH growled as he looked at his watch. It was almost lunch time. He contacted his office with the Bluetooth device in his truck.

"Sheriff's office."

"Reed, is everyone still at the office?"

"Yes, sir."

"Great. I'm going to get lunch for everyone. We need to have a working lunch today. If someone needs to leave, have them go now and be back as soon as possible."

"Yes, sir. By the way, you had a visitor this morning," Reed informed him.

"Who was it?"

"It was a woman from an agricultural insurance company. She wanted to talk to you about some of those wheat field fires."

"What did you tell her?" Wade asked.

"I told her that you were out, and I wasn't sure when you'd be back. She didn't leave a message but said she'd be back. She didn't leave her name," said Reed.

"I guess I'll worry about her if she shows up again," Wade said.

"Also, Megan Ford's attorney called. He wants to look at some old case files."

"Did he look online?"

"He said that he needed to see the actual files rather than what has been posted online."

Wade sighed, "When is he coming?"

"He'll be here at four o'clock. I vote for pizza, sir," said Reed.

"What?"

"Pizza for lunch, but it's just a suggestion."

Wade laughed, "Pizza it is, then."

Wade arrived with lunch as promised and went directly to the conference room. Reed locked the door and put the phones on hold while everyone filled their plates.

While they ate, Wade shared the information in the lab report and told them about the discussion with Chief Gaines.

"Reed, take Odom with you and visit all the stores in town that sell the supplies like those used by the arsonist. Find out if anyone has bought large amounts or is making the same purchases often," Wade said. "Maybe we'll get lucky and catch him on video buying the stuff."

"Yes, sir," the men said in unison.

"Dodson and Marina, contact the post office, Fed Ex, and UPS. Find out if they've made any large or regular deliveries of the supplies. If they have, find out where they were delivered and where they came from."

"Yes, sir," replied Dodson.

Marina nodded.

"Maddie, you'll run the office."

"Yes, sir."

"Chief Gaines is going to fax a roster of the firefighters. We need to check all of them in detail. When it comes in, Maddie and I will get to work on it. We'll need to find out where they were right before and during the arson fires," added Wade.

"Sir," Maddie said. "I heard from Lodge this morning. He's been released to return to work on Monday. He's on light duty only until his collar bone heals."

"That's good news. He can run the office, and the rest of us will be free to solve this case. I'll be here the rest of the afternoon unless something else comes up. I understand we have one appointment to see old case files. That's all I have for now. Enjoy your lunch. If you don't like pizza, blame it on Reed," Wade joked before taking a big bite.

Everyone began their assigned tasks as soon as lunch was finished. Wade was sitting at his desk reading the lab report again when Maddie tapped on his door.

"Come in, Maddie."

"Ms. Pruitt is here to see you," said Maddie. "She said she doesn't have an appointment, but she hopes you have a few minutes. This is her card."

Wade looked at the card and said, "This must be the woman that came by earlier and talked to Reed. Has the fax from Chief Gaines arrived yet?"

"Not yet."

"I was hoping it had so that I could put her off. Show her in but feel free to interrupt if the fax arrives," Wade said.

"Yes, sir," Maddie said with a grin.

Wade put the lab report he'd been reading into his desk. He stood as Maddie led the insurance investigator to his office.

"Hello, Wade," said Tiffany.

Wade could only stare in amazement.

"Wade?"

"What are you doing here?" he said when he recovered from the shock.

"I work for an insurance company. Two of our clients have filed claims to recover the losses they sustained in the wildfires. I'm here to investigate those claims," she informed him.

"Please, sit down," he said, indicating a chair. "I'm sorry about my reaction. I never expected to see you here."

"Didn't your deputy tell you I was coming?"

"He told me that a woman from an insurance company wanted to see me. I had no idea that it would be you," answered Wade.

"I should have left my name, but that wouldn't have given you a clue either. I married a man named Roger Pruitt in 2005 and moved to Breckenridge. We have an eight-year-old son together; his name is Ross. We divorced three years ago, but I kept the name of Pruitt for professional reasons."

"I see," Wade replied.

"Have you ever married?" asked Tiffany.

"No, I haven't. What do you need from me for your investigation?" Wade asked, trying to change the subject from personal to professional.

Tiffany was surprised at his abrupt return to business. "I'll need copies of your files for the wheat field fires at the Rich farm near Harrold and the Mayer farm near Lockett."

"Help yourself to some coffee. I'll get those copies for you. Maddie and I are the only ones in the office at the moment, and it looks like she has her hands full," Wade said as he left the office.

He located the files and began making the necessary copies. He was pondering how he was going to tell Lizzie about Tiffany when Maddie tapped him on the shoulder. He dropped the file he was holding and turned to face her.

Maddie tried to hide her amusement and said, "I would have done that for you."

"You were busy, and I needed some air," he said as he picked up the scattered pages from the floor.

"Who is she?"

"She's...we were...," Wade stammered, trying to find the right words. Finally, he sighed and said, "We were engaged a long time ago."

It was Maddie's turn to be surprised. She knelt to help retrieve the file and said, "What's she doing here?"

"She works for an insurance company. She's investigating some of the crop fires."

"Does Lizzie know about her?"

"Yes, I was trying to decide the best way to tell her about this visit when you ambushed me," Wade said with a grin.

Tiffany waited impatiently in Wade's office. She knew that he wouldn't be expecting to see her. It was obvious that he wasn't happy about her visit. She planned to be in town for a few days and had hoped to spend some time with Wade.

She wondered who he was seeing and how long they had been together. She vaguely remembered someone standing with him when she visited his family reunion. It was so dark that she couldn't really see the woman. She wished she knew more about her competition.

Wade finally returned with the requested copies and handed them to Tiffany as he asked, "How long are you going to be in town?"

"I'll be here for at least a week. It depends on how long it takes to wrap up my investigation," she answered with a smile. "Maybe we could have dinner while I'm here and catch up."

"I'm pretty busy right now. I'm shorthanded and looking for the person that's been setting fires all over the county. I spend what little free time I have with Lizzie."

"Who's Lizzie? Is that the woman you're dating?"

"Yes, it is. I'm not sure what you're hoping to find in your investigation. The fact is that we have an arsonist setting fires all over the county. He set both of the fires in question. His latest fire caused a death."

Lizzie was in town to shop and run errands. She thought she'd stop by the office to see Wade before driving home.

"Hi, Maddie," she said as she entered the sheriff's office. "Is Wade busy?"

"Oh...Lizzie...hi...yes...he's in the middle of a meeting with an insurance investigator," Maddie answered nervously. "I'll let him know you're here."

Lizzie was a little confused by Maddie's response but only said, "Thanks."

Wade answered the phone on his desk. He raised his eyebrows when Maddie informed him that he had a visitor. He abruptly ended the meeting.

"I'll have to cut this short. There's an urgent matter that needs my attention," he said as he stood and indicated that Tiffany should leave.

Tiffany frowned and sashayed through the office toward the main door. Lizzie watched as she exited the building. She managed to keep her anger and jealousy under control when Maddie indicated that Wade was now available. She smiled and walked directly to Wade's office, and quietly closed the door.

"Lizzie, let me explain," Wade began.

"I'm listening," Lizzie said as she plopped into the now vacant chair and crossed her legs.

"I didn't know she was in town until she walked in," Wade said as he sat down and told Lizzie everything that had transpired.

"I understand and can deal with the fact that she's here on business. I don't like it, but I'll deal with it." Lizzie told him. "I can't deal with the fact that she may be hoping to get close to you."

"That isn't going to happen," Wade assured her.

"I'm sorry; it was such a shock to see her coming out of your office," Lizzie said.

"I was just as surprised when she walked in," Wade said. "What brought you to town today?"

"I had some errands and went to see Jan and Darcie. I decided to stop by to see you before going home." Lizzie paused before continuing, "There's something that I need to tell you."

"What's wrong?" Wade asked with concern.

Lizzie took a deep breath before saying, "In light of the conversation we just had, this is a terrible time to bring it up, but…Jan told me that Drake came home to be with the family and help as much as he can since Ben Wagner had that stroke."

"How long will he be here?" Wade asked cautiously.

"Jan said that he's moved back permanently," Lizzie told him.

"I see," said Wade, obviously unhappy about the situation.

"There's one more thing," Lizzie said apprehensively. "Drake stopped to see the baby as I was leaving. We had a short conversation, no more than a minute. He was playing with Darcie when I left. I doubt that I'll see or hear from him again."

Wade sat in silence for a moment before saying, "There's nothing we can do about the two of them being in town. We'll just have to try and avoid them."

"What do you suggest?" Lizzie asked.

"I can leave instructions that I'm out of the office if Tiffany calls or comes by here. That won't be as easy for you. There's no one to run interference at the inn," Wade pointed out.

"That's true. I'll see if my folks can help with that, but I don't think he'll come to the inn. He's too busy with his dad right now. I need to get going; call me later," Lizzie said with a smile as she stood.

Wade rose and walked around the desk before kissing her and holding her tight. "You can count on it," he said.

Lizzie had no more than left the parking lot when Graham Shaffer and Megan Ford arrived. Maddie showed them to his office while Wade brought in an extra chair.

"What can I do for you?" Wade asked as he sat down.

"We would like to have access to some old case files," the attorney began. "My client, Miss Ford, would like to see the actual file pertaining to her father's arrest and subsequent death. I would like to see the file of another client. His file was not available online."

"We've been shorthanded and haven't had the time or

personnel to get many of those files uploaded," Wade explained. "Do you happen to have the case numbers?"

"Unfortunately, we don't, but we have the names and approximate dates," Graham answered. "Collin Ford was arrested during the summer of 1991. We understand he committed suicide while in custody."

"I'm sorry to hear that. My condolences, Miss Ford," said Wade.

"Thank you," said Megan as she dabbed away an imaginary tear.

"Jameson Monroe was arrested in the fall of 2002," added the attorney.

"Both of these cases were before my time," said Wade as he wrote down the information. "They're probably in the storage facility. It might take a while to find them. How soon would you like to have them?"

"As soon as possible," replied Mr. Shaffer. "I gave your deputy the information when I made the appointment. Is it possible the files have already been located?"

"I'll find out," he said to his guests as he picked up the phone and buzzed Maddie's desk. "Do you happen to know if Reed brought any case files from the storage facility?" he asked and listened to Maddie's reply. "Good, we'll get started on those right away," he said and ended the call.

"I'll check Reed's desk and be with you in a moment," he said to his guests.

"You represent Jameson Monroe?" Megan asked with a sneer. "What did he do?"

"I'm not at liberty to discuss his case," replied Graham. "Do you know him?"

"We went out a few times," Megan answered but said no more.

Wade returned a few minutes later with both files in hand. "Here they are. I'm sorry, but you'll have to make the copies yourselves. Deputy Clifton and I have some urgent business to attend to, and no one else is here."

Megan began to complain, but Graham patted her hand and said to the sheriff, "That's perfectly all right."

"Let me show you to the copy machine, and I'll leave you to it. You can leave the files with my deputy when you've finished."

"Thank you, Sheriff. We'll be out of your way as soon as possible."

CHAPTER FOURTEEN

WADE and his deputies met in the conference room later that afternoon to compare notes.

"Deputy Gordon Reed and Deputy Clint Odom, did you find out anything at the liquor stores?" Wade asked.

"The highest alcohol content liquor sold locally is Everclear. There are two types. One is a hundred-and-fifty-one proof and is more than seventy-five percent alcohol. The other is a hundred-ninety-proof at ninety-five percent alcohol. Both are sold a bottle or two at a time primarily to customers between the ages of twenty-one and twenty-five," reported Odom.

"There are others with a high alcohol content sold, but usually in small quantities. They don't keep many of those in stock because they don't sell often," added Reed.

"There aren't any regular large quantity purchases, but there are a few customers who buy smaller amounts frequently," said Odom.

"We have copies of the surveillance videos for the past two weeks from one of the stores. We haven't had the opportunity to watch those yet," Reed said.

"Why only one store?" asked Wade

"It was the only one with a working security camera," Reed replied with a smirk.

Wade shook his head, "Our perpetrator could have purchased the alcohol in another town and brought it with him. It was a long shot, but I was hoping we'd get lucky and discover large local purchases. He could be buying online. Deputy Craig Dodson and Deputy Marina Gonzalez, what did you learn in your investigation?"

"We visited with the local United States Post Office, United Parcel Service, and Federal Express," Gonzalez began. "None of them have had any large shipments of alcohol to deliver."

"UPS does have an occasional small delivery," Dodson reported. "There is one address they deliver to frequently. We visited the person at that home. It's an elderly woman who is home bound. She believes a shot of whisky every night helps her sleep. Her son orders it for her and has it delivered to her house every couple of weeks."

"It doesn't appear likely that our firebug has his alcoholic accelerant delivered. That would lead me to conclude that he doesn't order online. He probably buys elsewhere. Deputy Maddie Clifton and I have been looking into the firefighters' backgrounds. Deputy Clifton will give the report."

"We did background checks on every member of the fire department based on the fact that some of the firefighters themselves believe that the arsonist might be one of their own. The profile given to us by Chief Gaines stated that our arsonist is likely a male between the ages of fifteen and thirty. He's probably unmarried and lives alone."

"That profile could fit a lot of people," Odom pointed out. "It fits me!"

"We'll discuss that later," said Wade with a smirk.

"Oh, but there's more," said Maddie. "He could possibly have a criminal background. He could also have issues with substance abuse and or psychological issues."

"The city does an extensive criminal background check on all new hires," said Wade. "That tells me that if our arsonist is a firefighter, he's never been caught."

"There are four members of the fire department who fall into the age range and live alone. Chris Quintero, Kanden Kyzer, Alan Nichols, and Lucas Fields," Maddie informed them.

"Kyzer doesn't fit the profile anymore," said Wade. "Unless I'm mistaken, he was recently married at the inn. He was probably on his honeymoon during some of the fires. I'll check with Chief Gaines to be sure."

"We plan to interview these three or four possible suspects before interviewing the remainder of the department," added Maddie.

"Does anyone have anything to add?" asked Wade. When no one spoke, he said, "I'd like for Reed and Odom to get started on the security camera footage. Gonzalez and Clifton will look into Nate and Joyce Tucker's background. We need to know if there are any enemies that might have set that fire. Dodson and I will interview the possible suspects from the fire department."

Reed and Odom watched two hours of footage from the security camera before Odom suddenly said, "Can you back that up?"

"What did you see?" Reed asked as he backed up the recording.

"Right there. Do you see that guy?"

"Where did he come from?" Reed pondered aloud and backed the recording up a bit more.

"He's wearing some warm clothes for this time of year," Odom pointed out.

"I don't think he wants to be noticed. See how he slipped in behind that group of guys."

"The hood is over his head, and he's keeping his face low. He doesn't want to be seen. Did he buy anything?"

Reed sped the video up to see the man in the hoodie follow the same group of guys to the cash register. He put a bottle and some cash on the counter. The cashier spoke to him, and he pulled his wallet from his pocket to show his identification. The cashier shook his head and pointed to something out of camera range. He took the bottle off the counter and pointed to the door.

"I'll bet he was underage, trying to blend in with the older men," Odom said. "I thought we were onto something for a minute."

"I did, too. I'll print this out and verify our conclusions," Reed said. "Wait, maybe we are onto something. The age range is fifteen to thirty. This kid could be our firebug. But if that's the case, he probably doesn't buy the alcohol."

"He either steals it, or someone else buys it for him," said Odom. "Didn't the Tuckers' neighbor says she saw someone wearing jeans and a hoodie?"

"I'd have to check the report to be sure, but I believe you're right," said Reed with excitement.

Odom glanced at the recording as it continued to play. "There's something familiar about that guy," he said, pointing at the screen. "His face isn't very clear, though."

Reed tried but was unable to get a good image of the man's face. They watched as he purchased a pint bottle of Bacardi 151.

"That's one of those liquors on our list," said Reed. "I wonder if he shows up on the video again."

The two deputies watched the entire recording but didn't see the man again. Reed printed the blurry image.

"Let's see if that liquor store owner can tell us about these two," said Reed.

Ten minutes later, the two deputies were interviewing the owner of the liquor store.

"This kid had one of the worst fake IDs I've ever seen. He probably didn't realize at the time that I know his daddy," said the store owner. "I doubt that he'll try that again anytime soon."

"Do you know the boy's name?" asked Reed.

"I don't know his first name, but his last name is Copeland. His dad's name is Bruce."

"Do you happen to know this man?" Odom asked.

"It's not a very good picture, is it? I've been telling my wife that we need a better security camera."

"It looks like he bought a bottle of Bacardi 151," Odom pointed out.

"I don't sell much of that stuff," said the store owner. "I don't think he's a regular customer. I haven't sold any of that liquor since then."

The deputies said thank you and went on their way. Reed looked up Bruce Copeland and found an address. A man in jeans and a t-shirt was mowing the lawn when they stopped in front of the house.

"Mr. Bruce Copeland?" asked Reed.

"Yes, what can I do for you?"

"We understand you have an underage son who recently attempted to buy alcohol. We'd like to ask him a few questions."

"Are you planning to arrest Dean for trying to buy a bottle of booze?" Copeland asked in surprise.

"No, sir. We need to talk to him about another matter," Odom replied.

"He's in the house. Do we need an attorney?"

"That's your right if you would like to have an attorney present. You're welcome to be in the room while we talk with him."

"I want to know what this is all about before I allow you to see my son," said Copeland.

"Dean was identified on a security recording from the liquor store he visited recently. His appearance in the recording matched the description of a person seen at one of the recent fires in the area."

"Are you talking about the fire that killed that farmer? You think Dean might have been responsible?"

"We don't know, but we wouldn't be doing our jobs if we didn't follow every lead."

"I'll take you to him. I know he didn't do it, but I'd like you to shake him up a little bit."

The deputies questioned Dean and verified his alibi before returning to the office. They shared their findings with the rest of the team in the conference room.

"We identified the male in the video footage as sixteen-year-old Dean Copeland," Reed began. "He was with his family at Lake Kemp at the time of the Tucker fire."

"That's good work," said Wade. "What did you find out about the Tuckers?"

"The farm was part of Mr. Tucker's inheritance when his parents' passed away," began Gonzalez. "There's a truck payment and a small amount of credit card debt. I found nothing that would indicate a financial reason for the fire."

"The Tuckers have no criminal history," said Maddie. "They've both lived in this area their entire lives and were married shortly after graduating high school. There's nothing to indicate an issue with neighbors or business associates."

"I didn't think there would be," said Wade and nodded at Dodson.

"We interviewed the three firefighters who fit the profile. Chris Quintero works on the B shift and can account for his whereabouts before and during the fires. Lucas Fields was working a second job during all of the fires. He's been working nights at the hospital when he's not on duty with C shift at the fire department."

"That leaves us with Alan Nichols," said Wade. "He works the A shift. He can't or won't account for his whereabouts for any of the fires. That makes him our prime suspect."

"Do you think Nichols is hiding something or being obstinate?" asked Reed.

"I believe it's a bit of both," answered Wade. "I have the feeling that he likes to know things but doesn't share that information unless it will benefit him in some way. He may be hiding something. I don't know if he's protecting himself or another person. He may be protecting some piece of information."

"I've dealt with him before," Dodson said. "He's the kind of guy who says what he thinks a person wants to hear. He uses any information he gains against that person. He acts like a friend the entire time he's planning to stab someone in the back."

"We'll need some concrete evidence before the judge will give us a search warrant. We'll interview the remainder of the fire department tomorrow. Maybe someone will have information that we can use."

CHAPTER FIFTEEN

CACUS SAT IN THE DINGY, run-down farmhouse he had found and wept. He hadn't been able to eat or sleep since the last fire. When he had learned that the farmer had died, he went to his safe house and took out his journal.

June 5, 2015

I don't know what to do! I never meant to hurt anyone! Why did they have to come home? That poor man wouldn't have been burned if they had only stayed away. He should have stayed in the truck instead of trying to save the animals. He should have driven away.

It wasn't my fault. It was his fault! No one had been there all weekend. How was I to know they would come home?

No one will believe me. The sheriff and the fire department will try harder to find me now. I overheard some farmers talking about watching for strangers around their property.

Maybe, they'll stop looking for me if I stop for a while. Yes, that's what I'll do. I'll stop for a while. I'll gather more supplies. I'll choose another canvas. Maybe, I'll find a new town.

I need to be more careful. My new neighbor notices everything. I told him that I sometimes work a second job. Maybe, he'll think I've been work-ing. I need to go back now. I need news about the investigation.

Cacus closed his journal and gathered a few of his belongings. He drove away from the house, leaving a cloud of dust in his wake.

* * *

Graham Schaffer was in his office early the next morning. He wanted to get started on the case files he had copied at the sheriff's office. He'd be visiting his other offices later in the week and wanted to have these cases well in hand before he left.

He spent the morning reading through every page of Collin Ford's case. He made notes as he read each page. The attorney thought about interviewing the people mentioned in the file, but memories fade over time, and it had been almost twenty-five years since the last fire and Ford's death.

He went through the file and his notes three times. The medical report stated that there were no marks on Collin Ford's body other than those consistent with hanging. According to the transcript of the interview, Ford confessed before the questioning began. His confession had not been coerced.

Graham looked at every possible angle that might help him clear the man's name. Everything indicated that Collin Ford was, in fact, guilty.

Graham considered calling Megan right away. He dreaded telling her what he had learned. He knew she'd be disappointed. He didn't want to see his precious Megan cry, but he thought it would be best to tell her in person. He decided to tell her while they were at dinner that evening.

He put the Ford file aside and looked at Jameson Monroe's case file. The attorney wondered why Megan would have dated such a man. Monroe was arrested in 2002. He had been charged with assault with a deadly weapon. He was found guilty and sentenced to fifteen years in prison. He was released on parole four months ago. He was now being accused of a similar crime.

Jameson had admitted to Graham that he was guilty of the previous charge. He had been working a lot of late nights. One night, he decided to take off early to surprise his girlfriend. He walked in to find her in bed with another man. He went to the closet, took out his baseball bat, and beat the man as he ran for the front door.

His attorney at the time had suggested he claim temporary insanity. The judge and the jury didn't believe it. He was convicted and sent to prison.

Jameson told Graham that he had seen his former girlfriend at a local restaurant two weeks before the charges were made. He said that he didn't speak to her or go near her. He had not seen or spoken to her since then, but she was now accusing him of assault. He swore that he was innocent and could prove it. He was with another woman at the time he was to have assaulted his former girlfriend.

Graham thought it was a good sign that he hadn't yet been arrested. That would change if the police weren't able to verify his alibi soon. He needed to find out what evidence they had against Mr. Monroe in this case. He also needed to find the woman that Monroe claimed to have spent that evening with.

The woman wouldn't be easy to find. She was a female truck driver on a cross-country run. She stopped at the local truck stop for fuel and a meal. Jameson was sitting alone in a booth. There were no empty tables, so he offered to share his table with her.

They ordered their meals and talked a little about the weather and the life of a truck driver. When they had finished eating, he invited her to his apartment for the night. He thought it was about ten p.m. when they left the restaurant. She left at sunrise the next morning. Security cameras confirmed his story about leaving with the woman but nothing more.

Graham needed someone to watch that truck stop. The woman

might stop there again. He picked up the phone and dialed the number of the Vernon Daily Record. He placed a help wanted ad for immediate employment.

He then called the police department and asked if they had a photo of the woman from the security cameras. He made an appointment to pick up a copy of the photo that afternoon.

Graham arrived for his date with Megan promptly at seven. She looked lovely, and he decided to wait until the evening was over to tell her the bad news. They had a nice dinner and pleasant conversation.

He walked her to her door and kissed her goodnight before saying, "Megan, my dear, I have something that I need to tell you."

"Is it about my father's case?" Megan asked.

"Yes, yes, it is. Maybe we should sit down," he said as he led her to the porch swing.

"Tell me," she said excitedly as she sat down. "I told you he was innocent!"

"First, there was no record of a suicide note in your father's file," Graham told her. "The investigation into the incident showed that the sheriff's department followed every protocol. No one had any reason to suspect that he was suicidal."

"Of course, they'd say that. They were trying to cover up their mistakes," Megan said.

"There was one other inmate there that night. His statement confirms that everything was done that could be done," said Graham.

He took a deep breath and held her hand before he continued, "Megan, I've looked through the case file and taken into account every possible alternative. I have no doubt that your father started that fire.

"No!" Megan said. "He couldn't have!"

"He was identified by an eyewitness," continued Graham. "His fingerprints matched those found on the gas can left at the scene. He was only charged with one count of arson. There had been no evidence linking him to the previous fires. Had he not confessed, he would not have been charged with the others."

Megan contained herself while Graham talked. When he finished, she said, "That's going to make it harder to clear his name, isn't it?"

"It will be impossible," Graham told her.

"Impossible?" Megan stood. "Impossible!" she screamed. "What kind of lawyer are you?"

She picked up a vase and threw it at him. He ducked as it sailed toward his face and shattered on the wall behind him. She screamed obscenities as she pulled a hanging flower pot from the porch railing and threw it into the yard.

"You must be the worst lawyer in the state. You couldn't get me off, and you aren't able to clear my father. Where did you get your degree? The Law School of Losers and Idiots! Have you ever won a case?"

Graham was stunned by her reaction. He knew she'd be upset but hadn't expected this tirade. He was momentarily speechless.

"Well? What good are you?" Megan said as she glared at him.

"Megan, I'm sorry. I know you're disappointed, but there's nothing more I can do."

"I never want to see you again," Megan screamed as she kicked a cushion off of the porch swing.

"Megan, please…," he began as she flung a garden gnome in his direction and stomped into the house.

CHAPTER SIXTEEN

"GOOD MORNING, SHERIFF," Lodge said with a grin as Wade entered the office.

"Good morning. It's good to have you back," Wade replied. "Are you sure you're able to work?"

"It might be a challenge with this sling, but I was ready to come back when I was released from the hospital," Lodge joked. "My release from the doctor and the mail are on your desk."

"It's my understanding that Baker is due back next week. The two of you will be running the office in shifts as long as you're on light duty," said Wade.

"That's fine with me. It's nice to have something to do instead of lying on the couch watching old movies. That sounds like fun until you can't do anything else," said Lodge.

"Have you met our new hires?" asked Wade.

"I met Gonzalez when I came in this morning. I haven't met Odom yet."

"He's been working closely with Reed and Dodson on this case. You'll probably meet him sometime today."

Wade began to walk away but stopped and said, "Send Maddie, Dodson, and Reed in to see me when they get here, please."

"Yes, sir," answered Lodge.

Wade walked to his office, feeling as if a weight had been lifted from his shoulders. He wasn't sure he'd know how to handle a fully staffed department, but he was looking forward to it.

He still hadn't heard from the county commission about hiring another deputy. He picked up the phone and called Wendell Johnson. The commissioners would be meeting in a couple of days, and he wanted to make sure the department's needs were on the agenda.

"Mr. Johnson, this is Wade Adams," he said when the phone was answered.

"Hello, Sheriff. What can I do for you?"

"I wanted to touch base with you again about hiring another deputy."

"Oh yes, how are the two new hires working out?"

"They're doing fine. They're both a good fit for our department. Have you given any more thought to my request to hire the third applicant as well?"

"I have it on the agenda for the meeting this week. I can't make any promises, but I don't expect any opposition from the other commissioners," Johnson assured him. "Have your injured deputies returned to work yet?"

"Lodge came back today, and Baker is due back next week. They'll both be on light duty and running the office for a while," answered Wade. There's something else that I'd like for the commission to consider."

"Oh?"

"I'd like to recommend that Deputies Clifton, Dodson, and Reed each receive a commendation. They've all been working particularly hard. They've voluntarily been working double shifts and on their days off to keep the department running smoothly during our recent dilemma. I believe that they deserve some official recognition for it."

"I agree. I'll put your recommendation on the agenda."

"Thank you, Mr. Johnson," said Wade as he ended the call.

Wade sat at his desk and read Lodge's medical release. Satisfied that everything was in order, he filed it away. He noticed an unusual envelope while going through the mail. There was no postage or postmark and no return address. Only the words *Sheriff Adams* were scrawled across the front.

"Did you want to see me, Sheriff?" Maddie asked through the open door.

"Yes, come in and have a seat," Wade said, indicating the chair across from him. "When is your next scheduled day off?"

"I'm scheduled for Thursday, but I can work if needed," answered Maddie.

"No, Deputy Clifton," Wade began. "I don't want you to work Thursday. I appreciate how hard you've been working. You've kept this office running and sacrificed your own time to do it. Now that Lodge is back and our new hires are trained, I want you to take some extra time off."

"Thank you, sir," Maddie said happily.

"Dodson and Reed will also get some extra time off, but you have the first choice. I want you and Drew to decide what weekend you want and put it on the calendar. We'll be fully staffed when Baker comes back next week. Hopefully, there won't be any need for you to work so much again," said Wade with a smile.

"This means a lot, Wade. Thank you. I'll call Drew right away," Maddie said as she left the room.

Wade walked to Lodge's desk and showed him the envelope, and asked, "Was this in today's mail?"

"It must have been slipped under the door last night. It was on the floor when I got here this morning. I thought it was strange, but I got busy and didn't think about it again."

"I think I'd better open this in the lab," Wade said.

Wade took the standard precautions in the lab before he carefully opened the overstuffed envelope. Inside were copies of two obituaries, nothing more. One was for the recently deceased Nate Tucker, and one was for a man that Wade didn't know. Wayne Bowers, a former Vernon resident, died six months earlier in Wichita Falls. *Was someone trying to tell him something? Were the two deaths connected?*

He left the envelope and its contents in the lab after making a copy of Bower's obituary. He asked that they be checked for prints and anything else that might tell him who sent it.

He needed to know more about the death of Wayne Bowers. He returned to his office and made several phone calls to the Wichita County Sheriff's Department and the Wichita Falls Police Department. He eventually learned that Mr. Bowers had been killed in a car accident. There had been no reason to suspect it was anything other than an accident.

Wade couldn't shake the feeling that someone was sending him a message. He called Joyce Tucker to make sure she was home before driving to see her.

"I'm sorry to bother you again," Wade said when Joyce opened the front door. "I wanted to show you this in person."

"What is it?"

"Does the name Wayne Bowers mean anything to you?"

"No, I don't remember hearing that name before."

Wade showed her the obituary with the man's photo, "Does he look familiar?"

Joyce studied the photo before saying, "No, I don't know him. Was he killed in a fire, too?"

"No, ma'am. He was killed in a car accident before Christmas."

"What does he have to do with Nate?"

"I don't know. I was hoping you could tell me."

Wade said goodbye and drove back to town.

Tiffany drove into the parking lot as Wade got out of his truck. He had managed to avoid seeing her again, but there was no way he would be able to avoid her this time. Tiffany smiled and waved.

"Hello, Tiffany," said Wade with a reluctant smile.

"I'm so glad to finally catch up with you," she said as she got out of the car. "There's someone I want you to meet." She opened the passenger door, and a young boy stared up at Wade.

"This is my son, Ross," she told Wade. "He pretends to be a sheriff all of the time. I thought it would be nice for him to meet a real sheriff."

Wade smiled down at the young man and shook his hand, "It's nice to meet you, Sheriff Ross."

"Are you a real sheriff?" the boy asked.

"Yes, I am," answered Wade.

"My sitter had to leave town for a family emergency at the last minute," Tiffany informed him. "I had no choice but to bring Ross with me. I told him that if he was good that I'd bring him to meet a real sheriff. I hope you don't mind."

"I never turn down a meeting with a fellow sheriff," he said. "Would you like a tour of my office?"

"Yes, sir," Ross replied with a huge grin on his freckled face.

Wade led Tiffany and Ross inside. Maddie gave the boy a toy badge that they kept on hand for such occasions. The tour ended in Wade's office. Ross climbed into Wade's lap and asked about everything he could see. Wade couldn't help but smile at the little boy's enthusiasm.

Wade noticed the time and realized that Lizzie would soon be there for their lunch date. "Sheriff Ross, I have an important meeting to attend. I'll escort you out."

"Are you going to catch a bad guy?"

"Probably not this time," laughed Wade.

"Thank you for taking the time to show us around, Sheriff Adams," said Tiffany as they stood beside the car. She indicated that her son should say thank you as well.

"Thank you, Sheriff," said Ross as he shook Wade's hand.

Lizzie was getting out of her jeep when she noticed Wade beside his truck. She waved, but he didn't respond. As she got closer, she saw Tiffany and a little boy get into a car parked beside Wade's truck and drive away. She couldn't help but notice the wistful look on Wade's face.

Lizzie felt the green-eyed monster of jealousy crawl up her back. She managed to control her temper as she said, "Hi, sweetheart."

Wade turned and smiled at her, "Hi, baby."

As he pulled her into a hug, he could see the fire in her vivid blue eyes and realized that he was in big trouble.

"Lizzie, let me explain," he began.

"'I'll avoid Tiffany,' you said. 'I'll have my calls screened and be out of the office when she shows up,' you said."

"I have avoided her," Wade answered angrily. "She drove up behind me. I didn't know she was here until it was too late.

"You didn't seem to be in a hurry to get away from her," Lizzie retorted.

"She brought her son with her. He wanted to meet a real sheriff."

"I suppose you just happened to have that toy badge for him in your pocket."

"I gave him a tour of the office, Lizzie. What was I supposed to do?"

"Avoid Tiffany! That's what you're supposed to do!"

Lizzie went back to her jeep and drove away.

"Fine, I'll just have lunch alone!" Wade shouted as he got into his truck and slammed the door.

CHAPTER SEVENTEEN

LIZZIE'S ANGER hadn't subsided by the time she arrived at the inn. She got out of her jeep and slammed the door. She mumbled under her breath as she went inside the house.

"That was a quick trip," Lois said as she turned and saw the expression on her granddaughter's face. "What's wrong, Lizzie?"

"Wade and I just had a huge fight," Lizzie replied angrily.

"I'm sorry, honey," Lois said as she hugged Lizzie.

"I'm so mad at him. I haven't felt like this since..." Lizzie stopped.

"Let's sit down, and you can tell me all about it."

Lizzie obeyed and told her grandmother everything that had happened. When she had finished, she asked, "What am I going to do, Granny?"

"Do you trust Wade?"

"I trust him, but I don't trust her," Lizzie said emphatically.

"That makes no sense at all."

"Why not?" asked Lizzie in surprise.

"You either trust him, or you don't."

"But...," Lizzie began.

"There are no buts, Lizzie," said Granny. "If you trust Wade, then you have to trust him no matter who tries to get his attention. He isn't some weakling who is easily led by the opposite sex. He's a grown man responsible for his own actions. No woman can sway him if he doesn't want to be swayed."

Lizzie was silent as her grandmother continued.

"I know it's hard for you to trust after your experiences with Drake and Rob. Don't judge Wade based on those past relationships. He's a different person. Trust him until he gives you a reason not to."

"What if he still loves Tiffany? What if he chooses her? What will I do then?" asked Lizzie with tears in her eyes.

"You'll pick up the pieces just like you've done before and get on with your life."

Lizzie thought about her grandmother's words. "I know you're right. Part of me wants to walk away, and part of me wants to work things out. Either way, I'll have to deal with this situation. Thank you, Granny."

"Come on," Lois said with a grin. "I'll help you unload the jeep before I leave."

"Oh no! I forgot all about shopping."

Lois laughed, "It sounds like you need to make another trip to town."

Lizzie grinned, picked up her keys, and hurried to the jeep. She returned two hours later. She gasped when she went into the kitchen. There on the counter was a vase with two dozen long-stemmed yellow roses. There was no card attached, but she was sure she knew who had sent them. She smiled as she dialed Wade's number.

"Sheriff's office, Deputy Lodge speaking."

"Hi, Brandon. This is Lizzie. It's nice to hear your voice again. How are you?"

"Hello, Fletcher! I'm doing great."

"Is Wade busy? I couldn't get him on his cell."

Lodge chuckled, "His cell is out of service at the moment. Let me see if he's available. Hold on."

"Adams," Wade answered abruptly.

"Hi, Wade. Is this a bad time?" Lizzie asked.

"It is if you're going to yell at me again," said Wade.

"I didn't call to yell. I want to apologize for my behavior this morning and for ditching you at lunch. I'm sorry that I lost my temper," said Lizzie. "Why don't you come for dinner tonight so that I can try to make up for lunch? I'll make all of your favorites."

"That sounds like a plan. What time?"

"Whenever you're ready. Thank you for the flowers. They're gorgeous."

"What flowers?"

"The two dozen roses that you sent."

"I didn't send flowers."

"You didn't?" asked Lizzie because she didn't know what else to say. "There was no card, so I naturally assumed they were from you."

"Is that why you called to apologize?" Wade asked with irritation.

"No, I was going to apologize anyway." Lizzie retorted.

"I'm sorry; I don't want to fight again," Wade sighed wearily.

"I don't either. Will I still see you for dinner?"

"I'll be there."

The call ended, and Lizzie stared at the flowers. *Who could have sent them?* She called her grandmother and asked if she had taken delivery of the flowers. No one in her family knew where they came from or when they came.

Lizzie thought about just enjoying the flowers, but her curiosity was too strong. She knew Wade would also want to know who had sent them and why.

She called both flower shops in town. No flowers had been delivered to the inn from either store, and no one had carried out two dozen yellow roses.

Lizzie was deep in thought when Dan came into the kitchen. They had been friends since they were in high school. He started working on the farm and at the inn shortly after the inn opened.

"Lizzie, did you find the flowers?" asked Dan Hayes as he came into the kitchen.

"Yes, I did! Are they from you?"

"No, I found them on the front porch earlier today. I brought them in and put them in that vase. I didn't want them to wilt before you saw them. I'd say Wade knows exactly what you like," Dan said with a grin.

"He does, but he didn't send them. Was there a card with them?"

"He didn't?" Dan asked in surprise. "I didn't see a card, but it could have fallen out."

"Whoever it was must have brought them out in person," said Lizzie.

"Who else would know what your favorite flowers are?"

"Anyone who knows me very well," laughed Lizzie. "You, Wade, my family..." Lizzie paused. "I think I might know who sent them. If I'm right, Wade isn't going to be happy."

"Do you mean Drake?"

"Yes," said Lizzie.

"Nope, Wade's not going to be happy at all," said Dan. "I'm going home. I'll see you tomorrow."

Lizzie said goodbye to Dan and quickly dialed Wade's number. He still wasn't answering his cell phone. She dialed the office.

"Hello, Lizzie," answered Wade.

"I tried calling your cell. Lodge said it's out of service. What happened?"

"I'll tell you about it later. What's up?"

"I think I might know who sent the flowers. You aren't going to like it."

"Drake?"

"I don't know for sure," Lizzie said. She told him what she had discovered and what Dan had told her. "What time do you think you'll be here for dinner?"

"I'll leave here in about an hour. I should be at your place by six-thirty."

"I'll have dinner ready."

Wade arrived promptly at six-thirty. He noticed that the roses were on the check-in desk. Lizzie usually put flowers that he sent where she would see them frequently. He was pleased to see that she hadn't done the same with those.

Lizzie had dinner on the table. She had made all of his favorites as promised. They sat down to eat and had a pleasant conversation. Lizzie apologized again for her behavior. He apologized for not sending Tiffany away.

"You were going to tell me what happened to your cell phone," Lizzie prodded.

"I have a new one," said Wade.

"Wasn't the one you had only a few months old?"

"Uh huh," mumbled Wade as he quickly took a bite. "This is really good pie."

Lizzie sensed that there was a really good story behind the cell phone issue and asked, "Why did you need a new one?"

"You aren't going to let this go, are you?" Wade asked.

"Nope," said Lizzie with a grin.

"If you must know," Wade began in mock annoyance. "I was angry when you left, so I decided to go to lunch solo. My phone must have fallen out of my pocket at the exact moment that I slammed my truck door. I heard a strange noise and opened the door to see what it was. Pieces of the phone fell like rain onto the pavement."

"Oh, Wade, I'm so sorry," said Lizzie trying not to laugh.

"It's not your fault. I lost my temper and didn't pay attention to what I was doing. Lodge has been giving me a hard time about it all day," said Wade as he laughed. "It's funny now but not at the time."

The couple enjoyed their dessert and discussed watching a movie together when the office phone rang. Lizzie excused herself to answer it.

"Paradise Creek Inn, how may I help you?"

"Hi, Lizzie. This is Drake."

"Hello, Drake. How are you?"

"I'm good. How are you doing?"

"I'm fine. What can I do for you?"

"I just called to see if you found the flowers that I left on your front porch."

Wade walked into the room and whispered that he needed to leave. He had gotten a text that there was another fire. Lizzie signaled for him to wait.

"Yes, I did. They're lovely. Thank you, Drake," said Lizzie as she looked at Wade. She knew right away that they were about to have another fight.

"I wanted to deliver them to you in person because I wanted to tell you that I've moved back to the area. I'm living with Mom and Dad for now. Mom needs help with the farm and with Dad."

"I'm sure they're glad to have you home with them," said Lizzie while she looked at Wade.

Wade's cell phone rang. He looked at the caller id and knew he had to answer. He went back to the kitchen and answered the call. When he returned, Lizzie was holding the flowers in her hands and smiling.

"I thought you said that Drake was too busy to come to the inn. I thought you said you probably wouldn't see or hear from him again," said Wade angrily. "You don't seem to be very upset that Drake sent the flowers. Did you have a nice conversation with him?"

"What do you mean?"

"Never mind, I don't have time to argue about this now. There's another fire. I have to go."

"Will you call me when you're finished?"

"I don't know, maybe. I have to go."

Wade walked out the front door without another word.

Lizzie waited for what seemed hours before Wade called. She heaved a sigh of relief when she saw his number on her caller id.

"Wade, I'm so glad you called."

"I'm sorry I had to leave so suddenly," Wade replied.

"Was anyone hurt at the fire?"

"No, thank goodness. This one wasn't arson. It was accidentally set by an overturned barbeque grill. No structures were damaged, and no one was hurt."

"Oh, that's a relief," said Lizzie.

"I'd have called sooner, but I was working traffic control, and it took the fire department a while to put it out."

There was silence for a few minutes while they both tried to decide on the best way to bring up the subject of Drake.

Finally, Wade asked, "What did Drake have to say?"

"He wanted to know if I'd gotten the flowers and to tell me that he has moved back. He's living with his parents to help with Ben's recovery and the farm. He asked if we could get together for dinner sometime. I told him no."

"I see. What were you thinking when you were holding those roses?" Wade asked, dreading the answer.

"It doesn't matter now. I threw them out right after you left," Lizzie replied.

Wade didn't like the answer, but he was too tired to argue. "Lizzie, I'm sorry, but I'm exhausted. It's been a long day. I'm going to say goodnight. I'll talk to you tomorrow." He hung up before Lizzie could reply.

CHAPTER EIGHTEEN

THE NEXT MORNING Lizzie woke to the sound of her cell phone ringing.

"Hello," she answered groggily.

"Are you still asleep?" Jan asked.

"I was. What time is it?"

"It's just after eight o'clock. Are you okay? You don't usually sleep this late."

"I'm fine. I was up late last night. Wade worked traffic control at a fire and couldn't call until it was out."

"I heard there was another fire. Was anyone hurt?"

"No."

"That's good. The reason I'm calling so early is that Faith and I decided it was time we had lunch together. Do you want to join us?" Jan asked.

"When and where?"

"How does a burger at our usual place sound today at eleven-thirty?"

"That sounds great," said Lizzie, now fully awake. "I'll call you if something comes up and I can't make it."

"Okay, see you then."

Lizzie got up and showered before making the decorations for the upcoming birthday party. She should have made them yesterday, but she still had enough time to get everything done. She was almost finished when she heard a tap on the back door.

"Miss Fletcher, your power may blink on and off for a while. It would probably be a good idea to back up all of your computer files and unplug your computer just in case," the foreman told her.

"How long do I have to back things up?"

"You probably have about thirty minutes. We have some heavy-duty power tools that might overload your circuits. I'll come back and make sure you're ready before we get started."

"Thank you. I'll back it up right now."

Lizzie immediately backed up the office computer. She saved all of the appointments, bookings, and records to a thumb drive. She put the drive in the pocket of her jeans before she unplugged the computer and everything in the office. She didn't want to lose any equipment due to power surges. She also unplugged every television set in the inn, just in case.

She dialed her parents' phone number.

"Mama," she said when Ellen answered, "I'm going into town to have lunch with Jan and Faith. Do you need anything?"

"No, I can't think of anything. Tell the girls hello for us."

"I will. I'll call you when I get home."

Lizzie located her keys and her bag before going outside. She found the foreman and told him that he could use the power tools when necessary. Then she climbed into her jeep and drove to town.

Jan was already at the restaurant when Lizzie arrived. They sat in a corner booth and placed their orders. Faith sat down beside Jan and made her order. The three women were enjoying their food and conversation when they heard a familiar voice.

"Hello, ladies. May I join you?"

Drake didn't wait for an invitation. He sat down next to Lizzie and helped himself to one of his sister's French fries.

"I didn't know you were coming to town. Is Dad okay?" asked Faith.

"He's fine. Mom sent me to get her prescription refilled. Dad loves the burgers here, so I thought I'd take some to him," replied Drake. "It's a happy coincidence to find the three of you here together."

Lizzie looked at the time on her cell phone and said, "I'm sorry to have to break this party up, but I need to get back to the inn. Drake, will you let me out, please?"

"You have to leave already? I just got here," he teased.

"Yes, I have a client coming to the inn. It would look pretty unprofessional if I wasn't there when she arrived."

Drake reluctantly stood and let Lizzie out of the booth. She paid for her food and turned to leave, bumping into Drake.

"I thought I'd walk you out," he said.

"That's not necessary. Goodbye."

Drake followed her to the parking lot and opened the jeep door for her. She got in without a word and started the jeep.

"Why are you so unfriendly today, Lizzie?" Drake asked as he closed the door.

"I told you last night. I love Wade. I'm not interested in a relationship with you."

"We can't even be friends?" Drake asked mockingly.

"No!" Lizzie replied angrily and drove away.

Drake stood in the parking lot and watched her drive away. This wasn't going to be as easy as he thought.

Lizzie hated lying to Jan and Faith, but she knew if she didn't, she'd be stuck there sitting beside Drake until he decided to leave. She thought about going to Wade's office to tell him what had happened, but she didn't want him to think she was spying on him. Instead, she stopped on the side of the road and called his cell.

"Hi, Lizzie. Can I call you back? I'm in the middle of something right now," Wade said when he answered the phone.

"Yes," Lizzie replied. "Call me when you can. I need to tell you something."

Lizzie's cell phone rang as she parked her jeep at the inn.

"Lizzie, what was that all about?" Jan asked when Lizzie answered the phone.

"I'm sorry, Jan. I didn't mean to run out on you and Faith, but being seen sitting next to Drake was a recipe for disaster."

Lizzie explained about the tension in her relationship with Wade. She explained about the fight, the flowers, and the phone call from Drake.

"Does Drake know how you feel?" asked Jan.

"Yes!" Lizzie answered. "I told him last night and again today. I've been trying to tell him that I'm not interested ever since I moved back here. He doesn't listen."

"In all honesty, Lizzie, you seemed to be pretty interested at Ben and Carol's anniversary party and especially during our baby shower," Jan pointed out. "He may not listen or believe you because you've been sending mixed signals."

Lizzie was silent. She was surprised and hurt by her cousin's words.

"Lizzie, are you still there?"

"Yes!"

"I'm sorry if I've hurt your feelings, but if you think about it honestly, you'll know that I'm right."

"I wasn't dating Wade either of those times. I had hoped that Drake and I could be friends because I didn't want to lose you or Faith."

"Drake may be my brother-in-law, but you're my cousin. You're the closest thing I have to a sister. You won't lose me," Jan replied.

"What do you think Faith will say about this mess?"

"I don't know. I'll talk to her and let you know. I need to get back to work. I'll talk to you later."

Lizzie thought about what Jan had said. She remembered the anniversary party. She had just recovered from her breakup with Rob. She and Wade didn't start dating until Drake had gone back to

Colorado. During the baby shower, she was hurting and missing Wade. Both times she took comfort in what she wanted to believe was nothing but friendship. She had been a fool.

However, there was no excuse for Drake's behavior today. She had done nothing this time that could be considered a mixed signal. She was willing to take the blame for their past meetings but not this one. Today was all on Drake's shoulders.

Lizzie was angrily making birthday party decorations when the power blinked. The foreman tapped on the back door. She motioned for him to come in.

"The power may be on and off until we've finished for the day. I'd wait until we leave to plug your computer back in," he advised.

"Thank you," she said as her phone rang, and he waved as he went out the door.

"I understand you had an interesting lunch today," Wade said irritably.

"Yes, I did. Did someone already tell you about it?"

"I heard something about it," he said.

Lizzie told Wade about lunch and the phone conversations she had had. When she finished, she asked, "What did you hear?"

"Lodge was getting lunch and saw the two of you talking in the parking lot. He was laughing about the expression on Drake's face when you drove away and left him standing there." Wade paused before adding. "It's hard to avoid people sometimes, isn't it?"

"Maybe he got the message this time," Lizzie said irritably. "Will I see you tonight?"

"I think I'll stay in town tonight. I have to do laundry and a few other things around the house."

"I guess I'll talk to you later then," Lizzie said, disappointed.

Wade returned to his work and was interrupted by the intercom on his desk.

"Sheriff, Tiffany Pruitt is here to see you," Lodge informed him.

Wade swore under his breath. He had forgotten to tell Lodge that he didn't want to see or talk to her.

"I'll be out shortly," he said to Lodge's surprise.

Wade took a deep breath and went into the lobby to talk with Tiffany.

"What can I do for you today?" Wade asked formally.

"I've finished with the insurance cases and wanted to see if you'd like to have dinner before I leave," Tiffany said with a smile. "Ross would love to see you again."

Wade glared at Lodge, whose jaw had just dropped. Lodge noticed the look and quickly returned to the work on his desk.

"No, thank you. I have a previous engagement."

"That's too bad, but we'll have lots of time to get together. I've accepted a job at an insurance agency here in Vernon."

"You're going to be living here?" asked Wade with surprise. "Tiffany, it was nice to see you again and to meet your son. But I'm in love with Lizzie. You and I will never have anything more than a professional relationship."

"What makes you think that I want anything more from you?" Tiffany said, embarrassed.

"I'm just letting you know how I feel. I don't want to mistakenly lead you to believe otherwise," Wade said firmly.

Tiffany stared at him angrily. She seemed to want to say something but couldn't find the right words. Instead, she turned on her heel and stormed out of the office.

Wade looked at Lodge, who was grinning like a Cheshire cat. "Who was that?" he asked.

"Someone that I forgot to tell you that I don't want to talk to or see," Wade said. "She's an insurance investigator."

Lodge looked at him in disbelief.

"We were engaged a long time ago," Wade added reluctantly.

Lodge whistled and said, "It seems to be a red letter day for exes. First, Lizzie's bothers her at lunch, and now yours shows up here. What are the odds?"

"I've been wondering that myself," answered Wade as he went back to his office.

CHAPTER NINETEEN

KYLE JENSEN HAD BEEN PATROLLING Highway 287 between Vernon and Chillicothe since his shift began at three that Sunday afternoon. The day had been uneventful, and he was bored. He'd made only two traffic stops so far. He hoped the remainder of his patrol was more exciting.

The most excitement he'd had on the job lately was while arresting Megan Ford. He gingerly touched the healing scratches on his face as he thought about that night. He had heard about Megan but had never met her. Now that he knew who she was and what she was capable of, he wouldn't be caught off guard again.

Trooper Jensen pointed his radar gun at a northbound eighteen-wheeler and sighed. The trucker wasn't speeding. Word had probably gotten out about his location. He looked at his watch and realized that it was time for his dinner break. He started the engine and drove onto the highway.

Khari Wilson smiled when she saw the Texas State Trooper walk in the door of the Chillicothe Dairy Queen. They had been flirting for months, but the big man had yet to ask her out. She had decided it was time she took matters into her own hands. She walked to the counter and gently nudged the teenaged cashier away so that she could take Kyle's order.

"Well, hello, handsome. Do you want your usual today?" she asked in her sweetest voice.

Kyle smiled and winked. "You know me too well. I may have to change things up a bit next time just to keep the mystery alive."

Khari rang up his usual Triple Belt-Buster with bacon and cheese combo with an extra-large iced tea. She always gave him her employee discount just to sweeten the deal. She took his money and watched him as he walked toward a booth.

She delivered his meal and sat down opposite him. "Kyle, you've been coming in here for a while now. Maybe one of these days, when we're both off work, we could get to know each other better," Khari said with a smile.

"What did you have in mind?" Kyle asked with a grin.

"Oh, I don't know. We could go to a movie or have dinner someplace together. You could even come to my place for dinner and a movie."

"I'll be working swing shift for several weeks. The next time I'm scheduled for the day shift, I'll give you a call, and we'll have dinner," he assured her. "There's only one problem."

"What's that?" she asked.

"I don't have your number," Kyle said.

Khari took a napkin from his tray and wrote her phone number on it. She pushed it toward him as she stood.

"I've got to get back to work. Don't lose that number," she said while wagging her finger at him.

"I'll put it right here next to my heart," he said as he stuffed it into his shirt pocket.

Trooper Jensen's evening was slightly more interesting. He made several traffic stops for speeding. He worked an accident caused by a teenager while texting and driving. He was thankful that no one was seriously injured this time.

The remainder of his shift consisted of watching and thinking.

He thought about his life up to this point in time. He'd grown up in Vernon and always wanted to be a police officer like his grandfather. There weren't any openings in the Vernon Police Department when he'd finished at the police academy in Wichita Falls. He joined the Wilbarger County Sheriff's Department instead. He was a deputy for several years but had decided that he wanted to try something different.

His letter of resignation was already typed and ready to submit when Sheriff Morton announced his retirement. He thought about it for almost a week before deciding that he'd like the job. Wade Adams also wanted the job.

He wasn't happy with the decision the county commission had made to have a special election. Although he liked Wade, he had been with the department longer and felt he should have been given the job. He applied with the Texas Department of Public Safety after he lost the election and turned in his resignation as soon as he was accepted.

There were no hard feelings between him and Wade or the rest of the department. He had needed a change. Until recently, he had been satisfied with his current situation. He wasn't sure another career change was what he wanted this time.

He thought of things he'd like to do and things he'd like to have in his life. He thought about Khari Wilson. It might be nice to settle down with a good woman and have a couple of kids. He didn't think Khari would be the right woman for him. His thoughts were interrupted as a pickup truck flew past him. His mind was back in the present in an instant.

Trooper Jensen's shift was finally over. He stopped at the Allsup's on Main Street in Vernon on his way home. He filled the gas tank of his patrol car before going inside.

"Hi, Kyle," called the clerk as he entered the store.

"Evening Ellie," he replied. "How's it going tonight?"

"It's been pretty quiet. Did you get gas on you?" she asked as she wrinkled her nose and pointed at the hem of his left pant leg.

"I let my mind wander and overfilled the tank a little," he said as he looked down to survey the damage.

"How many burritos do you want tonight?" Ellie asked with a smile.

"I think four of the beef and bean burritos will be enough," he replied as he walked toward the cooler.

He returned with a six-pack of Bud Light and watched as she dropped four burritos into the deep fryer.

"Ellie, do you fry a fresh batch of burritos for every customer?" he asked with a grin.

"I will if a customer asks me to do it, but I don't usually volunteer," she answered with a shy smile. "I don't want you to eat stale burritos after a long shift."

Kyle tipped his hat and said, "Thank you, ma'am."

"I've told you a dozen times that I'm not old enough to be called ma'am," she said playfully.

"You're right; I'm sorry. I guess I'm still in work mode," he said as he took out his wallet. "Thank you, Ellie. I really appreciate it. There's nothing better than a fresh Allsup's burrito."

"You're very welcome," she said with a beaming smile.

"Do you ever work a day shift?" he asked.

"I don't very often. I like the peace and quiet of this shift."

"Would you be interested in meeting for lunch before work sometime?" he asked.

"Yes, I'd like that."

"You're always here when I'm headed home. What hours do you work?"

"I'm here at three and off by midnight,"

"Do you want to meet at the steakhouse tomorrow?"

"I can't tomorrow, but I'm free the rest of the week," Ellie assured him.

"Okay, how does Friday at noon sound? We'll have a little time to talk before we have to be at work," Kyle suggested.

"I'll be there."

"Great! I'll see you later," Kyle said, gathering his purchases.

"Goodnight," said Ellie with a smile.

Kyle lived south of the city limits on Highway 183. He thought about Ellie Rozzell as he drove toward his house. He compared her in his mind to Khari Wilson. He liked both women, but of the two, he was more attracted to Ellie. He wanted to know more about her.

His thoughts were interrupted when he noticed the motion sensor light blink on at his home. He knew that it was probably triggered by an animal, but he remained cautious. He surveyed his property as he drove into the drive and parked near his back door. It was open.

Before getting out of his car, he removed a flashlight from the glove box and his service weapon from its holster. He got out slowly, leaving his car door open. He crept to the back door and listened. He carefully opened the door wider and quietly went inside. He cautiously checked every room of the house. He didn't relax until he was sure that he was alone.

He could still smell gasoline as he retrieved his midnight snack from the patrol car. He decided to change out of his uniform and wash up before eating. His stomach growled as he settled in his recliner and turned on the television. He cracked open a beer and scrolled through his list of recorded programs. He ate while he watched the latest episode of *Counting Cars*.

Outside, a lone figure stood far enough away to avoid the motion detector but close enough to see every move the trooper made through the living room window. He had stood in that place every night for the past week. He watched as the man inside did the same thing night after night.

Kyle Jensen fell asleep in his chair soon after completing his meal. He slept soundly and was unaware that smoke filled his home as fire consumed the firewood he kept on the back porch. Soon the blaze grew large enough to attract the attention of a passerby who called the fire department.

Sirens pierced the night air as the fire engines raced to the scene.

The entire house was in flames. The fire department battled the blaze for several hours. It was finally under control when the sun began to peek over the horizon.

Firefighter Chris Quintero sat down to catch his breath and noticed the car near the back door. The paint was scorched and peeling on one side, but it was obviously a highway patrol car. He signaled to his partner Kanden Kyzer.

"Kyzer, do you see this?" he asked as he pointed to the car. "Do we know who lives here?"

"We can probably find out pretty quickly," answered Kyzer.

The two men approached Chief Gaines. He turned and saw the look of concern on their faces.

"What's wrong?"

"There's a highway patrol car parked near the back door. There's a good chance that the patrolman is inside the house," said Quintero.

"We thought it would be a good idea to find out who lives here," added Kyzer.

Chief Gaines sighed and hung his head before saying, "I'll make the call. You two can start searching the house."

"Yes, sir," they said in unison.

Both firefighters secured their personal breathing apparatus before going into the still-burning house. They entered through the back door and found themselves in the kitchen. The room was filled with smoke making it difficult to see. They followed the wall with their hands until they found a doorway to their right. They moved carefully through the smoke and stepped over debris. This appeared to be the living room.

They stopped and turned to each other before moving toward the shape in the center of the room. A body lay in what appeared to have been a recliner. It was burned beyond recognition.

Kyzer pointed to the living room window, and Quintero nodded. They would take the victim out through the large opening rather than through the narrow smoke-filled kitchen. They broke the glass and struggled to get the body through the window. Fire-fighters outside the window joined in the effort. Once outside, the EMTs took charge of the victim while the remainder of the team returned to battle the blaze.

Chief Gaines had discovered the identity of the victim. He had met Kyle Jensen a few times but hadn't known him well. He dreaded making the call to the DPS and Sheriff Adams.

CHAPTER TWENTY

WADE WAS SLEEPING SOUNDLY when a loud noise invaded his dreams. He looked at the clock. He still had an hour before he had to get up. He slapped the alarm button, but the noise wouldn't stop. Finally, he realized the noise was coming from his phone.

"Adams," he answered with a yawn.

"Wade, this is Leo Gaines. I'm sorry to wake you. We're fighting another fire."

"How bad is it?"

"It's bad. We have another fatality," Leo said. "The property belongs to State Trooper Kyle Jensen. We believe Jensen died in the fire."

"Are you sure it's Kyle?"

"We aren't absolutely certain, but the body was found in the living room. The victim had been sitting in a recliner in front of the television. I'm sorry, Wade."

"I'm on my way."

Wade swore as he quickly dressed and hurried to his truck. He stomped on the accelerator as he turned on his emergency lights. He was dealing with a myriad of emotions. Kyle Jensen had been his co-worker and his friend, but more than that, Kyle was his brother, a part of the law enforcement brotherhood.

There are no words to describe the true meaning of the word brotherhood. Trusting each other and having each other's back in dangerous situations is something that only those who have experienced it can understand. Fellow officers are co-workers, friends, and extended family, but the bond goes much deeper and is often stronger.

"Kyle," Wade said as he stared through the windshield. "I don't know if you can hear me, but I promise you we'll get this guy!"

Wade arrived as the victim's body was being loaded into the van. Dr. Hughes spoke to him before getting into the driver's seat.

"I'm sorry about your friend, Wade."

"Thanks, Doc. Is there anything you can tell me?"

"Not at the moment. I'll start on the autopsy right away. I know that every law officer in the county will want answers as soon as possible."

"I appreciate that," Wade replied.

Chief Gaines was giving instructions to his team when Wade found him.

"This fire was different," Leo said. "It didn't start as a grass fire. It started at the house. He used gasoline this time instead of alcohol. We can still smell it in some areas. He poured gas all the way around the house before igniting the wood pile. The only similarity is that B shift is on duty."

"Did you find anything inside?" asked Wade.

"We'll have to wait to search in there," Gaines said, jerking his thumb toward the still-burning house.

Wade began searching the area. He took out his smart phone and photographed the area as he walked slowly around the house. He expanded the circle each time around. He found a trail in the short grass. He followed it until the narrow trail ended in a trampled circle of dust and vegetation. He was approximately twelve yards from the house.

Wade searched the ground thoroughly. It looked as if someone had knelt down to rest at some point. There was an impression in the dust that may have been someone's knee. There were foot prints, but they weren't clear.

Why was someone standing here? Wade looked toward the house and realized that he was facing what was once the living room window. Someone stood here watching and waiting.

Wade stood deep in thought. *Why had the arsonist changed his pattern? Did he run out of his usual supplies? Why did he decide to burn a house, and why this house? Why Jensen?*

"Did you find something?" Leo asked as he approached Wade.

"It looks like someone was standing here watching Kyle. I'd say someone stood here often based on the trail I followed to this spot."

"I don't like the sound of that," said Leo. "It's safe to search through what's left of the house now."

The fire had destroyed any fingerprints or biological evidence that may have been inside the house. The remains of the television and recliner were in what was once the living room. Two empty beer cans were found nearby.

"Why did Kyle just sit here when the fire started?" Wade wondered aloud. "If I smelled smoke, I'd be trying to find the source. If I saw fire, I'd be trying to put it out or call the fire department."

"It looks like he had a couple of beers. Maybe he was sleeping," Leo pointed out.

"Wouldn't the smoke detector have been loud enough to wake him up?"

"That depends. He may not have had a smoke detector, it may not have been working properly, or he could have been a sound sleeper."

"There's one way to find out about the first two scenarios," said Wade.

The pair searched areas where a smoke detector is commonly

placed. Leo found it hanging in the hallway outside the bedroom. The batteries were missing, and the sound device was broken.

"This didn't happen in the fire," said Leo as he held the broken device for Wade to see.

"This was no random arson and no accident," Wade said angrily. "This is murder. Someone wanted Kyle dead."

Wade stopped to see Dr. Hughes later that morning before going to his office. He hoped the medical examiner would have some useful information for him.

"Hello, Sheriff," said the doctor. "I haven't finished the autopsy yet. I'm waiting on dental records."

"I understand. What have you found so far?"

"I believe he had a meal before he died. What was left of his stomach contained traces of some type of spicy food. I could smell chili powder. He was probably sleeping when the fire started. He died of smoke inhalation before the fire reached his body."

"That's some consolation. At least he wasn't in pain when he died," Wade said.

"I'll let you know when I've made a positive identification."

Wade called his team to the conference room when he returned to the office and said, "Before we begin, I'd like to welcome Deputy Calvin Baker back."

"Thank you, sir. It's good to be back," replied Baker with a smile.

"He and Lodge will run the office in shifts until they're released to regular duty."

Wade shared what he knew before giving them instructions, "This is a murder case, and we need to investigate it as such. The killer used fire as the murder weapon. Who had motive? Who had opportunity? I want to know everything there is to know about Kyle Jensen. I want to know if his death is connected to the death of Nate Tucker.

"Gonzalez and Reed, I want you to dig into Kyle's personal life. Look into his background, financial records, love life, the works.

Odom and Maddie, I want you to go through his DPS career with a fine-toothed comb."

"Yes, sir."

"Dodson and I both worked with Trooper Jensen when he was a deputy sheriff. We'll talk with his family and look into our department records. Find out if Kyle had any enemies. Find out who those enemies are and what they were doing between midnight and three this morning. Find out anything that will help us catch this guy." He paused a moment before adding, "I know that most of you didn't know Kyle Jensen very well. He was a fellow peace officer. I'd appreciate it if you'd join me in a moment of silence in Kyle's honor."

The entire team worked with a vengeance to find the man responsible for their colleague's death. Wade had arranged for lunch to be delivered to the conference room to thank them for their efforts. When they had finished eating, Wade began the meeting.

"I want to thank y'all for your hard work and support."

"Yes, thank you," Dodson added.

"What do we know about Trooper Jensen's personal life?" Wade asked.

"He was single, never married, and had no children," said Gonzalez. "He wasn't dating anyone. There was nothing in his financial records to indicate a problem. He owned his home and had lived there for many years. He was late with the mortgage payment once several years ago. He drove an older model pickup that he had paid off without any issues. He had one credit card with a low four-figure balance."

"I traced his movements on the night of the fire," Reed added. "He was patrolling Highway 287 between Vernon and Chillicothe on the three to eleven shift. He ate a burger at the Dairy Queen in Chillicothe. The information in the autopsy report led me to believe that Jensen must have stopped somewhere after his shift. I tried to think of a place that would be open when his shift ended. I discovered that he stopped often at the Allsup's store on Main Street. He bought gas, burritos, and a six-pack of beer. He also made a lunch date with the clerk, Ellie Rozzell."

"Had they been seeing each other long?" Wade asked.

"No, sir. It would have been their first date," replied Reed. "Khari Wilson, the woman that I spoke with in Chillicothe, commented that they had discussed going out but made no definite plans. Neither woman knew about the other. I've verified the whereabouts of both women at the time of the fire."

"Nothing in his personal life to be concerned about," Wade observed. "What about his career?"

"We looked into every arrest he made as a state Trooper," Odom said. "We've eliminated all but one possible enemy."

"You're not going to like it," Maddie said. "It's his latest arrest, Megan Ford."

"Have you talked with her yet?" asked Wade.

"Yes, sir," replied Maddie. "She claims to have been at home asleep at the time. Her mother vouched for her."

"Miss Ford has been known to leave without her mother's knowledge," Wade pointed out. "I talked with Jensen's family and co-workers. No one knew of any enemies that he might have had. Dodson, what did you find in our records?"

"I looked into every case that Jensen was involved in while he was a Deputy Sheriff. Many of those people are still in jail. Some of them are deceased. I've verified the movements of all but four of those remaining. Two of those four live outside of our area. I have law enforcement there working on locating them. The remaining two are Noah Burns and Able Slayton."

"What were the charges against them?" Wade asked.

"Slayton was charged with assault with a deadly weapon," said Dodson. "Burns was charged with felony drug possession and assault of a peace officer."

"Let's bring those two and Miss Ford in for questioning," said Wade. "I'd like for those of you working late tonight to gather the necessary information. We'll talk with them all tomorrow. I believe it may take several of us to bring Miss Ford in."

"It may take all of us," replied Dodson as he rubbed the fading bruise on his arm.

Dodson and Odom were tasked with bringing in Able Slayton for questioning the next day. The man sat nervously, waiting for the interview to begin.

"Mr. Slayton, I'm Sheriff Wade Adams. I've been looking over your record."

"I don't know what this is about, but I've stayed out of trouble since I got out of prison," said Slayton.

"I'd like to know where you were when Kyle Jensen died," said Wade bluntly. "Where were you between ten o'clock Sunday night and six o'clock Monday morning?"

"Who's Kyle Jensen?"

"He was one of the deputies who arrested you twenty years ago," Wade replied. "You threatened his life that day. I want to know if you carried out the threat."

"Hold on! I don't know anything about that. I was angry that day. I said a lot of things. I don't even remember this Jensen guy. I've been working on a construction job for the past month in Arkansas. I got back into town yesterday."

"Can you prove that?" Wade asked with a tone of disbelief.

"Call my boss," Slayton said. "He'll tell you I was there."

"What's his name and number?"

Wade left the room to make the call. Slayton waited nervously for his return.

"Mr. Slayton, thank you for your time and assistance," said Wade when he reentered the room. "You're free to go."

Noah Burns was brought in by Deputies Reed and Clifton. He calmly waited in the interview room.

"Mr. Burns, my name is Sheriff Adams. I've been looking over your record."

"I've been clean and sober for a long time now, Sheriff. Those records are part of a past that I'm not proud of," said Burns.

"You're here today because I need information," said Wade.

"What kind of information? I'll be happy to help if I can."

"I understand that you attempted to strangle Deputy Kyle Jensen when you were arrested."

"Someone told me that I did," replied Burns with a pained expression. "I was pretty high at the time. I don't remember anything about the arrest or the attack on the deputy. I read about his death in the paper. I'm so sorry."

"Where were you between ten Sunday night and six Monday morning?"

"I work as a counselor for teens battling addiction. I was counseling a teenager and his parents. It was a long night," said Burns.

Burns gave Wade the necessary information to verify his whereabouts and was soon allowed to leave.

"Two down and one to go," said Wade. "Where is Megan Ford?"

"I've called and verified that she is currently at work," said Maddie.

"I think Dodson should sit this one out. Her lawyer would love an excuse to file charges against him and the department," Wade said. "Whoever brings her in is risking bodily injury, so I'll ask for volunteers."

Maddie said, "I'll go. She may be better behaved with a woman."

"I wouldn't count on that, but thank you," said Wade.

"I'll go," said Odom. "I'm curious about Miss Ford."

"Thank you, Odom. I'll be going as well," said Wade. "We'll take two vehicles and leave in fifteen minutes."

Wade asked his deputies to wait nearby while he spoke to Megan. He didn't want to alarm her with a show of force. They were to move in if necessary. To everyone's surprise, she responded to the request to accompany them to the Sheriff's office very calmly.

"Do I need a lawyer?" was her only response.

Megan calmly sat in the interview room while Wade read through her file once again. "Miss Ford, thank you for being so cooperative," Wade began. "You're here today to answer some questions regarding Trooper Kyle Jensen."

"I don't understand what his death has to do with me," Megan replied.

"Your encounter with Trooper Jensen was rather violent, to say the least," Wade pointed out.

"I was drunk that night. I remember what happened, but it's like it was all a bad dream," Megan said, making sure her story matched the story told to the district attorney. "I was surprised to hear about his death. That was horrible."

Wade looked at Megan with a raised eyebrow before asking, "Where were you between ten Sunday night and six Monday morning?"

"I was at home all night. I went to bed at eleven and woke up when my alarm went off at six-thirty."

"Can anyone verify that?"

"My mother was home, too. She'll verify that I was there."

"Miss Ford," Wade began. "You and I both know that your mother isn't always aware when you leave your house."

"What are you implying?" Megan said angrily.

Now this is the Megan I was expecting. Wade looked directly at Megan, "I'm saying that unless your mother was in the room watching you sleep all night, she isn't able to verify your alibi."

"Alibi? I need an alibi?" screamed Megan.

"You physically assaulted Trooper Jensen a few weeks ago. He's now dead, murdered. You're the only suspect who can't prove where you were at the time of his death," Wade said calmly.

Megan was speechless. She stared at Wade in disbelief as she processed what he had said.

"You're free to go for now, Miss Ford, but don't leave the county," Wade said as he stood and opened the door.

CHAPTER TWENTY-ONE

CACUS STARED out the front window of his living room. He watched his neighbor, Tanya Balderas, as she parked her car and walked to her apartment.

"I'm sorry, my darling," he whispered to the empty room. "I haven't made anything for you lately. Soon, my darling, soon."

He went to the apartment building office after Tanya had moved out of his sight. He made a pot of coffee and glanced at a newspaper that his manager had left on the table. He gasped when he noticed the headline, *Arson to Blame in Death of State Trooper*.

That can't be right! When did this happen? He sat down at the table and read the article. He couldn't believe what he was reading. *A house fire claimed the life of State Trooper Kyle Jensen early Monday morning. Chief Gaines had no doubt that the fire was intentionally set. It is likely the same person responsible for other fires in the area.*

Had someone found his secret place? Was someone trying to set him up? He'd have to wait until his lunch break to find out. At noon, he quickly got into his truck and drove to the run- down house.

June 17, 2015

I don't know what's happening. I haven't created any art since that poor farmer died. Now, someone else is dead. I didn't set that fire. At least, I don't think I did. Could I have started it without remembering? Has the giant taken over more completely than before?

Nothing is missing. Everything is just as I left it. There's no sign that anyone else has been here. It couldn't have been me.

Is someone trying to blame me or take credit for my work? Who? I don't have time to figure it out now. I have to get back to work.

He closed the journal, left it on the dresser, and drove back to town.

* * *

Graham Shaffer smiled as he looked out of his office window. He watched rivulets of water cascade down the glass. At long last, it was raining.

He was pleased with the rain, but he was more pleased with himself. He had located the woman from the truck stop in the Jameson Monroe case. She vouched for Monroe, and the district attorney had no choice but to drop the case.

Graham had been looking into the possibility of filing a lawsuit for damages against Monroe's former girlfriend. He'd need to discuss the suit with Monroe before he moved forward. He picked up the phone and dialed Monroe's number. They needed to work together to determine what losses Monroe experienced as a result of the false charges.

A rumble of thunder brought the attorney back to the present. *This rain should help the wildfire situation.* A flash of lightning lit up the room, and a rumble of thunder immediately followed. *Unless, of course, lightning causes one*, he thought as he settled behind his desk.

Graham was scheduled to be in his Austin office on Monday. He'd decided to leave early so that he could take care of some personal business. He wanted to be caught up with his work before the end of the day.

He needed some office help. He wanted to hire someone who would keep the office running while he was away. He didn't have many clients at the moment, but he hoped that would soon change.

The attorney picked up the phone and again placed an ad for immediate employment in the classified section of the local newspaper. He'd start accepting applications when he returned later in the week.

Graham was working at his desk until a clap of thunder rattled the walls of his office. He looked out the window to see Megan Ford crossing the parking lot. He quickly stood and went to greet her at the door.

"What a pleasant surprise!" he exclaimed. "What brings you here in such weather?"

"I need to talk to you about something," she said. "Do you have the time now, or should I make an appointment?"

She was wearing a pair of jeans that could very well have been painted on and a low-cut blouse that was more appropriate for a night of bar hopping. Her walk through the rain made her clothes cling to her body all the more. Shaffer couldn't take his eyes off her.

"Please, come in," he said as he guided her to a chair. "What do you need to talk to me about?"

"I want to apologize for my behavior the last time that we spoke," she said sweetly. "I was very disappointed about what you had to tell me. I overreacted, and I'm ashamed of myself."

"That's quite all right, my dear. Let's forget it ever happened."

"That's very kind of you. I'd like for us to be friends."

"There isn't any reason why we can't," replied Graham. "Why don't we have dinner tonight and talk things over?"

"I need to talk to you about a business matter, not a personal one," Megan began. "Would it be possible to come to an agreement so that I could contact you as needed for legal situations?"

"Yes, that could be arranged," Shaffer answered cautiously.

"I'm willing to pay for your services as long as they aren't too expensive," she said as she bit her lip and looked at him hopefully.

"What type of situations do you anticipate?" he asked.

"I don't expect anything to happen," she replied.

"Megan, you'll have to tell me what's going on if you want my help."

"Yesterday, the sheriff and two deputies came to see me at work. They hauled me to the sheriff's office and asked me questions about Kyle Jensen's death. My boss wasn't happy about the situation."

"Did they?" Surprised, Graham leaned back in his chair. "Were you charged with anything?"

"No, the sheriff asked where I was that night. I told him that I was home asleep. Apparently, my mother's word for it wasn't good enough. He said I was free to go but told me not to leave the county."

"I understand why they would want to question you after your last encounter with the trooper. Did you ask for an attorney?"

"I asked them if I needed one. They said it was my right if I would like to have an attorney present. I thought about calling you, but I was too embarrassed."

"I gather that you're a suspect in the death of Trooper Jensen, but they don't have the necessary evidence to make an arrest. I think we should come to an agreement," he said decisively.

"Thank you, Graham," Megan said with a smile.

Half an hour later, the retainer agreement was signed. They agreed that Graham would be available to Megan at any time for legal advice or representation. She would pay a small fee and any expenses he incurred on her behalf for each occurrence.

The rain had stopped by the time Megan left Graham's office. He was quite pleased with the outcome of their meeting. He would have been happier if she had agreed to go out with him again. However, he was quite sure he'd be seeing her often as her attorney.

CHAPTER TWENTY-TWO

WADE SAT AT HIS DESK, reading the latest lab report. The lighter he had found at the Tucker farm had no viable prints. The envelope and obituaries he had received in the mail had no prints or DNA.

The evidence from the fire that killed his friend was no help. The smoke alarm had no prints. There was nothing left outside to give them a clue.

They did have two suspects. Megan Ford didn't fit the profile at all, but she had no alibi for the time of Jensen's death. He knew Megan well enough to know that she'd do almost anything to get revenge. Was she really angry enough over her arrest to kill a man? It's possible she burned his home but didn't know he was inside. That didn't explain the broken smoke detector. Did she start the other fires? Was it all part of a plan to hide her real target?

The other suspect, Alan Nichols, worked for the fire department on A shift. He fit the profile, and he couldn't or wouldn't prove that he hadn't started any of the fires. He had no known connection to Kyle Jensen. Nichols was hiding something; he was sure of it.

Wade slammed his desk drawer shut in frustration. He had no

evidence and no leads. He'd have to wait for the arsonist to make a mistake.

"Is this a bad time?" Baker asked cautiously as he leaned on his crutches in the doorway.

"No, I'm just blowing off a little steam," Wade replied with a grin.

"Today's mail just arrived. I thought you'd want to see this one right away," Baker said as he handed Wade a large manila envelope.

Wade examined it closely. It was addressed to Wade personally, with no return address. This one had postage and was postmarked in Bowie, Texas, two days earlier.

"Thank you, Baker," said Wade. "I'll be in the lab for a few minutes."

Wade opened the envelope when he was certain that it was safe. He found a photo of Kyle Jensen at his home and a photo of a woman that Wade didn't know inside. He made copies of both photos and asked the lab to run their usual tests.

He was deep in thought when he returned to his office. *Why the photos and obits? Are they connected? If so, how? Who is sending them?*

Wade was startled when the phone on his desk rang.

"Sir, Zach Weis is on line one for you," Baker informed him. "He says it's urgent."

"Who is Zach Weis?" asked Wade.

"He's a local farmer. He said he's found something that you need to see."

"Thanks, Baker," he said before answering the incoming call.

"This is Sheriff Adams. What can I do for you?"

"Sheriff, I believe someone is living in my uncle's old house," said Weis.

"What makes you think so?" Wade asked patiently.

"Nobody has lived in that house for more than twenty years. The only thing I keep there anymore is farm equipment that I don't have room for at my place. I noticed tracks in the mud that shouldn't have been there. They go from the road right up to the barn."

"Did you go inside the barn or the house?" Wade asked.

"I looked inside the barn. It was too dark in there to see much. I looked through the door of the house and could see foot prints on the floor. I decided I'd better call you before I found someone, or they found me."

"You did the right thing, Mr. Weis. Give me directions and your address. One of my deputies and I will be there right away."

"It'll probably be easier if you come to my place," said Weis. "I'll lead you to the old house from here."

"Baker, try to find out everything you can about this woman," said Wade. "This photo was in the envelope along with one of Kyle Jensen. Recruit some help from the others. Dodson and I are going to see Mr. Weis. He wants us to check an old building."

Zach Weis led Wade and Dodson to the old house. There were two sets of tracks from the road to the old barn. One set matched the farmer's pickup. Weis opened the barn doors, and the three men peered inside. The tracks continued into the barn.

"This plow has been moved," said the farmer. "I parked it in the middle so it would be easier to hook up next time."

"It looks like it was moved so that someone could park in here," Dodson observed.

"Tell us about this house," said Wade.

"The farm has been in the family for four generations," began Weis. "The house was originally built for a hired hand. My uncle was the last person to live in it. My dad kept the house in pretty good shape as long as he was able."

"When was the last time you stopped by here?" asked Dodson.

The farmer thought for a minute and rubbed the gray whiskers on his chin, "I don't know for sure. It was probably last fall when I parked that plow in the barn."

"How is the house laid out?" Wade asked.

"This door goes into the kitchen. There's a door from the kitchen to the living room and another from the living room to the bedroom. There used to be a door to the outside from the living room, but that was covered over years ago."

"There's only one way out of the house?" Dodson asked.

"Unless you use a window like we did when we were kids."

"Is there any electricity in the house?" Wade asked.

"No, there's no water or gas either," replied Weis.

"I'd like for you to stay here until we're sure no one is inside," said Wade.

"It's probably a good idea to watch for snakes while you're in there," said the farmer.

Wade shuddered as he remembered his last encounter with a snake. He stepped onto the porch with his gun drawn. He gently pushed the door open and peered inside.

It was dark, too dark for this time of day. The sheriff and his deputy took flashlights from their belts. There were tracks in the dust on the floor. The windows were boarded up on the inside.

Wade avoided cobwebs as he went inside first. He stopped at a door at the opposite end of the kitchen. Dodson led the way into the living room. Wade fought the urge to laugh as Dodson tried to brush a cobweb from his face.

Wade opened the door to the bedroom. The entire room had been cleaned and dusted. There were no cobwebs and no dust on the floor. The bed was made. A red composition notebook lay on top of the dresser. When they were sure that no one was inside, Wade went to speak with Zach Weis.

"Mr. Weis, there's no one inside, but someone has been staying here," said Wade. We'd like your permission to search the house and the area around it."

"Do what you need to do, Sheriff," replied Weis.

Wade went back inside, and the two officers began to look around. Wade went to the closet. On the shelf inside, he found a box full of empty water bottles and a funnel. There were rows of different-sized containers of liquid on the closet floor. He took a glove from his back pocket and carefully turned one so that he could see the label. It was a bottle of Everclear. The sizes of the bottles varied from pint-size bottles to one-and-a-half-liter bottles. The type of liquor varied as well, from different types of Vodka to Bacardi 151 and Everclear.

"I think this is probably where our arsonist is hiding out," Wade said.

"How do you want to handle this?" asked Dodson

"Let's photograph everything and leave it as we found it," said Wade. "He'll probably be back here soon if he stays with his pattern."

"Do you want to try to lift any prints?"

"I'll see if I can lift one from one of those liquor bottles toward the back. I don't want our firebug to notice anything. We'll take a few of those water bottles with us too."

Dodson photographed the room while Wade lifted prints.

"Wade, I think you'd better see this," said Dodson.

Wade turned to see what had Dodson so concerned. He had opened the notebook with his pen and was reading the first entry. Their suspicions were confirmed. The arsonist was indeed hiding here.

"How did he come up with a name like Cacus?" asked Dodson.

"I'd really like to take that with us, but it might tip him off," Wade replied. "How do you feel about a stake out?"

"We're going to need a good place to hide and some supplies," Dodson answered with a sigh as they left the house. He hated stake outs.

"Mr. Weis, I'd like to have some deputies here," said Wade. "Is there a place where they can watch without being seen?"

"We'll need a good place to hide a vehicle, too," added Dodson.

"There's a barn down the road," replied the farmer. "It has a loft with a window facing this direction. You might be able to see the house from there if you have some binoculars."

"Does that barn belong to you as well?" asked Wade.

"It does, and you have my permission to use it. I store bales of alfalfa in there, but you should have room to park your truck. I'll show you if you follow me over there."

Mr. Weis reluctantly returned to his home. Wade had explained to the farmer that too much activity in the area might alert the arsonist to their presence. Dodson settled down for a long wait as Wade promised to send relief and supplies soon.

Wade returned to the office and immediately went to the lab. He left the prints he had collected and the water bottles for analysis. He asked Reed and Odom to join him in his office as he passed their desks.

"We're pretty sure we've found where our firebug has been hiding. Dodson is out there now, keeping an eye on things. I'd like for the two of you to gather supplies and make any arrangements you need to relieve him. You'll be out there for several hours. Let me know when you're ready. I'll have a map and the coordinates ready for you. There's no physical address."

"Yes, sir," Reed said. "We'll need the night vision setup, won't we?"

"Most likely," Wade replied. "You'll need to take two vehicles as well. Dodson needs a way back, and I'd rather you weren't out there without transportation."

Wade dialed the fire department after his deputies left his office.

"Chief Gaines," the fire chief answered.

"Leo, we've found where the firebug has been hiding," said Wade with excitement. "We found bottles of alcohol and plastic water bottles."

"Did you bring it back?" asked the fire chief with equal excitement.

"I brought back a few things and left Dodson out there watching the place."

"I'm on my way."

Chief Gaines arrived at the sheriff's office in record time. Wade took him to the lab to show him what he had collected. He told him about the journal as they walked.

"Cacus? What kind of name is that?" asked Leo.

"According to that journal, he was a fire-breathing giant in Roman mythology. I haven't looked into it for myself yet," answered Wade. "My lab people haven't had time to gather much information from these yet, but this is one of the water bottles. He had a box full of them."

"Wade, half my people use water bottles like these," Leo said with worry.

"A lot of people use this type of water bottle. It may not be a firefighter."

"Have you eliminated all of my crew as suspects?"

"All but one," answered Wade gravely. "Let's go back to my office, and I'll fill you in."

Wade informed the fire chief about the evidence and the suspects. He also informed him about the strange mail he had been getting as he showed him a photograph.

"Leo, do you recognize this woman?"

"No, who is she?"

"I don't know," Wade answered with a sigh. "It came in an envelope today with a photo of Kyle Jensen."

"I'd better get back to the station. Let me know what happens with that stake out," said Leo as he stood."

"Which shift is on duty now?" Wade asked.

"B shift. We might be busy tonight if he doesn't turn up at that house," answered Leo as he waved goodbye.

Wade found the coordinates for Reed and Odom. He noticed that Odom used a similar type of water bottle. He gave them the information and sent them on their way. He quietly went to the lab and motioned for one of the technicians to join him.

"Yes, sir?"

"I'd like for you to very discreetly compare any prints you find to the ones we have on file for Deputy Odom right away," Wade said. "I don't want any record of it unless they match. If they do, tell me and only me immediately."

"Yes, sir."

CHAPTER TWENTY-THREE

SHERIFF WADE ADAMS paced the floor of his office. He had too much on his mind to sit still. *Who was the woman in the photograph? What connection did she have to the fire victims or Wayne Bowers? Did Cacus send the envelopes? If not Cacus, then who? Why? Who is Cacus? Megan Ford, Alan Nichols, Clint Odom, or someone else?*

Wade sat at his desk and pressed his fingers against his temples in an effort to relax. He tried to clear his mind in hopes that something would start to make sense.

"Sheriff," Baker said through the open door. "I know who the woman was."

"Was?" asked Wade. "Is she dead?"

"Yes, sir. Her obituary is in this afternoon's paper," Baker said as he handed the newspaper to Wade.

"Della Wallace died after a lengthy illness," Wade read aloud. "Do you know what sort of illness?"

"I called Dr. Hughes," answered Baker. "She happened to be one of his patients. She's been battling emphysema for several years. She died in the hospital early yesterday morning."

"Was there any chance someone helped her to an earlier death?"

"I asked him that. He said he was with her when she passed away."

That's one mystery cleared up," said Wade. "We need to find out how she was connected to the others."

"I've searched school records, business records, and church records. I haven't been able to find anything connecting them," said Baker. "Lodge has been checking military and hospital records. He hasn't found anything either, as far as I know."

The phone rang on Wade's desk. Baker discreetly left the office as Wade said, "Adams."

Wade hung up the phone and went directly to the lab. The lab tech Jesse Marez was waiting for him.

"Sheriff, I tested all of the water bottles. There were two sets of prints on each. One set of prints is a match for Odom."

Wade hung his head and said, "Damn, I was afraid of that."

"His prints were only on one of the bottles," added Marez.

"Who do the other prints belong to?"

"They belong to firefighters Alan Nichols and Tonya Balderas," said Marez. "The other set matches the prints you lifted from the liquor bottles."

"Let's keep this between us until I've had a chance to talk to those people. I don't want anyone accidentally tipping them off."

Wade was on his way back to his office when Dodson returned.

"Did you see anything?" asked Wade.

"A couple of rats and a snake in the barn, but nothing at the house," Dodson replied.

Wade grimaced, "That doesn't make me any happier about my shift."

"I didn't think it would," said Dodson with a grin.

Lodge was whistling as he arrived for his shift.

"Lodge, do you think you can handle a surveillance assignment?" asked Wade. "We'll call for help if anything happens."

"That beats office work any day," replied Lodge.

"We'll relieve Reed and Odom in a few hours. Until then, I'd like for you to find Tonya Balderas and Alan Nichols for me."

"Yes, sir."

"I'll be in my office. I need to make a phone call and relax before we leave."

Wade sat at his desk and picked up the phone. He smiled when he heard Lizzie's voice.

"Hi, are you on your way?" Lizzie asked when she answered the phone.

"Honey, I'm sorry. I'm not going to make it tonight," Wade answered.

"Oh…I see."

"We might have a break in the arson cases. We found an old house where our firebug may have been hiding. I'll be taking my turn watching in a few hours. If we're lucky, this could all be over tonight," he said excitedly.

"Okay, I understand," she answered sadly.

"I promise I'll make it up to you," Wade said with concern in his voice.

"Promise me you'll be careful," said Lizzie.

"I will. I'll call you later."

Wade was napping when Lodge tapped on his door.

"I'm sorry to wake you. I found Tonya Balderas. This is her address," Lodge said as he handed the address to Wade. "I haven't been able to locate Alan Nichols yet."

"Is Gonzalez here yet?"

"She came in a little while ago."

"Send her to see me, please. She can go with me to interview Ms. Balderas."

Marina Gonzalez was eager to show her new boss that she was competent in all aspects of police work. She was waiting for Wade at the door by the time he had his hat and keys in hand. Wade informed his deputy why they were going to visit the firefighter as he drove.

Wade knocked on the apartment door while Marina stood on the opposite side. Tonya opened the door, clearly expecting to see someone else standing there.

"Hello, Sheriff. What can I do for you?"

"Ms. Balderas, this is Deputy Gonzalez. We'd like to ask you a few questions."

"Certainly, come in." Tonya looked at them both curiously before saying, "May I ask what this is about?"

"Do you use water bottles with a sport top?" Wade asked.

"Yes, I keep them handy. Why?"

"May we see one of them?" continued Wade.

Tonya went to the refrigerator and brought a full bottle for Wade to see. "What's going on?"

"We've discovered several water bottles in a location that we believe the arsonist is using. Your prints are on one of the bottles we tested," Wade said as he watched her closely.

"My prints! How many bottles did you test?" she asked in surprise.

"I'd rather not say at this point in time," Wade replied.

"I have these bottles everywhere. They're in my car and my locker at work. I have some in my locker at the gym. Anyone could have picked one up from the trash or when I wasn't looking."

"Can you verify your whereabouts at the time of each of the fires?"

"I was on duty and helped fight those fires. You can look at the duty logs. I check in at seven in the morning, and I don't leave before seven the next morning."

They were interrupted by a knock on the front door.

"That's my date for the evening," added Tonya tearfully. "Are we almost finished here?"

"Yes, for now," said Wade. "Please, keep our conversation confidential until we've talked with some others about the evidence that we've found."

Wade opened the door and stood face-to-face with Alan Nichols.

"Mr. Nichols, I'd like to ask you a few questions," said Wade recovering from the surprise.

"What's this all about?" Nichols asked.

"I'd like to know what kind of water bottles you use," replied the sheriff. "Do you buy the ones that have a sport top?"

"Yes, I use these," Nichols said as he held a bottle for the sheriff to see.

"We found your prints on some identical bottles found at a location believed to belong to the arsonist," Wade said as he enjoyed the look on Nichols' face.

"So what? Anyone could have picked up a bottle that I've used."

"Can you verify your whereabouts at the time of the fires?"

"I've already told your people that I was home alone."

The sheriff and his deputy excused themselves and left the couple standing in the doorway. Nichols watched deep in thought as Wade's truck left the parking lot.

"What did you think?" Wade asked Marina as they drove back to the office.

"I'd say she was shocked and upset. She's right, though. Anyone could have picked that bottle up from anywhere."

"She was on duty at each of the fires," said Wade. "I'd like for you to find out if she left for any reason other than fire department business."

"Yes, sir," said Marina. "Isn't her date one of our suspects?"

"Yes, he is," answered Wade. "I wonder how long it will take Ms. Balderas to figure that out. Find out how long they've been seeing each other. Lodge and I will be on stake out tonight. Call me if you find anything that can't wait until tomorrow."

"Yes, sir."

Wade's cell phone rang as they arrived at the office.

"Sheriff, this is Reed. Someone is entering the old house."

"I'm on my way," said Wade excitedly.

Wade called Dodson and picked him up on the way to join the others. He drove behind the barn as Reed and Odom climbed out of the loft.

"Is he still in there?"

"Yes, we haven't seen any other activity," answered Reed. "He parked a beat-up old truck in the barn and went into the house."

"Let's roll the vehicles in there quietly. He can't see outside, and there's only one way out," said Wade.

The four officers crept to the door. Reed and Odom waited outside while Wade and Dodson quietly went in.

A slim man, wearing jeans and a black hoodie, stood over the dresser. He was pouring liquor from a glass container into one of the plastic water bottles. A butane lighter was in his back pocket.

"Keep your hands where we can see them," Wade ordered.

Startled, Cacus dropped both bottles. The glass bottle shattered on the floor. Reed and Odom rushed in to assist in the arrest.

The sheriff and his deputies collected evidence. Cacus quietly sobbed as he sat on the bed in handcuffs.

"What's your name," asked Wade.

"I am Cacus!" the sobbing man said forcefully.

"What's your real name?"

"I am Cacus!" he repeated.

"It says here," began Dodson as he looked at the man's driver's license, "that your name is Michael Clark."

"Michael Clark, you're under arrest for arson and the murders of Nate Tucker and Kyle Jensen," said Wade.

"I didn't mean to kill anyone. The farmer was an accident. I don't know anything about the other man's death."

Dodson read Clark his rights and led him to the truck. All of the evidence from the house was loaded into the back of the truck. Clark didn't resist arrest and was silent during the ride to the sheriff's office. He remained silent as he was escorted to an interrogation room.

"Lodge, call Dr. Hughes and ask him to join us. I'd like his opinion about our arsonist. Dig up anything you can find on Michael Clark, also known as Cacus," said Wade. "I'll be in my office when you have something."

Odom watched the man through the two-way mirror and said, "Wasn't he on the tape from the liquor store?" he asked Reed.

"I'll pull it up and print another copy," replied Reed as he left the room.

Wade sat at his desk reading the journal while he waited for information from Lodge. Reed handed him a copy of the photo he had printed from the video tape.

"Mr. Clark was caught on the liquor store security camera. He was buying the bottle of Bacardi 151 that was found in the house."

"That's a good catch, Reed."

"Thank you, but I didn't catch it. Odom did."

Wade took a deep breath and said, "I need to see Odom for a few minutes."

"I'll send him in," said Reed.

A few minutes later, Odom tapped on the office door, "Did you want to see me?"

"Come in," said Wade as he pointed to the empty chair in front of the desk. "We have some things to discuss."

"We do?"

"Your prints were found on one of the water bottles that we brought back from the house this afternoon. Do you have any idea how that might have happened?"

Clint Odom stared open-mouthed at his boss. He wracked his brain, trying to come up with a logical reason, but he had nothing.

"I have no idea," he finally replied. "I use those bottles on a regular basis, but I always dispose of them."

"Where do you use them?"

"I have some in my car and at my apartment. I have a couple of them at my desk. How could he have gotten hold of them?" asked Odom.

"That's one of the things we're about to find out," said Wade as Lodge handed him the report he'd been waiting for.

Dr. Hughes and all available members of the sheriff's department watched through a two-way mirror as Wade began the interrogation.

"Mr. Clark...," Wade began.

"My name is Cacus!"

"All right, Cacus. I'm going to ask some questions, and you're going to answer them truthfully. Where did you get the water bottles and the alcohol?"

Michael Clark, a.k.a. Cacus, remained silent for a few minutes. He looked into Wade's eyes and down at the table.

"Let's try another one," said Wade. "Why did you burn those fields?"

There was still no response.

Wade decided to try another tactic, "I understand that your mother recently passed away. I'm sorry for your loss."

"Thank you," Michael mumbled.

"I know you miss her. You lived with her, didn't you?"

"Yes. She helped me."

"How did she help you?"

"She would get the medicine I needed from the doctor," answered Michael.

"What kind of medication did she get for you?" asked Wade.

"I don't know. It helped me keep the giant under control."

"Do you know which doctor prescribed the medication?"

"No."

"She was a nurse, wasn't she?" asked Wade.

"Yes."

"Is it possible she took the medicine you needed from the hospital pharmacy?"

"No, Mother would never steal. The bottles she brought were small with only a few pills in each."

"Do you have a job?"

"Yes, I'm the maintenance man at the Riverside Apartments."

Odom slapped his forehead with his palm and said, "That's why he looks so familiar. He's the maintenance man where I live. He lives next door to me."

"Did you collect the water bottles from the garbage at those apartments?"

"Yes."

"Where did you get the liquor?" Wade asked.

"I took some from the apartments that needed repair work. I bought the rest," the arsonist replied.

"I've read your journal," Wade informed him. "You talk about someone that you call my darling. Who are you talking about?"

"She's a firefighter who lives in my building. Her name is Tonya."

"Do you set the fires for her?"

Cacus began to emerge again. "The fires are my masterpieces. They are works of art for my darling."

"Why did you use liquor?"

"Different amounts and kinds of alcohol burn with different colors and intensity," he said, looking Wade in the eye.

"Did you choose your locations for the same reason?"

"Each canvas produces a different result."

"Why did you kill Nate Tucker?" Wade asked.

"It was his fault," said Michael. "He came home too soon. I only wanted to burn the hay stacked outside. I never wanted to hurt anyone."

"What about the fire that killed Kyle Jensen?"

"I didn't start the fire that killed that man. After the farmer died, I stopped my artwork. I didn't want to accidentally kill anyone else!" Cacus said adamantly.

"What were you planning to do tonight?"

"I was going to destroy it all!"

Wade said nothing as he placed the photos and obituaries on the table in front of the prisoner. He waited while Cacus looked at them.

"Who are these people?" Cacus asked.

"Did you send these to me?"

"No."

"You don't know them?"

"No."

Wade placed another item on the table, "Does this notebook belong to you?"

"Yes."

"Do you have a partner, or do you work alone?"

Cacus answered indignantly, "I work alone! Only I can create such masterpieces."

Wade gathered all the items from the table and left the room. His deputies met him in the hallway.

"Let's get him in lock-up. I want a twenty-four-hour watch on him. Gonzalez, call the judge and get a search warrant for his apartment. We'll search that first thing in the morning," Wade directed. "The rest of you go home and get some rest. Tomorrow is going to be a busy day."

"Sheriff," Lodge began. "There's another fire."

CHAPTER TWENTY-FOUR

DAN HAYES TAPPED on the back door of the inn. Lizzie smiled and waved for him to come inside.

"Hi, Lizzie. I'm going home and thought I'd see if you need me to pick up anything before I come back in the morning," he said.

"I can't think of anything I need. Aren't you going home earlier than usual?" Lizzie teased.

Dan gave her a shy grin and said, "I have a date tonight. I need to get cleaned up before driving back to her place for dinner."

"Is it anyone I know?"

"Probably, but I'm not going to tell you anything yet. I want to wait for a while to see how it goes."

"Where does she live?" Lizzie prodded.

"She lives in Lockett," answered Dan. "That's all I'm going to say on the subject. If we keep talking, you'll have me telling you every detail."

"OK, I understand," Lizzie laughed. "Have a good time."

"See you in the morning," said Dan as he grinned and walked out the door.

Lizzie looked at the clock. Wade would be there soon for dinner.

She went to the pantry and gathered what she needed. She smiled when her cell phone rang, and she saw Wade's face on the screen.

Lizzie hung up the phone and stared at the dinner ingredients on the counter. Wade wasn't coming. He would be working tonight instead. She was disappointed and worried. She had hoped that they could resolve the tension between them this evening. She was concerned about their relationship and Wade's safety.

They had had minor disagreements from time to time but nothing like this. They had been having frequent arguments since Drake moved back to the area and Tiffany came to town. Drake had made no secret of wanting to reignite their past romance. It was obvious that Tiffany would like to rekindle the flames with Wade.

Lizzie put away the food she had planned to prepare and sighed. It would have to wait until another time. She hoped it wouldn't be too late for them. She believed they could get past this if they just had the chance to talk about it.

Lizzie tried to find something to take her mind off of her worries. She had already prepared everything for the weekend event. She looked at the calendar for the month. There was nothing else that she needed to do.

She tried reading, but she was too restless. She played solitaire on her laptop until she realized that she couldn't concentrate on that either. Maybe, a walk would help take her mind off her troubles.

Lizzie strolled around the grounds and then to the pond. She walked by the pool and considered soaking in the hot tub. That didn't appeal to her either.

She decided to walk through the construction area. The roof and outer walls were framed. It wouldn't be long before they were finished. Then the plumbing and electrical work would begin. The work was being done more quickly than she had expected. At least this part of her life was going well.

She went back inside and found a movie that she thought might keep her mind occupied. She changed into her pajamas and put the movie in the DVD player in her room. She drifted off to sleep before the movie was over.

Outside the inn, someone approached through the darkness.

Dan Hayes said goodbye to his date and walked to his truck. He looked at the sky and paused for a minute, enjoying the colors of the sunset. He climbed inside and started the engine. He suddenly realized that what he saw couldn't possibly have been the sunset. It had set hours ago. He turned in his seat and looked again at the sky.

He started his truck and drove onto Highway 70 toward the yellow-orange glow in the distance. It appeared to be southwest of Lockett. He knew it was a fire, but he couldn't be sure about the size and exact location until he got closer.

As Dan drove, he realized that the fire was in the general direction of the Fletcher farm. He called the fire department but was unable to give them an exact location. He told the dispatcher to have them follow the glow. He agreed to let them know when he found the fire.

Dan couldn't believe his eyes as he grew closer to the Fletchers' land. There was no doubt that the fire was near the inn. He called the fire department and stomped on the gas. He could see that the inn was already in flames before he crossed the bridge. He called James and told him that the inn was burning. He drove onto the patio, slammed on his brakes, and went inside to find Lizzie.

Lizzie had been dreaming about Wade.

"Wade, are you hot?" she asked but got no answer.

"Is it hot in here?" There was still no answer. She reached for Wade, but he wasn't there.

She woke with a start. She sat up but couldn't see anything. Her room was filled with a dense darkness. She began to cough as she got out of bed.

Suddenly, her bedroom door burst open.

"Lizzie? Are you all right?"

"I'm here! What's happening?"

"The house is on fire. We have to get out of here."

They made their way to the kitchen by trailing the walls with their hands and relying on their memories. Their eyes burned and watered. Their throats and lungs felt as if they would explode. They dropped to the floor in an effort to escape the relentless black smoke that filled the inn. They crawled to the back door and onto the patio. Lizzie could hear her parents calling.

"Lizzie! Lizzie, are you okay?" Her mother screamed as she ran toward her.

"Yes…thanks to…Dan," Lizzie coughed.

"Are you okay, Dan?" Ellen asked.

He could only nod his answer while coughing.

"Is anyone else inside?" James asked.

"No," Lizzie answered hoarsely.

Lois led Lizzie and Dan away from the house and toward the pond. They lay on the ground and gasped for fresh air as they watched her family spring into action. They used the water hose from the lawn and buckets filled with water from the swimming pool. Their efforts had little effect, but they kept trying.

Lizzie was lightheaded and nauseated. It seemed to her that she was still dreaming as she watched the others fight the flames with anything they could find.

The firefighters immediately went to work to extinguish the blaze when they arrived. Lois and Ellen led the EMTs to Dan and Lizzie. They were immediately taken to the ambulance and given oxygen.

"I'm all right! I don't need to go to the hospital," Lizzie insisted. "What if someone gets hurt and needs the ambulance more than I do."

"Her vital signs aren't bad," said Tonya Balderas to her partner. "She might be right. Someone could get injured while we're gone."

"Miss Fletcher, I'll make a deal with you," said Rashad Weaver. "We'll wait, but you have to use the oxygen mask. If your vital signs decline, we're taking you to the hospital with no argument."

"It's a deal," Lizzie said before she began to cough again.

"I'm okay," said Dan pulling the oxygen mask from his face. "I need to talk to your boss."

Dan didn't give the EMT's a chance to argue and walked away. He spoke with Chief Gaines briefly before he got into his pickup and drove away. Dan later returned, pulling a water tank behind the pickup. The fire chief directed him toward an area of the fire where the extra water would do the most good. Ellen and Lois helped the EMTs tend to the tired firefighters as best they could, while James helped Dan.

Finally, the fire was under control. Lizzie watched as the exhausted crew took turns resting and fighting what remained of the fire. She was startled when someone spoke to her. It was a fireman she had not seen approaching. The fireman's voice was muffled by the breathing device.

"Miss Fletcher, are you hurt?" he asked.

"No, I'm sure this is just a precaution," she answered, pointing to the oxygen mask. "Do you know what caused the fire? Was it arson?"

The fireman only nodded. He had taken a step toward her with an outstretched hand when their conversation was interrupted as Wade rushed to her side.

"Lizzie! Thank God you're alive. Are you hurt? Let me look at you?"

"I'm okay. I'm so glad you're here," she said as she fought back the tears.

"I came as soon as I heard. Is your family okay?" Wade asked with worry on his face.

"Yes, they're fine. They're here somewhere helping."

Wade held her tight and kissed her forehead. Chief Gaines cleared his throat as he stood nearby.

Wade turned toward the chief and said with a big smile, "We got him, Leo."

Gaines slapped Wade on the back and laughed, "That's the best news I've heard in a long time."

"You caught the arsonist?" Lizzie asked in confusion. "One of the firemen told me this was arson."

"We haven't had time to determine the cause of this fire yet," Chief Gaines replied with a frown. "Who told you that?"

Lizzie looked around. She saw the man she had talked with walking away from the scene. "That's him over there," she said and pointed.

"Miss Fletcher, all of my people are working to put out this fire. I don't know who that is, but I'm going to find out."

"I'll go with you," said Wade.

Chief Gaines called to the unknown fireman. The man began to run when he realized he'd been discovered. The two officers chased him until they lost him in the dark.

The sheriff and the fire chief didn't speak as they walked back toward the inn. They were each lost in their own thoughts as they caught their breath. They stopped to discuss the situation before rejoining Lizzie and her family near the ambulance.

"You said you got the arsonist." Leo Gaines asked.

"Yes, we did," answered Wade. "He confessed to every fire except the one that killed Kyle Jensen."

"That would explain why the evidence from that scene didn't match what we found at the rest," Gaines observed. "Are you thinking what I'm thinking?"

"I am if you're thinking we have another fire bug."

Chief Gaines nodded. "We'll know more after we've determined the cause of this one, but I have a feeling that our second arsonist just outran us."

"I have that same feeling," Wade said.

"I'll look into what caused this one personally," Chief Gaines said as they walked toward what remained of the Paradise Creek Inn.

CHAPTER TWENTY-FIVE

THE FIRE WAS FINALLY OUT. Lizzie couldn't see much in the dark. She knew the inn was damaged, but she couldn't tell how badly.

"Miss Fletcher," said Rashad Weaver. "It's time to take that ride to the hospital."

"I think Dan should go, too," said Ellen. "He drug Lizzie out of the house and hasn't stopped coughing since."

"It sounds like she means business," said Tonya Balderas as she led Dan to the ambulance. "We'd better humor her and make sure you're okay."

"Mrs. Fletcher doesn't mess around when it comes to injuries," Dan replied with a grin as he tried to hide a cough.

Dan and Lizzie were taken to the hospital as a precaution. Wade followed the ambulance and stayed by Lizzie's side. The sun was beginning to peek over the horizon when the trio returned to the inn.

"Lizzie, I'm sorry I wasn't here for you during the fire," Wade said sadly.

"Wade, you were trying to stop the fires. How could you have known?"

"That's just it! I should have known! I should have been here!"

"You're here now," said Lizzie with a smile.

"But I can't stay, Lizzie. I have to catch this guy. He could have killed you."

"I understand that you need to catch him," Lizzie replied. "But I'm afraid we'll lose us in the process."

"I don't want that to happen," said Wade as he pulled her close. "I need to look around for any evidence that might have been left behind. I'm sorry, but it can't wait."

"I know," said Lizzie. "I have work to do that can't wait either."

The Fletchers, Wade, and Dan stood with their arms around each other as they surveyed the damage. The inn wasn't a total loss, but it was severely damaged. The majority of the new construction had burned, leaving only the concrete foundation. The southwest corner of the house had sustained major damage from the fire. The rest of the inn was damaged by smoke and water.

The construction crew arrived as the Fletchers stared at what remained of the inn. They had been unaware of the fire until they drove upon the scene.

Wade approached the foreman and said, "I'd appreciate it if you and your crew would hang back for a while. My team is on the way. We'll be searching the area for any evidence that may have been left behind."

"Of course, Sheriff," replied the foreman. "Was anyone hurt?"

"No, thank God!"

"We'll work at another site today," said the foreman. "I need to talk with Mr. Fletcher or Miss Fletcher before we go."

While the foreman spoke with James, Wade began searching the area. Lizzie's mind whirled with all that needed to be done. She'd have to cancel every guest and event for the foreseeable future. She'd have to refund any deposits that had already been made.

She felt sick to her stomach at the thought of the events that were scheduled for this month. The weekend guests didn't concern her as much as those who had scheduled events. Would the wedding parties be able to find another venue? She had to contact those people now. She was thankful that she had taken the precaution of saving everything to a thumb drive.

"Where's that thumb drive?" she asked aloud as she tried to remember what she had done with it.

"What are you talking about?" Lois asked.

"I saved all of our records to a thumb drive," answered Lizzie. "I have to find it."

"Is it that important?" Ellen asked.

"It's very important, especially if the computer has been destroyed. Everything is on there: our calendar of events, names and numbers of guests and clients, and all of our financial records."

"Oh my Lord!" said Lois as she realized what Lizzie was trying to say. "We'll have to contact all of those people."

"Especially the wedding party for this weekend," Lizzie pointed out.

"It might help to retrace your steps," suggested Ellen.

"Good idea, Mom," Lizzie said as she closed her eyes and went through the process again in her mind. "I put it in my pocket! The jeans I wore that day are in the laundry basket. Do you think it's safe to go inside?"

James had called the insurance company and missed the conversation the women had been having. "Why do you need to go inside?" asked James.

"The most important reason is to find the thumb drive," Lizzie told her Dad. "I'm going to need to get some clothes, too."

"The insurance adjuster is on his way. Can it wait until he's finished?"

"Daddy, I have to cancel the wedding scheduled for this weekend as soon as possible."

"I hadn't thought about that," James said. "I'll go. Tell me where it is."

"It would be faster for me to go, Daddy. I know exactly what I'm looking for."

"Okay, but I'm going with you."

James and Lizzie carefully passed through the back door and made the trek to the laundry room. Fortunately, that room had little damage. Lizzie located the jeans she needed and retrieved the thumb drive.

She moved the laundry basket into the hallway before they went to her room. Lizzie gathered all of the clothing she could carry and stuffed it into the laundry basket. She went back to gather her essentials and her most treasured possessions.

"This will have to do for now, Daddy," said Lizzie. "Let's get out of here."

"Are you sure you don't want to take the kitchen sink, too," James teased.

"I'll get that next time," said Lizzie with a grin.

Lizzie explained that she needed to start making phone calls right away so that their clients might have time to make other arrangements for their weddings. She said goodbye to Wade and went to her parents' house.

Wade was searching the grounds around the inn. He knew what he was looking for this time. He found a place across the road where someone had waited and watched. He knew that Lizzie's private quarters couldn't be seen from there. Someone might have been able to see the glow of her bedroom lights from that position. He wondered who stood there and why.

He found a good shoe print in the soft soil and photographed it with his cell phone. He continued to scan the ground while he waited for his team. He watched the Fletchers as they struggled to deal with the loss. His heart ached for them. Their main source of income was now gone. Thankfully, they hadn't lost Lizzie as well.

"Sheriff, where should we start?" Dodson asked, interrupting Wade's thoughts.

"I've been concentrating on the area in front of the house. Have someone search the rest of the grounds. I need to check something inside."

"James, can you tell me where the smoke alarms are located?" Wade asked as he walked toward the family.

"It would be easier to show you," said James.

The two men cautiously went inside the house. There were three smoke alarms. One was in the upstairs hallway. One was in the main entrance, and the other was in the hallway between the kitchen and Lizzie's room.

They found the alarm near Lizzie's room where it should be. Wade took it down and opened it. The batteries had been removed, and the sound device had been broken.

"I don't understand. I replaced the batteries in all of the detectors when the time changed. Did someone do this deliberately?" asked James, with fear evident in his voice.

"It looks that way," said Wade gravely. "I'm going to need to talk with all of you as soon as we've finished our search. I'll check the other unit if you'd like to go outside for some fresh air."

"I'll meet you outside," James replied.

"Wade, are you in here?"

"I'm in the lobby area, Leo."

Leo shook his head as he made his way toward Wade, "Is that what I think it is?"

"A broken smoke detector," replied Wade. "There's another one in the same condition in the kitchen area. I can't get to the one they had upstairs."

"I'm sure it's been tampered with, too," said Leo. "It looks like it's the same person who set the Jensen fire. Gasoline was poured all over the construction area and on the adjoining side of the house. He either ran out of gas or was interrupted before he finished pouring."

"I found a place across the road just like the one at Kyle's place," Wade informed him.

"Call me when you get back to your office," said the fire chief. "I have lots of ideas that I need to sort through before I can put them into words."

Leo was about to leave when the insurance adjuster arrived. He spoke with the fire chief for a few minutes before he joined the Fletcher family.

"Hello, I'm looking for Mr. Fletcher."

"I'm James Fletcher."

"My name is Isaac Barnes. Your insurance company sent me," he said as he shook hands with James. "Would you tell me what happened here?"

"Dan Hayes was the first one here," said James. "Tell him what you saw, Dan."

Dan explained what had happened.

"Where is Miss Fletcher now?" Barnes asked.

"She's at our house making some necessary phone calls to guests and clients," Ellen replied.

"I'll need to speak with her when I've finished inspecting the house."

Dodson informed Wade that the team had searched the entire area. They found tire tracks across the bridge. It looked as if someone had parked there and walked toward the inn.

"We followed the foot prints to that spot across the road," said Dodson.

"That's good work," replied Wade. "I'd like for one of you to stay and take notes during the interviews. The rest will need to take the evidence into town and get started on it. The smoke detectors need to go, too. They've been tampered with," Wade added distractedly.

"I know I'm wasting my breath, but don't you think you should get some rest? You've been working for almost twenty-four hours. Let someone else take the lead."

Wade stared at Dodson as if he couldn't believe what he was hearing.

Dodson anticipated Wade's reaction. He placed his hand on the sheriff's shoulder and said, "Wade, you're too close to this one. Let one of us take the lead. We love Lizzie, too. We'll do everything we can."

Finally, Wade said, "You can take the lead, but I'm going to stay and take notes. There could be an answer here that will help us put the pieces together."

Dodson nodded and sent the rest of the team back to town with the evidence. Isaac Barnes was talking with Wade when he returned.

"You're absolutely sure it was arson?" asked the investigator.

"Yes, the evidence here matches evidence found at another fire earlier this month," Wade replied.

"Is it possible that the Fletchers started the fire in order to collect insurance benefits?"

Dodson interrupted when he saw the look on Wade's face, "No, sir, it isn't. This inn is a thriving business that the Fletchers depend on. They wouldn't risk their main source of income. More importantly, there's no way they would endanger their only daughter's life by setting a fire while she slept inside."

"I apologize. I seem to have crossed a line. These are questions that I have to ask in order to satisfy the insurance company," Barnes said as he wisely excused himself and began taking photos of the damage to the inn.

Dodson and Wade sat down at a patio table with the stricken family and Dan Hayes. Dan explained again exactly what he saw that led him to discover the fire and rescue Lizzie. He couldn't recall hearing the beeping noise of the smoke detectors and saw no one near the inn. No one heard or saw anything unusual.

"Does the name Alan Nichols mean anything to you?" Dodson asked.

"The name is familiar, but I don't believe I know him," said James while the others shook their heads.

"Did any of you know Kyle Jensen?"

They all replied that they did not.

None of them could think of anyone who might want to destroy the inn or hurt Lizzie. To their knowledge, they had no enemies.

"I suppose you could consider Megan an enemy," said Dan after listening to the others. "I can't imagine its true, but it wouldn't surprise me."

"That thought crossed my mind as well," Wade said.

"I haven't seen her around here, but she hates Lizzie," Dan replied.

"I'm sure we'll have more questions after we've sifted through the evidence. Please, call us if you think of anything," said Dodson. "We'll go talk with Lizzie before we start back to the office."

"Is it all right to start cleaning this mess up?" asked James.

"Start in the back if you don't mind," suggested Wade. "There is some evidence in front of the house that we may need to revisit."

Dodson waited beside the truck while Wade talked privately with the family. The two officers drove the short distance to the home of the elder Fletchers.

CHAPTER TWENTY-SIX

LIZZIE DIDN'T WASTE time unloading her jeep. She took only her phone, and the thumb drive into the house. She rehearsed what she was going to say to the bride while she waited for the computer to boot up.

"This is Lizzie Fletcher," she began when her call was answered.

"Hello, Lizzie," said the bride.

"I'm afraid I have some terrible news. I'm calling to let you know that the inn burned last night." Lizzie managed to sound professional and matter-of-fact as she spoke. "It's severely damaged. I'm so sorry, but we won't be able to host your wedding this weekend."

"Lizzie, I don't know what to say. I'm so sorry. Did you lose everything?"

"We haven't been able to get inside yet to see what we can salvage. Most of the damage seems to be in the guest areas."

"That means I'll have to find another place for the wedding and another caterer all in less than a week," said the bride as she realized what had to be done.

"The food may be okay since it was in the freezer and refrigerator. I'll let you know as soon as possible. It isn't safe to have the event here, but I'd be happy to cater as planned if you'd like," Lizzie offered.

"Lizzie, I need to talk to my mom. I'll let you know what we decide about catering," said the bride as she abruptly ended the call.

Lizzie took a deep breath and called the guests who had booked rooms for the following weekend. She had the same conversation with each one.

"I'll be happy to find other accommodations for you. I don't know how long it will be before we're operational again. The insurance adjuster and a construction company are here now assessing the damage. Thank you. I appreciate your understanding."

Lizzie thought about her current predicament after she had made the most urgent calls. She'd have to move in with her parents or find another place to live. It could be months before she'd be able to live at the inn again. She'd probably need to find a job as well. There would be no income if there were no guests.

She'd already spent the deposits for the next event. She hoped the insurance adjuster would take into account all those items that were damaged. The food might be salvaged if they could get it into cold storage in time, but the décor would be smoke damaged at the very least.

Her heart sank as she realized that all of the hard work they had put into making the inn a success was also lost. The longer the inn had to be closed, the harder it would be to get things back on track. The survival of the inn and the family's livelihood were in jeopardy. Lizzie hung her head and sobbed.

Dodson and Wade tapped on the front door. Lizzie wiped tears from her eyes before answering.

"Come in. Make yourselves comfortable. I need a minute, if you don't mind. Can I get you something to drink?"

"I'll get it," said Wade. "Do what you need to do."

Lizzie disappeared upstairs while Wade found bottles of water in the refrigerator. When she returned, Lizzie's face had been washed and her hair combed. She was still wearing the pajamas she had worn to bed the night before.

"I'm sorry about the way I'm dressed," she said. "All of my clothes smell like smoke. I'll have to put them in the washing machine."

"That's okay, Lizzie. We understand," said Dodson.

"Craig is taking the lead," Wade told her. "I'm going to listen and take notes."

"Okay," Lizzie replied.

Lizzie had seen no one near the inn that shouldn't have been there. She hadn't noticed anything unusual inside the house. She couldn't think of anyone who might want to destroy the inn or hurt her.

"Tell us about the firefighter that spoke to you," said Wade.

"I was sitting in the back of the ambulance near the doors," Lizzie began. "The EMTs were helping fight the fire."

"You were alone?" Dodson asked.

"Yes," answered Lizzie. "I didn't see him until he spoke to me."

"What did he say?"

"He asked if I was hurt. I told him I was fine and asked if the fire was arson. He nodded, and then Wade was there."

"Are you sure it was a man?" Wade asked.

"I'm pretty sure."

"Think back and picture this person in your mind," said Dodson. "Why did you believe it was a man?"

Lizzie concentrated, trying to remember every detail before she answered. "He was wearing a breathing mask. His voice was muffled, and I couldn't see his face. It wasn't a distinctive voice."

"How tall was he?"

"I remember that he wasn't as tall as Wade. He looked like he was an average-sized fireman."

"Does the name Alan Nichols mean anything to you?" Dodson asked.

"The name is familiar," said Lizzie. "He may have been involved in one of the events at the inn. I don't think I'd know him if I saw him."

"I understand you have had issues with Megan Ford," said Dodson.

"I suppose Megan could be considered an enemy," answered Lizzie. "I haven't seen or spoken to her since I stopped working for the Sheriff's department."

"Tell me about your recent disagreement with Drake Wagner," prodded Dodson.

Lizzie stared at him open-mouthed before looking at Wade. Wade seemed to be as surprised by the question as she was.

"We did have a minor disagreement the other day," Lizzie replied uncomfortably.

"Tell me what happened."

Lizzie told the deputy every detail. Wade already knew about the incident. She hoped hearing the details again wouldn't spark another argument.

"I'm going to repeat what you told me so that I'm sure I have it right," said Dodson. "You met Jan Wagner and Faith Foreman for lunch. Drake Wagner joined you unexpectedly."

"That's right," said Lizzie.

"You decided to leave, making the excuse that you had to meet a client. Drake followed you outside."

"Yes."

"How did he react when you told him that you weren't interested?"

"He wasn't happy about it," Lizzie replied.

"Was he angry enough that he might want to get even?"

"No, of course not," Lizzie said. "He doesn't have that kind of temper."

"Lizzie," Wade began. "Your relationship with Drake ended a long time ago. He may not be the same man he was then."

"Are you saying that you think Drake might have done this?"

"We're exploring all possibilities," said Dodson. "We have no leads. We have to start somewhere."

"I understand that," Lizzie began. "I just can't imagine that Drake would do such a thing."

The three sat in silent contemplation for a few minutes. Wade noticed an odd expression cross Lizzie's face.

"What's wrong, Lizzie?" he asked.

"I was remembering another time that I couldn't imagine someone doing such a thing. I was wrong then. Could I be wrong now?"

"Are you talking about the murders at the inn?"

Lizzie nodded.

"What's on your mind, Lizzie?" Dodson asked.

"Drake was here during the holidays while Wade and I were split up. He told me then that he wanted to put the past behind us and try again," Lizzie said as she glanced at Wade to gauge his reaction. "I told him that I was happy. The dream of owning my own inn was finally a reality, and I didn't want to give it up."

"Are you saying that he might have burned the inn so that you would reconsider his offer?" asked Dodson.

"The thought crossed my mind," admitted Lizzie. "But why would he start the fire knowing I was inside."

"Maybe, he planned to rescue you or take care of you," said Dodson.

"I don't like the man for obvious reasons, but even I don't think he would put Lizzie in danger," Wade confessed.

"This is just a thought; I'm not saying it's the case," said Dodson. "Maybe he had the mindset of 'if he couldn't have Lizzie, no one could.'"

Their conversation was interrupted by a knock on the door. Isaac Barnes had arrived to interview Lizzie. Dodson and Wade said goodbye and drove back to town.

Wade took Dodson's advice and went home to sleep for a few hours. He went to the office after lunch and called Chief Gaines as promised. He left a message when he was informed that the chief was out. Wade left his office and convened a meeting in the conference room.

"I'd like to start this meeting by saying that Dodson and I have come to an agreement about the Jensen case and the Fletcher case," Wade informed his team. "Some of you will be working with me on the Jensen case and some with Dodson on the Fletcher case. We'll be comparing notes periodically in both cases."

"We believe the Fletcher case and the Jensen case are connected based on the evidence found at both scenes," said Dodson. "We also believe there is a connection to Nate Tucker based on the mail that Wade received."

"We're going to start at the beginning and look at these cases from every imaginable angle," said Wade as he placed several photographs on the table for everyone to see. "We know how Nate Tucker and Kyle Jensen died. We know that Wayne Bowers died in a car accident and that Della Wallace died from emphysema. Last night there was an attempt to kill someone at the inn."

"What do you mean?" Reed asked. "I would assume that Lizzie was the target."

"She may have been," agreed Wade. "I was supposed to have spent the evening at the inn last night. It's possible that I was the intended victim."

"Was it common knowledge that you would be there?" asked Odom.

"I don't think so, but it is common knowledge that I'm there often," answered Wade.

"That would mean that this arsonist is targeting law officers," observed Gonzalez.

"It's a possibility that we need to consider," said Dodson.

"The first thing we need to do is find a connection between all of these people and our suspects," said Wade. "We've already established that Megan Ford and Alan Nichols have no alibi for the night of Jensen's death. We need to find out where they were last night."

"We have a possible third suspect," added Dodson. "Lizzie had a disagreement with Drake Wagner a few days ago. We need to know where he was last night."

"What about Wade's ex?" asked Maddie. "I'd consider her a suspect if Lizzie was the target."

"I hadn't thought of her, but you're right," answered Wade. "We need to investigate every possibility."

Wade and Dodson gave the team members assignments related to their discussion before changing the subject. It was time to discuss the evidence found.

"The smoke detectors had no prints," said Maddie. "They were in the same condition as those at the Jensen scene."

"The tire tracks match the tread pattern for Michelin Premier LTX," said Baker. "The vehicle was probably a truck or SUV. The shoe prints are consistent with a Wolverine brand hiking boot size ten-and-a-half."

"It's possible that the person responsible for Jensen's death and the fire at the inn was aware of Michael Clark's pattern," said Wade. "Our second firebug chose to burn the inn while the B shift was on duty to confuse us or implicate Clark. It's likely that he didn't know that Clark was in custody."

"We don't know if or when our second perpetrator will strike again," said Dodson. "We need answers as soon as possible."

The meeting was adjourned, and the team began their search. Chief Gaines arrived and was shown to Wade's office.

"I'm sorry I missed your call earlier," said Gaines.

"That's no problem, Leo. I know you're as busy as we are."

"I wanted to tell you this news in person anyway. We've been doing inventory this morning," said the fire chief. "We're missing some gear."

"Do you have any details?"

"I wrote it all down," Leo said as he handed Wade the information.

Wade looked at the information and said, "The shoe prints we found were size ten-and-a-half."

"That's the most common size we have. The rest of the gear is, too."

"Leo, how difficult is it to distinguish a man from a woman in full gear?"

"It's hard to know who is who. That's why we have names on the back of the jackets."

"What about the voices when wearing the breathing mask?" asked Wade.

"Most of the time, it's pretty easy. A man with a higher voice or a woman with a lower voice might be more difficult," Leo answered. "Are you thinking that it might have been a woman instead of a man that outran us?"

"I'm considering the possibility. Two of our suspects are women. One of them has no love for Lizzie. I'll add your information to the list of things we need to find," said Wade. "You look like you have something else on your mind."

"I've been thinking about this all day," Leo said. "The fire started after all of the Fletchers had gone to bed for the night. He had to know that the chances of the fire department arriving in time were slim to none. He also had to know that Lizzie was alone at the time."

"I have to admit that you have a good point," replied Wade. "I haven't been willing to consider that Lizzie might have been the intended victim."

CHAPTER TWENTY-SEVEN

THE NEXT MORNING the entire team gathered in the conference room. Wade's team started the discussion.

"Chief Gaines was here after our meeting yesterday," Wade began. "The fire department is missing a set of turnout gear. It was a spare set of the most common size they use." He paused for a moment before saying, "The chief pointed out the fact that this person was probably aware that Miss Fletcher was alone at the inn. That means that she was the intended victim and is still in danger."

"Do we need to arrange for protective custody," asked Odom.

"We'll offer that option, but I doubt she'll accept," Wade said with a grin. "She's working with her family and Dan Hayes to salvage as much as they can at the inn. She's well-guarded for the time being. To refresh our memories, Megan Ford and Alan Nichols have already been interviewed about the Jensen murder. Neither of them can provide a verifiable account of their activities that evening." The sheriff nodded at Maddie, indicating she should begin discussing what they had found.

"We started our search with suspect Megan Ford," said Maddie. "As we already know, she was arrested by Trooper Jensen and brought to jail, where Dodson took custody. She hired attorney Graham Shaffer to represent her in that case."

"Is she dating Shaffer?" asked Reed. "I saw them leaving the steak house together one night."

"I'll find out," said Maddie as she made a note. "Megan was once engaged to Drake Wagner. She blames Lizzie Fletcher for their breakup. She attempted to win Sheriff Adams' affections for a while."

"I remember that," grinned Baker. "She brought or sent packages of food almost every day."

Wade frowned at Baker and said, "Did you find anything else, Maddie?"

"Her mother, Roxanne, lives and works here in town. She has two sisters who live elsewhere. Her ex-husband Dan Hayes works for the Fletchers," said Maddie. "I also found a record of her father being arrested for arson years ago. He confessed and later hung himself in his cell."

"She came in with her attorney asking to see his file," said Wade. "They mentioned the suicide but didn't share any other details. What did you find out about Alan Nichols?"

"Alan Nichols has worked for the fire department for several years," said Odom. "Being a firefighter, he'd have access to any equipment they might have lying around. I discovered that his parents lived next door to Della Wallace before she moved to an assisted living facility. He may have known her. Nichols was related to Wayne Bowers. Bowers was his maternal grandmother's brother. I didn't find anything else case related. His parents live in Vernon. He has a brother who lives out of state."

"Tonya Balderas told us that he was her date when we talked to her," said Gonzalez.

"I'll add it to the list," said Maddie.

Wade noted the information and asked, "Anything else?"

"Tiffany Douglas Pruitt is divorced and has one son," said Gonzalez. "She currently lives in Beaumont, Texas, and until very recently worked for an insurance chain there. She will be working with a local agency in Vernon beginning next week."

"It occurs to me that Drake Wagner was probably acquainted with the Tucker family," said Wade. "I met them through Lizzie. It's likely that he did, too. Lodge, what did you find out?"

"I looked into the background of Michael Clark, aka Cacus," said Lodge. He's twenty-eight-years-old. He has no siblings. There's no record of his father. His last known living relative was his mother. She passed away at the end of March. Dr. Hughes thought that Clark's mother had enough nursing experience to recognize her son's symptoms. He also thought that she probably had access to medication samples based on Clark's description of the containers. I didn't find anything connecting him to Trooper Jensen. He's infatuated with Tanya Balderas, who lives in the same apartment building. He lived next door to Odom. I didn't find anything indicating he knew the other suspects or the victims."

"We found something interesting during our search," said Baker. "Trooper Jensen issued a speeding ticket to Nichols six months ago. Nichols argued that it had been a speed trap and took the case to court. He lost the case and had to pay a hefty fine plus court costs."

"Nichols didn't bother to mention that when we talked with him," said Wade.

"We found something else," said Baker. "Jensen also gave a speeding ticket to Drake Wagner in April. He hadn't paid the fine or contacted the J.P. about it as of yesterday afternoon."

"That's worth looking into," said Dodson.

"We searched the DMV records for vehicle registrations," said Gonzalez. "Miss Ford has a 2010 Honda Civic. Roxanne Ford drives a 2007 Buick Regal. Ms. Pruitt drives a 2013 Chrysler 200."

"It isn't likely that any of those cars have tires matching the tracks at the inn," Dodson pointed out.

"The registrations for Alan Nichols and Drake Wagner are more in line with our evidence," said Gonzalez. "Nichols has a 2014

Chevrolet Silverado pickup and a 1974 Corvette. Drake Wagner drives a 2009 Dodge Ram. His father also has a Dodge Ram registered as a farm truck."

"Any of those trucks might be the one we're looking for," said Wade.

"Reed and I talked with Miss Ford," Dodson said. "She claims to have been in Wichita Falls with friends at the time that the inn burned. We haven't been able to verify that. Tiffany Pruitt was in Dallas attending the wedding of her cousin."

"Mr. Nichols, on the other hand, says he was at home alone," added Reed. "We haven't been able to verify. We haven't made contact with Mr. Wagner."

"Odom and I will visit with the Tuckers and the Fletchers to see if they recognize or know anything about the information in the anonymous letters. We'll also talk to Nichols about them."

"We'll try to make contact with Wagner again," said Dodson. "Reed and I will drive to the Wagner place. We may be able to talk to his parents if he isn't there."

"I guess it's business as usual for the rest of you until we meet again this afternoon," said Wade.

Dodson and Reed drove to the Wagner family farm near Chillicothe, Texas. Drake was about to drive away in his truck when he saw their car turn into the drive. He turned off the truck motor and went to greet them.

"Hello, boys. What can I do for you?"

"Mr. Wagner, we need to ask you a few questions," said Dodson.

"Let's talk on the porch. It's cooler in the shade," said Drake as he led them to a round table on the covered porch. He leaned back in his chair and put his feet up on the railing.

Reed noticed that Drake's footwear was likely a match for the prints at the inn. He took advantage of the opportunity and said, "Those are nice boots. Where'd you get them?"

"I got them in Colorado. They're great for walking the mountain trails."

"Can you get them around here?"

"I'm sure you can. I had to order these. The biggest size in the store at the time was an eleven. It was faster to order a twelve online than to wait for their next shipment."

"I understand that you and Miss Fletcher had a disagreement recently," Dodson began. "Would you mind telling us what that was about?

Drake looked at the deputies in surprise. Finally, he answered, "I was going to ask her to dinner, but she didn't want any part of it. What happened?"

"Someone burned the Paradise Creek Inn last night," Dodson said as he looked directly into Drake's eyes.

Drake dropped his feet from the railing and sat up straight in his chair. "What? Is Lizzie okay? Was anyone hurt?"

"Everyone's fine," Reed informed him.

"Don't you think it was probably the guy that's been setting fires for weeks?"

"That person was in our custody before the fire started last night," Dodson replied. "Where were you last night, Mr. Wagner?"

"I was with Dad at the rehab center last night," Drake replied. "I've been there every night since he had his stroke. I'm sure the people that work there will tell you the same. I would never hurt Lizzie, but I'd like to get my hands on the person who burned her home and business."

"I'm sorry about your dad," said Reed. "How long has he been in rehab?"

"It's been a couple of months. My brothers and sister take turns staying with him during the week. I stay with him at night. He's probably going to be released today or tomorrow. Mom has been staying at my brother's place. She came home with me this morning to get Dad's room ready."

Reed took some papers from the folder he brought with him

and spread them out on the table. "Do you recognize or know any of these people?" he asked.

Drake scanned the documents and photos. "I knew Nate Tucker. I don't recognize the others."

"Not even this one?" Dodson said as he pointed to the photo of Kyle Jensen.

Drake looked closer, "No, I don't think so. Who is he?"

"That's State Trooper Kyle Jensen," said Dodson as he watched Drake's expression. "He stopped you for speeding not long ago."

"I forgot all about that!" said Drake as he remembered the incident. "I was on my way to the hospital to see Dad. That was right after he had his stroke. I need to take care of that ticket."

"Were you angry with Trooper Jensen about the ticket?" asked Reed.

"I wasn't happy about getting a ticket, but I was speeding. He was doing his job. Why are you asking about that?"

"Trooper Jensen died in a fire at his home," said Dodson. "We're checking all possible leads."

"I've been either at the hospital or here taking care of the farm since I've been back," said Drake.

Suddenly, the quiet of the morning was shattered by a loud explosion. The three men instinctively dove for cover. Their ears rang as they looked for the source of the noise. Fire and smoke billowed from Drake's truck.

Carol Wagner ran from the kitchen to the back porch, "Drake! What happened?"

"Mom, call the fire department," he said as he and the two deputies started toward the burning pickup.

They worked together to keep the fire from spreading while staying a safe distance away. They couldn't rule out another explosion. The Chillicothe Volunteer Fire Department arrived, and the three tired men returned to the porch. They stood and watched in silence while the firefighters worked to extinguish the blaze.

The Hardeman County Sheriff arrived as the fire department

was about to leave. He got out of his truck and strolled to the porch.

"Howdy, Drake," he said. "It looks like you've been having quite the barbeque today."

"It wasn't my idea," replied Drake.

"Craig, Gordon. It's been a while. How are things in your county?" Sheriff Roy Webb asked pointedly.

"We've been investigating fires and murders," answered Dodson. "We came to see if Mr. Wagner could help. We were about to leave when his truck blew up."

"The fire department found something they want me to see. Hang out here a minute, and I'll find out what's what."

"Today's incident is out of our jurisdiction. It may have been an accident. If it wasn't, it might be connected to our case," Dodson began. "I know this is bad timing, but if you're up to it, I have more questions."

Drake ran a shaky hand through his hair and sat down to ease the shaking in his knees. He looked at what was left of his truck. "Now is as good a time as any. It doesn't look like I'll be going anywhere this morning."

"Do you have any enemies?" Dodson asked.

Drake thought for a moment before he said, "The only person that I can think of is Megan Ford. I've been living in Colorado for years. I didn't have any enemies before I left here and haven't had time to make any since I moved back."

Drake stood as Sheriff Webb walked back toward the house. He was holding a small box attached to a wire in his hand.

"Do you recognize this?" he asked Drake.

"No, sir. What is it?"

"The fire chief thinks it's a triggering device. Tell me what happened."

When Drake had finished, Webb asked, "When was the last time you drove that truck?"

"I drove it home this morning from Wichita Falls. Mom and I got here about six."

"Did you see or hear anything unusual?"

"We both slept for a while. We were just starting our day when the deputies arrived."

"If you don't mind, I'd like to confer with my colleagues privately."

Drake nodded and went inside. Dodson and Reed walked with Webb away from the house. They told him about their current cases, and he shared his thoughts about the explosion and the triggering device. They agreed that the cases were likely connected.

"I'll send the report to you as soon as we know for sure what happened here," said Webb.

"We appreciate that," said Dodson as they walked back toward the house.

Drake was relieved to hear that they were finished for the time being. He watched as the lawmen drove onto the dirt road. It had been an eventful morning. First, he learned that he was suspected of setting fire to the inn and murder. Then, his truck exploded. He shuddered as he thought about what could have happened.

That afternoon, the team met again to share information and compare notes. Dodson and Reed began by reporting the explosion and what they had learned from their interview.

"The tires on the Wagner family vehicles were a different brand and tread pattern from the tracks found at the inn," said Reed. "The rehab facility in Wichita Falls verified that he has been there every night since Mr. Ben Wagner was admitted. He usually arrives before seven in the evening and leaves between six and seven in the morning after other family members arrive."

"We talked with Megan Ford when we returned," said Dodson. "She had been at work all day. We verified that with her supervisor. She clocked in at seven-thirty this morning. She didn't know anyone other than Jensen. I expected her to be pleased that there had been an attempt on Drake Wagner's life. Instead, she appeared to be quite upset."

"I was able to verify that she was in Wichita Falls at the time the inn burned," said Lodge. "She and a friend were at a bar from eight p.m. until it closed at two a.m."

"My source at the steak house tells me that Megan and Shaffer had dinner there two or three times," said Maddie. "He seemed to be enamored of her. The manager wasn't sure if she was really interested or leading him on. They haven't been there together lately. In fact, Megan's in there often with a lot of different men. She was there with Alan Nichols this week."

"Nichols seems to get around," said Gonzalez. "He's frequently been seen with Tanya Balderas and several other women at different establishments around town."

"Speaking of Nichols," said Odom, "Sheriff Adams spoke with him at the fire station. I had a tour of the station and discovered that he wears a size ten-and-a- half shoe and happens to own a pair of Wolverine boots. His truck tires also match the tread pattern. He went on duty at seven this morning."

"How far away is the Wagner farm?" asked Wade.

"I'd say fourteen or fifteen miles," Dodson answered.

"He could have had time to plant that device and get back in time if he had been there waiting," said Wade. "He admitted knowing both Della Wallace and Wayne Bowers. He said that he had no idea why someone would send the items to us. Mrs. Tucker and the Fletchers didn't know any of the people other than Nate, of course."

"I've been giving the person at the inn some thought," said Dodson. "Wouldn't Lizzie have noticed if the gear was much too big for the person wearing it?"

"I don't follow," said Wade.

"Megan Ford is a small woman. It would have been noticeable if she were wearing an average-sized set of turnout gear. Size ten-

and-a-half boots would have been hard for her to walk in, let alone run."

"That's true," said Wade. "Based on what we've learned today, we can eliminate Drake Wagner from our list of suspects for both the Jensen and the Fletcher cases. We can eliminate Megan Ford as a suspect in the Fletcher case. We can't eliminate her as a suspect in the Jensen case since we have no evidence to clear her. We also have no evidence to arrest her. I consider her as possible but not probable for the Jensen and Wagner cases. That leaves us with only one suspect who could have been responsible for not only the Jensen and Fletcher incidents but also today's explosion. Alan Nichols is our prime suspect."

"The speeding ticket could have been his motive for killing Jensen. What motive does he have to kill Lizzie or Drake Wagner?" asked Reed.

No one had an answer.

The meeting adjourned, and everyone was determined to find the evidence they needed to arrest Alan Nichols. Wade heard the front door open and turned to see Graham Shaffer stroll in.

"Sheriff Adams, I'd like to have a word with you," Shaffer said angrily.

"What can I do for you, Mr. Shaffer?"

"I want to know why your department has been harassing my client. Miss Ford called me in tears this afternoon."

Wade didn't invite the attorney to his office. Instead, he said, "Miss Ford is a person of interest in two separate cases. As we uncover evidence, naturally, we need to talk to her about it."

"I've instructed Miss Ford to contact me before she speaks with you or any member of your department again. It appears to me that the department is prejudiced against her, and I intend to see to it that she isn't arrested for a crime that she didn't commit."

"I thought it was unethical for a lawyer to date one of his clients," probed Wade.

"Miss Ford and I enjoyed a few social engagements. I was not representing her at that time," said Shaffer indignantly. "She came to my office recently and retained me as her attorney."

"You may not have time for any other clients," said Wade.

"Good day, Sheriff!" said Shaffer.

Wade returned to his office. He didn't have enough evidence to arrest anyone. He was worried that someone else would be killed before he could find the second arsonist. He was particularly worried about Lizzie. Why would someone want to hurt her?

Sheriff," Lodge said through the open door.

Wade looked at his deputy. He was holding another envelope in his gloved hand.

"This was with today's mail," Lodge said as he placed it on Wade's desk.

It was another large manila envelope addressed to Wade. Like the others, it had no return address. Wade immediately took it to the lab before opening it. This time there was an article about the opening of the Paradise Creek Inn and a note that read, *Ask Morton.*

CHAPTER TWENTY-EIGHT

"Ask Morton? What does that mean?" asked Lodge when Wade shared the information with his team.

"I don't know. This must have been sent the day of the fire," said Wade. "Someone is toying with us."

"What did the lab find?" asked Reed.

"They haven't finished with their tests yet, but I don't expect they'll find anything that wasn't on the previous letters."

"Whoever sent it seems to believe we'll know who Morton is," said Baker.

"Is Morton a first name or a last name?" asked Gonzalez.

"I knew a man when I was growing up named Morton Stapleton," said Odom. "Everyone called him Morty."

"I don't know anyone named Morton, first or last name," said Maddie.

"We don't even know if this Morton person lives here or somewhere else," said Wade.

Dodson had been sitting quietly, listening to the conversation. Finally, he said, "Maybe it means we should ask Rusty."

"Rusty?" asked Wade. Suddenly, he realized who Dodson meant. "Rusty Morton, why didn't I think of him?"

"Who is Rusty Morton?" asked Baker.

"Rusty was the Wilbarger County Sheriff before Wade was elected," answered Dodson. "Wade and I are the only two people still here that worked with him. Jensen was here too at that time."

"Maybe, this has something to do with revenge against the department," suggested Odom. "Jensen is killed. What better way to hurt Sheriff Adams than to hurt or kill the woman he loves."

"That doesn't explain the attack on Drake Wagner," said Reed.

"No, it doesn't. That attack may not be related to the other two," said Wade.

"I think we all need to be very careful, especially Wade and Craig," said Maddie.

"I'll try to get hold of Rusty," said Wade. "I'd like for the rest of you to find out if there are any other people named Morton who might have our answers. Find out if Megan Ford or Alan Nichols might be associated with anyone by that name."

Wade dialed the former sheriff's home number. He let it ring several times before giving up. Either Morton didn't have an answering machine, or it had too many messages. Hopefully, he had caller id. Wade tried Morton's cell phone number. It went right to voicemail. He sighed and thought about his former boss.

Rusty Morton had been the Wilbarger County Sheriff for years. He wouldn't have retired if his wife hadn't become ill. After she died, Rusty spent almost all of his time with his kids and grandkids. He was seldom home and rarely talked with old friends.

The phone on Wade's desk rang. He answered it quickly in hopes that the former sheriff might be returning his call.

"Sheriff Adams, this is Sheriff Roy Webb in Hardeman County."

"Hello, Sheriff Webb. What can I do for you?"

"I'm sure you've talked with your deputies about the explosion on the Wagner place," said Webb.

"Yes, sir, I have."

"The device we found under that truck was set to go off when the truck was started. I won't go into details other than to say that the device either malfunctioned or wasn't connected properly. Mr. Wagner is lucky to be alive. I'll send you a detailed report."

"Thank you, Sheriff," said Wade. "Is there anything I can help you with?"

"As a matter of fact, there is. Would you mind giving me an overview of the evidence found in your cases?"

Wade gave the Hardeman County Sheriff a quick summary of the evidence. He also told him that they had narrowed the list of suspects to one.

"That's interesting," said Webb. "I found a place near the Wagner's house similar to what you described. It looked like someone had stood and watched out of sight of the house. It was a well-worn area with a path leading to it."

"Were there any shoe prints or tread marks from a vehicle?" asked Wade.

"There were. I'll fax the photos to you when I fax the report."

"I'll let you know if they match," said Wade.

Wade went to the outer office and spoke to his team. "Sheriff Webb will be sending a fax of the report and some photos from the scene at the Wagner farm. It sounds like it might be the same perpetrator after all. The photos are of shoe and tire prints found in an area similar to those found at our two scenes."

"Have you talked to Rusty yet?" asked Dodson.

"I haven't been able to get hold of him. I'll keep trying," said Wade

"Maybe, we should go see him if you don't get hold of him soon," Dodson suggested. "Something doesn't feel right."

* * *

Rusty Morton was happy. It had been a long time since he felt like smiling and laughing. His kids were right. He had needed this trip. He was sorry that it was coming to a close.

His wife Lydia had always wanted to take a cruise. She died before they could make it happen. His son and daughter had suggested the trip. They said it would be in her honor. The whole family would spend a week on a Caribbean Cruise to celebrate Lydia's life and scatter her ashes at sea. It was what she would have wanted. He couldn't refuse.

He had had a wonderful time with his children and grandchildren. At times, it felt like Lydia was by his side, enjoying it all with him. He was going to miss them when he returned to the home he and Lydia had shared for forty years.

By the time the ship docked, he had made a decision. He needed to be near his family. It was time to let go of the past. It was time to move to a new town and start a new life. He wanted to watch his grandchildren grow up. He knew it wouldn't be easy to sell the house, but he knew it was the right thing to do. His family was thrilled when he told them of his decision.

It was late by the time their flight landed in Dallas. He was torn between spending more time with his family and going home to start the moving process. He wasn't looking forward to squeezing into Lydia's little car after that long flight. He decided to stay with his son for the night and drive home the next day.

He slept late the next morning and played with his granddaughter. It wasn't until he was loading the car that he realized his cell phone was still packed in his suitcase. He turned it on and noticed several missed calls. *Why would the sheriff's office be calling?*

* * *

Wade had tried several times that morning to contact Rusty Morton. He was worried. It wasn't like Rusty to ignore calls. He decided it was time to drive out to check on the former sheriff.

"Dodson, do you want to go with me to see Rusty?"

"Your truck or mine," Dodson said as he put on his hat.

"We'll take mine. Do you want lunch before or after we see him?"

Dodson rubbed his grumbling stomach, "Let's eat first."

They had a quick lunch and drove toward Lockett. Rusty lived near the old Lockett School. First-grade to eighth-grade students once attended school there. Lockett High School was located a few miles away. Board members eventually decided it was best to consolidate with the Vernon School District. The last Lockett High Senior Class graduated in 1970.

"His truck is here," observed Dodson as they drove up to Morton's house.

"I don't see Lydia's car," said Wade. "Maybe, he went somewhere in it."

"I doubt it. He always complained about how small and cramped it was," said Dodson. "He only drove it on long trips because it got good gas mileage."

"Maybe, he's on a trip, or maybe he sold it," Wade said as they got out.

They were almost to the front porch when Wade remembered that he'd left the file with the photos and obituaries in the truck. He went back to get them. As he opened the truck door, his cell phone rang. Dodson stepped onto the porch and rang the doorbell.

The explosion caused a shockwave that rattled the windows of houses more than a mile away. Neighbors began calling the sheriff's department to report what they had heard. Others called to report the fire.

Reed dialed Wade's cell phone. When he got no answer, he dialed Dodson's. He tried to call them several times between incoming phone calls. He knew something was wrong when one of the callers gave the address of the fire. It was Rusty Morton's home.

He felt that he needed to get to the scene right away. Unfortunately, he was alone in the office. When Maddie returned, he told her what he suspected and started out the door. Gonzalez was on her way in, and Lodge had just parked his car.

"Maddie needs help with the phones. She'll fill you in," Reed told Gonzalez as he ran toward Lodge.

"What's wrong?" asked Lodge as he got out.

"We need to get to Lockett fast," said Reed. "I'll tell you on the way."

The two deputies were horrified when they drove upon the scene. What was left of the house was in flames. Debris had scattered everywhere. Trees fifty yards away had been scorched. Some were burning. The fire department fought the flames in both areas.

They parked across the dirt road in order to control traffic. Reed saw Wade's truck as he directed a car away from the area. The Sheriff's truck was almost unrecognizable. It was covered in bricks and pieces of wood. All of the windows had been knocked out.

One of the firefighters tapped Chief Gaines on the shoulder and pointed toward the two deputies.

"Those trees are under control," said Gaines. "I'll need a couple of men to control traffic while I talk with the deputies."

Chief Gaines slowly walked toward Reed and Lodge. He dreaded telling them what they found. Two of the firefighters arrived at Lodge's car just before the chief did.

"I need a word with you both," he said. "These men will handle the traffic until we've finished."

Reed and Lodge followed the chief without a word. They steeled themselves for bad news. Chief Gaines stopped midway between the road and the burning house.

"I'm sorry to have to tell you this," the chief said. "Sheriff Adams is badly hurt and may not make it. We've called for the Medevac chopper. The deputy with him has been killed."

"Dodson is dead?" Reed swallowed hard and asked, "Do you know any details?"

"We haven't had time for that yet. Was there anyone else with them?"

"No, sir. There may have been someone in the house. They came to see Rusty Morton."

"If he was in the house, he was probably killed, too."

"May we see them?" asked Lodge stiffly.

"Sheriff Adams is in the ambulance. You don't want to see Dodson right now," Leo said with compassion.

The deputies took deep breaths as they walked toward the ambulance. The EMT moved aside. Wade was unconscious. His face was covered in blood. Slivers of glass protruded through his bloody shirt.

"Where was he when you found him?" Reed asked.

"He was near the back of his truck. The driver's side door was on top of him. It may be what kept him from being killed instantly."

"Where was Dodson?" Lodge asked.

The EMT looked at his partner before saying, "We think he took the brunt of the blast. We haven't moved him. He's over there."

Reed looked toward the place indicated by the EMT. He swallowed hard again and nodded. Lodge turned away and started back to the car. They could hear the helicopter as it approached.

"Where are they going to take the sheriff?" Reed asked.

"He's going directly to Wichita Falls."

Reed stayed by Wade's side until he was loaded in the Medevac unit. He thanked the EMTs and joined Lodge at the car.

"I called the office. Baker and Odom are on the way. Maddie and Marina are going to run the office. Maddie called Dr. Hughes. He should be here soon," Lodge said woodenly.

"Is Maddie going to call their families?"

Lodge nodded and hung his head.

Reed spoke to a fireman directing traffic, "Would you mind working traffic while we have a look around?"

"Go ahead. We've got this."

Reed and Lodge were taking their gear from the trunk of the car when Dr. Hughes arrived. They told him what they knew and walked with him to find Chief Gaines.

"Chief Gaines," Reed said. "We need to do our jobs if we're going to catch the person responsible. I know you don't advise it, but we need to see the body."

Leo Gaines nodded and led them to Dodson. The deputies hung back while Dr. Hughes examined the remains. When he had finished, they moved in to take the necessary photographs. Lodge had to walk away twice to vomit. Reed struggled to stay focused on the job. They helped Dr. Hughes place their friend in a body bag before moving to Wade's truck.

Baker and Odom arrived and began to search the surrounding area. When it was safe to search the remains of the house, Odom and Reed looked for evidence inside while Baker and Lodge sifted through the debris outside.

At first, all of the deputies were numb with shock and grief. The numbness gave way to pain and anger. Anger drove them to find answers. Anger kept them going into the wee hours of the morning. They would find who did this and make certain that person paid for what he had done.

The Fletchers had worked all day at the inn. They had cleared out the parts of the house that hadn't burned. They kept what could be saved and threw out everything else.

Lizzie had showered and was relaxing on the couch when her cell phone rang.

"Lizzie, this is Gloria."

"Hi, Gloria," Lizzie replied.

"I just got a call from Maddie Clifton. She asked me to call you. She had lots of other calls to make."

Lizzie sat up suddenly, very alert, "What happened?"

"Wade has been hurt. He's been taken by Medevac to Wichita Falls," Gloria's voice broke as she spoke.

"How bad is he?" Lizzie asked as she fought back tears.

Gloria sobbed, "He may not make it. We're leaving right now."

"I'll meet you there," said Lizzie as she fought back tears. "Mama, I have to go!"

"What's wrong?"

Lizzie told her family about the phone call from Wade's mother. They refused to let her go alone. They quickly gathered a few things and got into the car. They arrived at the hospital in record time, but they were not allowed to see Wade. They couldn't get an update on his condition since they weren't relatives.

Lizzie was frantic for news. Finally, his parents arrived. They were told that Wade was in surgery. His condition was critical.

Sean and Gloria shared what details they knew about the accident with Lizzie and her family. They were heartbroken to learn about Dodson's death. They cried and prayed together until the surgeon walked through the automatic door.

"Mr. and Mrs. Adams, your son is out of surgery. He's still in critical condition, but depending on how he does in the next few hours, he may have a chance. We had to remove a piece of metal that punctured his lung. We also removed his spleen and quite a bit of glass that was imbedded in his skin. He has a gash on his head that took several stitches. I'm most concerned about the head injury right now. He took a severe blow to the head. We'll keep him in ICU for a few days."

"When can we see him?" asked Sean.

"He's still in recovery. A nurse will come for you when he's settled in ICU."

"Thank you, Doctor."

Lizzie paced the floor, tried to read a magazine, went to the ladies' room, and then started the cycle all over again.

"Lizzie, would you mind calling the office to let them know how Wade is doing?" asked Gloria.

"I'd be happy to," said Lizzie.

She went outside to get some fresh air while she made the call. She felt a little better when she returned.

"We've asked the hospital staff to answer any questions you have about Wade's condition," Sean told her.

"Thank you," Lizzie said as she hugged him.

The two families kept watch together through the night. They continued to cry and pray together. Until they knew he would be okay, they refused to leave Wade.

CHAPTER TWENTY-NINE

WADE SPENT three days in the Intensive Care Unit. His body was healing, but he still hadn't regained consciousness. He had slipped into a coma.

Lizzie was beside herself. They had been arguing so much lately that she felt she was losing him. They hadn't had the chance to talk things over and work it out. Now, they might never get the chance.

She went to the hospital every day and sat with him for hours. She'd tell him how much she loved him and missed him. She read to him and talked to him while holding his hand or stroking his hair. When she left the hospital, she was restless and kept busy cleaning at the inn.

When Wade was moved from ICU to a standard room, Sean and Gloria had a hotel room nearby and took turns staying with him. They would discreetly find something to do so that Lizzie could spend time alone with him.

Lizzie sat in a chair beside Wade's bed and read to him. She leaned back and looked through the window of his hospital room. "Wade, it's the fourth of July. I can see the fireworks in the distance," she told him and described the colors and patterns.

Suddenly, she woke with a start. She had fallen asleep and had been dreaming of the past. She had been in this situation before. Rob had been in a coma when she last saw him.

Lizzie realized as she looked at Wade that he and Rob had some physical similarities. She had never noticed that before. Then she realized that Wade also had some physical similarities to Drake.

Lizzie thought about her past relationships. She had been completely in love with Drake. She remembered how much it hurt when he told her that he was going to propose to Megan. She later met Rob and fell in love with him. That, too, ended painfully when she discovered that her fiancé was already married.

Her relationship with Wade was different. She never felt that tingle when Drake or Rob touched her hand or brushed her hair from her face. She felt it every time Wade touched or looked at her. She had felt completely secure with Wade until Tiffany came along.

Tears streamed down her face as she finally realized what her grandmother meant. In spite of the similarities, Wade was not Drake or Rob. She knew that she didn't have to guard her heart anymore. She could trust him completely. If only he would wake up so that she could tell him.

Lizzie returned home and drove past the inn to her parents' house. Exhausted, she stretched out on the couch and slept soundly for the first time in days.

* * *

Reed had seniority and was now acting sheriff. He quickly had a new found respect for Wade. He had no idea what Wade did on a daily basis. The department was now short two people again. They had two deputies who still weren't totally familiar with the town or the county and two who were still recovering from injuries. He needed help.

He located the number for County Commissioner Wendell Johnson and made the call.

"Mr. Johnson, this is Gordon Reed with the Sheriff's department.

"Hello, Deputy. How are things going?"

"I could use some extra hands here. Would it be possible to hire that third deputy now?"

"I apologize. The commission approved the funds at our last meeting. I didn't have a chance to inform Sheriff Adams before he was injured," said Johnson.

"That's good news," replied Reed. "I'd also like to know if it would be possible to bring Lizzie Fletcher back temporarily."

"I'd say that's an excellent idea under the circumstance."

"Thank you, sir."

"How is Sheriff Adams?"

"There's been no change," replied Reed sadly.

"How's the investigation going?"

"It's practically crawling at this point."

"I understand being shorthanded makes it more difficult," said Johnson. "Keep us posted about the sheriff's condition."

Reed immediately dialed Lizzie's number when the conversation with Johnson ended. He hoped she'd be willing to help.

"Lizzie, this is Gordon Reed."

"Hi, how are you doing?"

"I had no idea how much work Wade does. I need your help, Lizzie."

"What do you need me to do?"

"Would you be willing to come back to work as an interim deputy?"

"Can I think about it for a while? I go to see Wade every day, and we're trying to get the inn back in shape."

"I understand if you'd rather not, but we really could use the help," said Reed. "I'm willing to beg and plead on my knees if you want."

Lizzie laughed, "I'll let you know by tomorrow morning. I need to talk it over with my family."

As soon as the call with Lizzie ended, Reed phoned Dashleigh Reynolds.

"Miss Reynolds, this is Gordon Reed with the Wilbarger County Sheriff's Department."

"Oh, hello, how are you?"

"I'm not doing so well right now. That's why I'm calling. We need another deputy. The funds have been approved. The job is yours if you're still interested."

"Well, I appreciate the offer, but I've already accepted another job. I've been working with the Gray County Sheriff's Department."

"I'm sorry to hear that," said Reed. He quickly realized that wasn't the right thing to say and added, "For our sake, that is. I'm happy that you've found a position."

Dashleigh giggled and said, "I understand, and thanks for considering me."

Reed called the team into the conference room. It was the first opportunity they had to discuss the evidence found at the scene.

Baker and Odom found shoe prints and tread marks matching those at the inn and the Wagner residence. They also found an area similar to the others where someone had been watching. Chief Gaines had watched closely for any extra firefighters but didn't see one. The device that triggered the explosion was attached to the doorbell.

"Rusty Morton had been on vacation with his family," Reed told them. "He came back to find his home destroyed and people from our department and the fire department all over his property."

"Did you talk to him about the note?" asked Maddie.

"He's going to stop by here later today. I'm not sure how much help he can give us. Dodson and Wade knew him pretty well and probably knew what to ask. I don't have any idea other than to show him that file."

"Dr. Hughes faxed his autopsy report to us," said Baker. "He determined the cause of death to be blunt force trauma as a result of the explosion. He did mention that it was instantaneous." The team was silent as they all remembered Deputy Craig Dodson and prayed for his family.

"Does anyone have anything else to share about this case? If not, I'll move on to the next item of business," said Reed. "The funds were approved to hire another deputy. I contacted Dashleigh Reynolds and offered her the job. She accepted another position and declined the offer. If you know anyone who would be a good candidate, please, tell them to apply. I also contacted Lizzie Fletcher and asked her to consider coming back to work with us as an interim deputy. She'll let me know in the morning."

"Won't that be an issue since she's involved with Sheriff Adams?" asked Odom.

"Ordinarily, yes, but since Wade is going to be out indefinitely, it shouldn't be an issue."

* * *

Lizzie discussed working for the sheriff's department with her family. There wasn't a lot more they could do at the inn until they heard from the insurance company. She had too much time to think. She needed something to do. She also needed the income.

There wasn't much money left after she refunded the deposits to those who had scheduled events at the inn. She had catered two weddings since the inn burned, but there was no other money coming in. She had to make do with staying at her parents' home and sleeping on the couch in the den.

Lizzie had considered looking for a job, but she wanted to be able to spend time with Wade every day. She discussed working with the sheriff's department with Wade's parents. They thought it was a good idea and promised to contact her immediately if Wade's condition changed. The deciding factor was the experience she had with Gloria.

Gloria hugged Lizzie and then stepped back. Her hands were

still on Lizzie's shoulders as she looked directly into Lizzie's vivid blue eyes and said, "Get the person who did this to our Wade."

Lizzie called Reed the following morning, "When do you want me to start?" she asked.

"Yesterday," replied Reed. "Seriously, as soon as you can would be great."

"I'm on my way."

Lizzie was happy to have something to occupy her mind and her hands. She was running the office when Rusty Morton came in. Reed asked her to send him to the conference room.

"Reed, I'm sorry that I didn't make it yesterday," said Morton. "I got tied up with my insurance company."

"That's understandable," said Reed. "Lizzie, would you mind staying and taking notes while we talk?"

Lizzie found a notebook and sat down. Reed spread the papers from the file over the table and explained why they needed his help.

"I knew Nate Tucker and Jensen, but I don't recognize these others," said the former sheriff. "Ask Morton. What are you supposed to ask?"

"We don't know," replied Reed solemnly.

"Are you sure I'm the right Morton?"

"We weren't, but I thought you were the most logical person to start with. It seems that we were right based on what happened at your place."

"Could I make a suggestion?" asked Lizzie.

"Who are you, little lady?"

"I'm sorry. I should have introduced you," apologized Reed.

"My name is Lizzie Fletcher," she said, extending her hand.

"Lizzie has worked with us before as an interim deputy when we were shorthanded."

"I bet I know your dad," Morton said with a grin. How is old James?"

"He's doing well."

"I was sure sorry to hear about your business."

"Thank you, now about that suggestion."

"What's on your mind?" asked Reed.

"I've been reading through all of the evidence. That note might have been written to lure someone from this office to the scene. The case notes said that someone had been watching nearby. He may have been watching long enough to know that Sheriff Morton wasn't home. He obviously broke into the house. He would have had to in order to rig the doorbell to explode."

"Is that what I heard?" asked Morton.

"You heard the explosion?" Reed asked in surprise.

"I was talking to Adams on the cell phone and then kablooey."

"You talked to Wade?" asked Lizzie.

Morton explained why he hadn't answered any of Wade's calls. He had ten missed calls from his former deputy and decided he'd better get in touch with him.

"The phone rang once before he answered. I asked him what was so urgent. I'm not sure that the last word was out of my mouth when the loudest noise I've ever heard blasted through the phone."

"Wade must have been beside his truck when the house exploded," said Reed.

"How do you know that?" asked Lizzie.

"If the call had come while he was on the porch, they would have known that Sheriff Morton wasn't home. Dodson would have walked away with Wade. If they had both been in the truck when the phone rang, Dodson wouldn't have been on the porch either."

"That would explain why he survived," said Lizzie. "If he had been on the porch with Dodson...," Lizzie said, unable to finish the sentence.

Reed swallowed hard before he continued, "Were Adams and Dodson the intended victims, or is anyone from the department a target?"

"Why were Adams and Dodson the ones to go to my place?" asked Morton.

"They wanted to go because they were the only people in the department that knew you and had worked with you," replied Reed. "They were concerned when you didn't answer Wade's calls. Every person in that file is either dead or a fire victim."

"Maybe, this guy knew that," said Morton.

"How could he know?" asked Lizzie.

"It could be someone very familiar with the department," Morton pointed out. "It may be someone who's been around a long time or someone who knew us years ago."

"That still doesn't explain the connection with the people in that file," said Reed.

"It might if those people were connected to an old case," said Lizzie.

"I don't remember any of those people. If it was an old case, it was a long time ago," said Morton.

"Sheriff Adams said something before the explosion. 'Someone is toying with us.' Maybe these people have nothing to do with the case," said Reed. "These could have been sent to confuse the investigation and lure us where he wants us."

"That's a possibility," agreed Morton. "He's had you chasing your tails while he waits for the right moment to strike."

The trio sat quietly, contemplating Morton's last comment. Their thoughts were interrupted by the ringing of Morton's cell phone. After the call ended, Morton said, "I'm sorry I can't be of more help. I need to leave and take care of a few things. Feel free to call me if you have any more questions."

Morton left the office while Reed and Lizzie returned to their work. Reed was in Wade's office thinking about the case and all of the evidence when Lizzie tapped on the door.

"There's a woman here to see you."

"Who is it?" Reed asked.

"She said her name is Tracy," replied Lizzie. "She doesn't want to speak to anyone but you. She said it's about the fires."

"All right, send her in."

"Hello, Sheriff. I hope I haven't come at a bad time."

"It isn't a bad time, but I'm not the Sheriff. I'm filling in for him while he's away," answered Reed. "What can I do for you, Miss?"

"Please, call me Tracy," she replied. "I understand you've been questioning some of the firemen."

"Yes, ma'am, we have."

"I'm married to one of those firemen."

"I take it that you're here to verify your husband's alibi."

"Not exactly," she said as she fidgeted nervously.

Reed was surprised by that response and asked, "What do you want to tell me?"

"My husband works the B shift. He was working at the time of those fires."

"I see," said Reed as he mentally ran through the B shift roster. Only two men on that shift were married. He had met Kyzer and his wife during the course of the investigation.

Tracy took a deep breath to calm her nerves and said, "He doesn't want me to tell you, but since the sheriff was hurt, I think that I should. I need to tell you now that he didn't do it."

"Who didn't do what?" asked Reed.

"He didn't start those fires. He'd never do something like that," she said.

"Who wouldn't?"

"Alan Nichols. He was with me all of those nights," she said.

Reed wrote the information on a note pad as Tracy continued talking nervously.

"I bumped into Alan one evening while my husband was on duty. One thing led to another, and we spent the night together. We've been seeing each other when my husband is on duty ever since."

"Was he with you when Sheriff Adams was injured?"

"No, he was working that fire."

"I'll need to know times and places," said Reed.

"I thought you might," Tracy replied. "Here's a list."

Reed took the list from her and read it carefully before saying, "May I give you some friendly advice?"

Tracy nodded.

"I think it would be in your best interest to end things with Nichols and to tell Lynn."

Surprised, she looked at him and said, "No, he can't find out. I love him. I don't want to lose him."

"Mr. McClain won't find out from anyone in this office," Reed assured her. "However, I think it would be wise for you to tell him before someone else does."

"I'll think about it," she said as she stood to leave.

"You should tell him soon," Reed said. "Mr. Nichols has been seeing several other women. I know that at least one of those women likes to cause trouble."

"What? He told me I was the only one."

"I'd imagine that your husband thinks the same thing."

"Touché," she said as tears filled her eyes.

Reed escorted her to the door before he turned and kicked the counter in frustration.

CHAPTER THIRTY

LIZZIE GOT off duty and started the half-hour drive back to the farm. She wanted to get cleaned up before going to see Wade. She had time to think about the case while she was alone in the jeep.

Reed had met with the team that afternoon when everyone returned to the office. Maddie and Gonzalez had visited with Megan Ford about the latest incident. She had been at work at the time. That fact was immediately confirmed by her employer.

Odom and Lodge had investigated Alan Nichols' movements at the time of the explosion and discovered that he had been on duty and working the Morton fire. Reed took the opportunity to share his information.

"A woman came forward today to inform us that Alan Nichols was with her at the time of every fire prior to the explosion," he told them. "We're back at square one."

Lizzie's mind raced with questions. *Did Cacus really work alone? Was someone else using the previous fires to cover their own tracks? Was it a coincidence that Nate Tucker's obituary was one of those sent to Wade? Why were those envelopes sent to Wade personally instead of the department? Had Wade been a target all along? Was he supposed to have died with her at the inn? Were members of the department targets and the others decoys? Were they all targets? Was Tracy lying about being with Alan Nichols during every incident?*

She couldn't help the feeling that the people in that file were somehow connected to the recent events. All of the fires prior to and including the one that killed Nate Tucker were set by Cacus. The information in his journal confirmed his confession. He denied setting the fire that killed Kyle Jensen. His journal entry also confirmed that fact.

Lizzie suspected that someone took advantage of the opportunity to include Nate Tucker either to implicate someone or lead them to someone. But who?

Her mind was still racing when she parked her jeep at her parents' house. Faith's car was in the drive. She hadn't talked with Faith since the day they had lunch together. She was anxious to see her longtime friend. She gathered her things and hurried inside.

"Hi, Lizzie," said Drake.

"What are you doing here?" Lizzie asked, confused and annoyed.

"That's not much of a greeting," he joked.

"I saw Faith's car and was expecting to see her."

"She loaned me her car since my truck is in pieces all over Mom and Dad's yard."

"That still doesn't answer my question. What are you doing here?"

"I wanted to make sure that you're okay. I heard about the fire at the inn and what happened to Wade," Drake answered. "I'm so sorry, Lizzie."

"Thank you. Why didn't you just call to tell me that?"

"I wanted to see you," said Drake.

"Oh good, your home," said Lois as she brought in a glass of tea for Drake. "Do you want some tea, Lizzie?"

"No, thank you, Granny," Lizzie answered. "I was about to

change and go to the hospital to see Wade. Where are Mama and Daddy?"

"They should be home any minute. They went into town to talk with the insurance company. I need to see how dinner is coming along," Lois said, sensing the tension between the pair. "I'll be in the kitchen if you need me."

"Drake, I really don't have time to talk," said Lizzie. "I need to get to the hospital before visiting hours are over."

"I won't stay long," he replied. "I just wanted to tell you that I'm sorry about how things worked out between us. I'm sorry that I never called you or made an effort to make things right. I was too wrapped up in my life in Colorado. My life was good there, but it was missing something. I realized when Dad had his stroke what was missing. I realized what was really important."

"What are you saying?" Lizzie asked apprehensively.

"I'm saying the most important thing in life is family. I missed my own family while I was away. Now that I'm back and have them around me again, I realize that I'm still missing something. I want a family of my own. I want you to be a part of my life and my family."

Lizzie stared at him. She hadn't expected this and didn't know how to respond.

Drake continued, "Lizzie, I know that I have a lot to make up for. I'm willing to do anything. Is there any chance for us?"

"Drake," Lizzie began. "I'm sorry if I've misled you. This may be painful, but I need to say this plainly so that there is no misunderstanding. I loved you in the past. It's because of that past and my love for Faith and Jan that I wanted a friendship with you, nothing more than friendship. I'm in love with Wade now. Even if I weren't in love with him, there would be no chance for us. It's time to stop living in the past, Drake."

Drake hung his head and sighed, "Did I ever have a chance to win you back?"

Lizzie thought for a moment before she shook her head and said, "No, I'm sorry."

"I'm sorry, too," said Drake. "I blew it when I told you that I was going to propose to Megan didn't I."

"Yes, that was the end for me," Lizzie answered truthfully. "I'd have stayed by your side through anything, but you chose her instead. I trusted you until that moment."

"Can we still be friends?"

"I don't know. I'd like to but…"

"I know," Drake said with a sigh. "I haven't been acting like a friend, and I'm sure Wade wouldn't like it at all."

"No, he wouldn't."

"Goodbye, Lizzie," he said as he wiped a tear from his eye. "I guess I'll see you around."

"Goodbye, Drake." Lizzie fought her own tears as she watched him drive away.

"Lizzie? Are you okay?" Lois asked as she entered the room.

"I'm fine, Granny. How long had he been here?"

"He arrived a few minutes before you did," Granny replied. "I didn't know what to do, so I invited him in."

"It was for the best. I think we've finally come to an understanding." Lizzie hugged her grandmother and said, "I'm going to change and go to the hospital."

James and Ellen were walking in the front door as Lizzie was about to leave.

"Would you mind waiting a little while before going to see Wade?" Ellen asked. "We need to talk about the inn."

Lizzie reluctantly followed her parents to the kitchen and sat down at the table. Lois joined them, and the discussion began.

"We've talked with the insurance company and the construction company," said James. "The insurance will cover the cost of the repairs to the existing structure but not the addition. Luckily, the construction wasn't too far along, and we'll be able to cover that cost with a loan from the bank."

"Are we going to be back in business soon?" asked Lois hopefully.

"That's what we need to decide," answered James. "We have some options to discuss."

"What options?" Lizzie asked.

"We can start by making repairs to the main house and wait a while to continue the construction on the addition," said James. "We would be able to have the business operating sooner, but we still wouldn't have enough space."

"Another option is to have the repairs and the addition done at the same time," added Ellen. "It would take longer, but all of the construction would be completed. We would have the additional space we need without having to turn customers away."

"There's a third option," James began. "We could tear down what's left of the existing house and build a brand new inn."

"Was there enough insurance money to build a new inn?" asked Lizzie.

"No, but with the money that the bank is willing to loan us, we could make it work," answered Ellen.

"What sort of a timeline do we have?" asked Lois.

"The quickest option would be to repair the existing house. That would take at least three months if all goes according to plan," James told them. "The repairs and the addition could take up to six months."

"How long will it take to tear down and build new?" Lizzie asked.

"That depends," said Ellen. "We'll need to draw up plans for a new inn. It could take a year or longer. The best thing about a new inn is that everything would be new. The wiring, the plumbing, and the framework would be up to date. We wouldn't have to worry about repairing or replacing anything in the house itself for years to come."

"That would mean we'd be out of business for at least a year," said Lizzie. "It might be hard to build our business back up."

"We need to figure out how we'll manage financially while the inn is closed, too," said Lois.

"That's why we need to think about this very carefully before we make a decision," said James. "The construction company needs an answer by the fifteenth of this month. Otherwise, they'll have to start another job before they can get to us, and whatever we decide will take longer."

"I don't think we can afford to stay closed for an entire year," said Lizzie. "People will have forgotten about us. They'll book their weddings and events at other venues. There are lots of other places people can stay for the weekend. I'm afraid we won't be able to recover if we're closed that long. The house was renovated four years ago. I don't think anything needs to be updated right now."

"How are our finances?" asked Lois.

"They're tight after paying back the deposits for the next few months," answered Ellen. "They'll be tighter if we have to return more. I like the sound of a brand new building with no issues to worry about, but I don't think we should stay closed that long either."

"I'd say it's unanimous that we won't build a new inn," said James. "What about the other two options? Can we manage for six months?"

"I think we can," said Ellen. "I can go back to work for a while if necessary. Lizzie is already working. We should be able to manage."

"I vote for option two," said Lois. "All of the construction will be completed, and we can stop turning customers away."

"Lizzie, what do you think?" asked her dad.

"I think having the construction completed all at once is the best option," she replied.

"Let's think about it overnight. Once we've made the decision, there's no going back," said James. "We need to be absolutely sure this is what we want before I contact the builder."

Lizzie had a quick dinner with her family before driving to

Wichita Falls. She had so much on her mind that she missed the exit to the hospital. She took the next exit and backtracked until she found the parking lot. She pushed all thoughts about the case and the inn from her mind as she got off the elevator at the hospital. She wanted to concentrate on Wade tonight.

She walked to Wade's room and stopped. Someone was crying on the other side of the door. She braced herself for bad news and quietly pushed the door open. Tiffany stood at Wade's bedside, holding his hand.

"I was afraid that something like this would happen someday," said Tiffany as tears rolled down her cheeks. "I've wasted so much time. I never should have left you. I'm so sorry, Wade."

"May I help you?" Lizzie asked as she entered the room.

"This is a private conversation, if you don't mind," Tiffany said. "Who are you?"

"I'm Lizzie Fletcher. Who are you?" she asked, although she already knew.

"I'm Tiffany Pruitt. Wade and I were engaged at one time," she said with a smile.

"So you're Tiffany. Wade told me about you," Lizzie said as she stepped further into the room. "Why are you here?"

"That's what I'd like to know," Gloria said as she entered the room behind Lizzie.

"Oh, Gloria!" said Tiffany as she turned and embraced Wade's mother. "I'm so sorry I didn't come sooner. I just heard about what happened. I got here as soon as I could."

"You don't belong here," Sean said as Gloria pushed Tiffany away.

"What do you mean? Of course, I belong here. I love him!" Tiffany shouted angrily.

"What's going on in here?" asked a nurse investigating the reason for the noise.

"This woman is not allowed to see our son at any time," Sean informed the nurse.

"Miss, you'll need to leave before I call security and have you escorted out," said the nurse firmly.

"What? I can't see him, but she can!" Tiffany said, pointing at Lizzie. "I'm not leaving until she does."

The nurse left the room and called hospital security.

"You left Wade years ago. You have no business here," replied Gloria. "Lizzie has been a part of Wade's life longer than you were, and more importantly, he loves her."

"Do you love him as much as I do?" Tiffany challenged Lizzie.

Lizzie looked at Wade and back at Tiffany before saying, "I love him enough to stay with him no matter what happens. I won't leave him the way you did."

Tiffany was glaring at Lizzie when the security guard arrived. Gloria and Sean stood on either side of Lizzie with their arms around her as they watched the guard escort Tiffany to the elevator.

"You go in and sit with Wade," Gloria told her. "We need to talk with the hospital staff. We don't want Tiffany to show up here again."

Lizzie went to Wade's room and sat down beside him. She was stroking his hair and talking to him softly when the monitor alarms began to sound. Lizzie jumped up. She didn't know what was happening.

Nurses rushed in and asked her to leave the room. Gloria and Sean were running down the hall as the door closed, leaving the three of them to wait in fear.

They watched as doctors and nurses rushed in and out of Wade's room. Finally, a nurse ushered them to the waiting room and informed them that Wade was being taken to surgery. She told them nothing more before hurrying away.

Two hours later, Wade's doctor came out to tell them what had happened. A small sliver of glass had been missed during his previous surgeries. It caused internal bleeding that had gradually gotten worse. His blood pressure dropped and caused the alarm on the monitor to sound.

The doctor told them that Wade was doing well and that he would recover from the most recent surgery. He wanted to run more tests to make sure there wasn't another piece of glass waiting to cause more problems. The three of them cried with relief but couldn't relax until they could see Wade for themselves.

Lizzie sat with Wade for a while before she decided that she needed to go home. It was almost an hour back to the farm, and she wanted to be at work early. She needed to try to find answers to her questions. She said goodnight to Sean and Gloria and gently kissed Wade goodnight before she made the journey home.

CHAPTER THIRTY-ONE

LIZZIE ARRIVED at the sheriff's office and waited while Reed parked his truck. She wanted to talk to him while she had his undivided attention.

"Good morning, Lizzie," said Reed. "You're here early."

"Good morning. I have something on my mind that I'd like to discuss with you."

"Follow me to Wade's office. We'll talk while I have my coffee."

Reed poured himself a cup of coffee and offered Lizzie a cup. They both sipped the hot beverage before starting their conversation.

"What do you want to talk about?" Reed asked.

"I know that you need me to run the office while the rest of you work the case, but I'd like to do something else today."

"Are you bored with running the office already?"

"It's not that. I had an idea last night that I'd like to look into. I was awake most of the night thinking about it."

"What was your idea?"

"I'm not sure that the idea is ready to share yet," Lizzie replied.

"Would it be okay if I looked at all of the evidence again and tried to sort it out?"

"A fresh pair of eyes might be what this case needs," said Reed. "I've run out of ideas, and no one else seems to have any either. I'll ask Maddie to run the office today. Let me know if you come up with anything."

"Yes, sir," said Lizzie as she stood.

"You can finish your coffee first," said Reed with a grin.

"I want to get started right away. This is driving me crazy," said Lizzie. "I'll just take the coffee with me. Is it okay if I use the conference room?"

"Yes," Reed laughed. "On second thought, you don't need the coffee. You're already amped up."

Lizzie laughed and left the office to gather the files she needed. She spread everything out on the table in the conference room. She read each file carefully. Things weren't coming together like she had hoped they would. She took the photos of the victims and the suspects and placed them on the table. She located the photos that had been included in the anonymous letters and put them beside the other photos. She began to move the photos as she mentally talked herself through the evidence.

Rusty Morton is still alive. Nate Tucker was accidentally killed by Cacus. Wayne Bowers was killed in an accident, and Della Wallace died from emphysema. Lizzie arranged the photos in a column on the left side of the table. *Kyle Jensen and Craig Dodson were killed. Wade Adams was injured. Attempts to kill Drake Wagner and Lizzie Fletcher were unsuccessful.* She arranged those photos in the center of the table. *Megan Ford and Alan Nichols were the main suspects.* She thought as she placed those photos on the right side of the table.

She stared at the photos on the table for a few minutes before finding a sheet of paper and a pencil. She made a chart and drew lines connecting the names of each group of photos. Suddenly, she knew what had been bothering her.

Lizzie rushed to Wade's office and said, "Reed, I think I've figured it out. I need to talk to Megan Ford."

"We've all but eliminated her as a suspect, Lizzie," Reed replied.

"I know, but I really need to talk to her."

Reed looked at Lizzie for a moment before he answered, "Find out where she is, and I'll go with you."

"I already did. She's at home. Her mother sold their house, and they're packing to move."

"Are you going to tell me about this before we go?" Reed asked with a smirk.

"I'll tell you on the way," Lizzie replied as they quickly left the office.

Lizzie and Reed stood on the front porch of Megan's house and knocked on the door.

"Hello, Deputies," Roxanne said in surprise when she opened the door. "What can I help you with?"

"We'd like to speak to Megan, please," said Reed.

Megan was standing in the living room and heard the request. She walked to the door and said, "I've already answered all of your questions."

"We have a few more to ask," Reed replied.

"I'm not answering any questions without my attorney."

"Megan," said Lizzie. "We don't want to ask you questions because you're a suspect. We need to talk to you because you might be a witness."

"A witness?" Roxanne asked.

"I'm not answering any questions you have to ask, Lizzie Fletcher," Megan said angrily.

"Please, Megan. It's important," said Lizzie. "You may have information that could save someone's life, maybe even your own."

Megan and Roxanne were both surprised by Lizzie's words. They looked at each other. Megan nodded, and Roxanne invited them in.

"Is there a convenient place that we can use to show you some photos?" asked Reed.

"You can use the dining room table," said Roxanne as she led the way.

Megan sat in a huff at the head of the table. Roxanne sat beside her and watched as Lizzie placed the photos for them to see.

"I know that you've already been asked if you know these people," Lizzie began as she indicated the photos that had been sent in the mail. "I'd like you to look at them again. This time, think back to any encounter or connection you might have with them. Maybe you've seen them at work or at a restaurant. You might have spoken with them on the phone."

Megan looked at the photos and then back at Lizzie. "Is this some sort of trick? Are you trying to get me to implicate myself somehow?"

Lizzie gently placed her hand on Megan's shoulder and looked directly at her. "Megan, I know that there's some bad history between us. I give you my word that this is no trick."

"You also have my word," said Reed. "We believe that you may have information without realizing it that could help us solve this case."

"Why do you believe that?" asked Roxanne.

"Deputy Fletcher will explain as Megan answers her questions," replied Reed.

Megan sighed and said, "I'll answer your questions, but I'll call my attorney if I think it's necessary."

"Understood," said Reed.

Megan and Roxanne looked at the photos and the names attached to them. Roxanne had seen Della Wallace and Rusty Morton in the store where she worked but didn't know their names. Megan had seen Nate Tucker at her office but hadn't spoken with him.

"You don't have any personal connection with any of these people that you can recall?" asked Lizzie.

"No," answered Megan.

Lizzie removed those photos and placed photos of the victims on the table. She moved the photos as she spoke.

"Nate Tucker had a connection to my family. He had a connection to Wade and Drake because of my connection to him," she said as she put those photos side by side. "We know that the arsonist was responsible for Tucker's death, so I'll remove him from the problem. Jensen, Dodson, and Adams are connected through the sheriff's department. I'm also connected to them for that reason."

Lizzie continued moving the photos while she explained the connection between each of the victims. Finally, she came to the suspects.

"Megan, you are the only person connected to all of these victims. That's why you were a suspect. You couldn't have killed or attempted to kill any of these people because we've verified where you were during every incident except the Jensen case."

"I know that," said Megan. "What's your point?"

"I think I'm beginning to understand," said Roxanne with wide eyes.

"Megan, you are connected to all of these people. They may have been targeted because of you," said Lizzie.

Megan looked at Lizzie, finally beginning to grasp what Lizzie had been trying to explain to her. She paled and asked, "Why would someone do this because of me?"

"It's possible that someone is setting you up," said Reed. "Do you have any enemies that might want revenge? Is there anyone that would be willing to kill other people and implicate you in the process?"

Lizzie could practically see the wheels turning in Megan's mind as she thought about all the things she had done and the people she had wronged. Megan was so pale that her mother became concerned.

"Megan, are you okay?" Roxanne asked.

"I think I'm going to be sick," mumbled Megan as she ran for the bathroom.

She eventually returned, still pale and trembling. "I've made some enemies in my life. I don't know that any of them would kill someone over it."

"Will you give us a list of those people?" asked Reed.

"I'll try. I may not remember them all," said Megan honestly.

Megan listed the names of everyone she could recall that might consider her an enemy. Roxanne had no illusions about her daughter but was still surprised at the length of that list.

"Is Megan in danger?" she asked Reed.

Reed and Lizzie looked at each other for a moment before answering her question. "It's a possibility," said Reed.

"What?" Megan asked with alarm.

"You can prove where you were for each of the crimes. If someone was trying to frame you, they've failed. Whoever is responsible might resort to coming for you," Reed explained as gently as he could.

"What are you going to do?" Roxanne asked. "You have to protect my daughter."

"Normally, we would have a team of officers guard Megan around the clock," began Reed. "Unfortunately, we don't currently have the manpower to do that. That leaves us with only one option. I don't think you're going to like it."

"I'll do anything. What's the other option?"

"You'd be in protective custody… at the jail," answered Reed. "For your protection, you'd be in a cell isolated from the inmates, but you wouldn't be a prisoner. You'd be able to leave the cell, and your mother is free to visit," he explained. "We may even find some work for you to do in the office if you'd like, but you'd have to stay at the jail with us."

"Isn't there another way," asked Roxanne. "Couldn't some of the officers from the Police Department guard her?"

"That's not a good option, Mom. Some of the people on that list are police officers," Megan informed her.

"We could contact another agency outside the county and ask them to provide protection," said Reed. "That would take time, and you'd have a sizeable bill to pay when it's all over. It won't cost you anything to stay at the jail, especially if you work for us while you're there."

"Will I be able to take some personal belongings to make it a little less like being in jail?"

"Yes, but there is one thing you shouldn't do," said Reed. "You shouldn't tell anyone where you are or why you're there."

"I'll have to give my boss a reason for missing work," said Megan.

"Is he on that list?"

Megan sighed, "Yes, he is."

"We'll investigate him first," said Reed. "If we can eliminate him as a suspect, you can contact him."

"When does she need to go to the jail?" Roxanne asked.

"It would be best if she goes with us now," answered Reed.

Megan reluctantly gathered some clothes and personal items. She packed them in a small suitcase and indicated that she was ready. Reed and Lizzie escorted her to the truck. Roxanne waved goodbye with tears in her eyes and promised to visit every day. Megan only nodded and rode silently to the jail.

The team went to work immediately and investigated everyone on Megan's extensive list of enemies. Part of the team ran background checks while other team members visited with people on the list. They convened at the end of the day in the conference room to compare notes.

"How are the background checks coming along?" asked Reed.

"We've finished about a third of them," replied Maddie. "Nothing unusual has shown up so far."

"Where are we with the personal interviews?"

"We've talked with several of the locals on the list," answered

Lodge. "None of them are fans of Miss Ford. I don't know that any of them are bent on revenge."

"There were two people who got our attention," added Odom. "Alan Nichols was on the list. Since he's been a suspect all along, we questioned him a little more thoroughly."

"Did you learn anything new from Mr. Nichols?"

"Nichols dated Megan briefly," Odom replied. "He told us that he discovered she was much more high maintenance than he had expected. He stopped calling her after the third or fourth date. Apparently, Miss Ford was unhappy with the situation. She followed Nichols and his date into a local restaurant and created a huge scene. Nichols' date left him there and hasn't spoken to him since."

"Nichols seems to be a ladies' man," said Gonzales. "Is it possible that the woman who vouched for him was lying?"

"Anything is possible," replied Reed. "Let's check her background. There might be something there that would warrant talking with her again. Who else got your attention?"

"Jameson Monroe also dated Miss Ford briefly," said Lodge. "His description of her is what got our attention. They had gone to dinner in Wichita Falls. Megan saw something that she wanted in a store window and asked him to buy it for her. He told her that he didn't have that kind of money. He said, and I quote, 'she turned into a Bitchosaurus rex right there in front of God and everybody.'"

Reed laughed and said, "That's quite a description and an accurate one based on the stories I've heard."

"I'd say that's a perfect description," said Lizzie with a grin. "I've seen that first hand."

The meeting was adjourned after a few jokes and assignments were made for the following day. Lizzie expected Megan to be in the way and a general nuisance at the very least. She was surprised that Megan remained subdued and in the cell.

At the end of the third day, Megan approached Lizzie and asked, "Can we talk...privately?"

"Sure," answered Lizzie. "Let's find a vacant room."

Megan followed Lizzie to the conference room and said, "I expected this to be a lot nicer."

"Taxpayer money only stretches so far," replied Lizzie as she closed the door. "What do you want to talk about?"

Megan took a couple of deep breaths and said, "I've never done anything like this before, so please be patient. I may not be able to say what I want to say right away."

"Take all the time you need," Lizzie said with curiosity. "Do you want to sit down?"

"No, I think better if I'm moving around," replied Megan. She took another deep breath and said, "You could have just ignored your hunch and left me to deal with the consequences, but you didn't. You came to my house and explained everything so that I'd understand the gravity of the situation. After everything I've put you through, you still helped me. Why?"

Lizzie was surprised and at a loss for words. Finally, she said, "It was the right thing to do."

"Thank you, Lizzie."

"You're welcome," replied Lizzie.

"I'm sorry about everything," Megan continued. "It's my fault that you and Drake broke up. I thought he was rich. When I found out I was pregnant, I decided that he was wealthy enough to pay lots of child support. I knew he wouldn't remember that night. I never imagined that he'd propose. I should have said no, but I thought that would mean a good life with lots of money. I should have let it go the day that I found out he wasn't wealthy, but I didn't. When he broke off our engagement, I blamed you, but I knew it was my fault. I'm sorry for all the trouble that I've caused you and your family since then. I have no excuse. I was acting like a stupid schoolgirl. I hope you can forgive me."

Lizzie was completely surprised by Megan's confession and apology. She looked into Megan's eyes and saw no hint of anger or deceit. Finally, she said, "I accept your apology, Megan. It might take some time, but I'll forgive you."

Megan smiled and hugged Lizzie so tightly that she could hardly breathe. "Thank you, Lizzie," Megan said with tears in her eyes.

The two women left the conference room. Lizzie returned to her investigation, and Megan went in search of Reed. Megan tapped on the office door and waited for Reed to answer.

"Come in, Miss Ford. What can I do for you?"

"I was wondering if you have something that I can do to pass the time," Megan asked politely.

"I'm sure that we have enough work to keep you occupied for a long time," said Reed with a smile. "You'll probably be back at home before we run out of things for you to do."

Megan followed Reed to the outer office and waited patiently while he discussed things that needed to be done with Maddie. It was finally decided that uploading old case files would be the perfect job for Megan. She had the skills necessary for the job. For her protection, Megan was shown to a workstation where she couldn't be seen from the main lobby. A box of files ready to be uploaded was already in place. She happily went to work.

Reed was walking through the lobby when Graham Shaffer stormed into the office. "I demand to see my client right away!" he shouted. "Why has she been arrested, and why hasn't she been allowed to contact her attorney!"

"Mr. Shaffer, I'll be happy to answer your questions, but I prefer to do so in private," said Reed firmly.

Shaffer followed Reed into Wade's office and pounded on the desk. "I want to see my client immediately!"

"Please, sit down, Mr. Shaffer. Would you like some coffee?"

"No! I don't want coffee. I want to see Megan Ford!"

"You need to calm down before I'll be able to answer your questions," said Reed, deliberately antagonizing the man. "Won't you sit down?"

Shaffer glared at Reed and sat down. He took a deep breath and asked, "Why has Megan Ford been arrested?"

"What leads you to believe that Miss Ford has been arrested?"

"I called her home and spoke with her mother. She told me that Miss Ford would be at the jail for a while," Shaffer replied angrily.

"Did she say that Miss Ford had been arrested?"

"No, she didn't, but what other reason could there be for Miss Ford's presence here?"

"Miss Ford has not been arrested," Reed informed him.

"Then, why is she here?"

"She's working here," said Reed.

"Working here? That's impossible!"

Megan tapped on the door and asked, "May I come in?"

"Please do. I was just explaining to Mr. Shaffer that you're working for us and that you haven't been arrested."

CHAPTER THIRTY-TWO

REED AND MEGAN FORD explained to Graham Shaffer the reason for Megan's presence at the jail. He wasn't happy about it, but he understood. He volunteered to play a part in the charade if needed.

The team had investigated most of the people on Megan's list. All of those suspects could account for their movements for at least one of the incidents in question. They were again at a dead end unless something significant was brought to light from the few remaining suspects.

A few days later, another anonymous letter arrived in the mail. This time it was addressed to the Wilbarger County Sheriff's Department. Reed took the envelope to the lab and followed the same precautions that Wade had followed. Inside the envelope were a photo of Drake Wagner and a note that said, *Remember the Coleman case.*

No one in the office had any idea what the Coleman case was or when it occurred. Rusty Morton was called in again.

"Let me see that note," said Rusty as he sat in Reed's office. "Coleman… Coleman…nope, I've got nothing. It must have been years ago. It may have even been before I came to work here."

"Thanks for taking the time to come by," said Reed.

"You're welcome. I may not be available the next time you get a mysterious note," said Morton. "I'm moving to the Dallas area at the end of the month."

"We'll be sorry to see you go," said Reed. "Would you mind if we call you if we get another note?"

"Sure you can. It will give me something to think about," replied Morton. "Have you looked in the old files for that case?"

"I have a deputy looking for it in the storage facility now. We found nothing by that name here in the office," said Reed.

"How is Adams doing?"

"There's been no change," replied Reed. "Everyone's concerned. It's been more than two weeks, and he's still in a coma."

"I'll keep him in my thoughts and prayers. Good luck finding Coleman. Let me know how this all turns out," said Morton as he left the office.

"Reed, doesn't that letter bother you?" asked Baker.

"It does a little," Reed replied. "Whoever sent it is well informed. That bothers me the most."

"You don't think it could be someone we know, do you?"

"I'm beginning to think that it could even be one of us," said Reed gravely.

Lizzie had been searching through the old files at the storage facility for two days. She was tired, dirty, and ready to go home. She decided to look through one more section and leave the rest for the next day. She moved the rolling ladder over to the section labeled 2000-2005. She climbed the ladder and took the top box. Her foot slipped on her way down the ladder. She caught herself but accidentally knocked another box off the shelf. The box seemed to explode when it landed. Files were scattered all over the floor. She sighed in frustration as she climbed down the ladder and began to pick up the files. *I may as well check this box now.*

Most of the files had stayed intact because the pages had been fastened to the folder. She looked at each name as she put them back in the box. She set aside the loose pages and files that had not been fastened. She planned to put them back together before filing them away.

She had repaired three of the scattered files when she noticed something interesting. The page on top of the stack had Nate Tucker's name on it. She picked it up and looked at it carefully. It was a list of jury members at a trial. The list included the names of Wayne Bowers, Nate Tucker, and Della Wallace.

Lizzie was so excited that she almost knocked the box over and spilled its contents again. She searched the page for anything that would lead her to the file it belonged in. She knew it wasn't one of the files she had repaired. She began to sift through the remainder of the stack until she had located the correct file. Thankfully, most of the pages were still inside.

She flipped through the file and shouted, "Yes, this is the one!" She grabbed her keys and ran to her jeep, leaving the other files and boxes where they were.

"Reed! I found it!" Lizzie said excitedly when she returned to the office.

Everyone stopped what they were doing and stared.

"I found the file," Lizzie said. "It explains everything!"

The team met in the conference room and examined the contents of the folder. Listed inside were the names of all the jurors for the case and the judge who presided over it.

"Look at this," Maddie exclaimed. "Jensen and Dodson escorted the suspect from the courthouse to the jail."

"That explains why they were targets. How do Wade, Lizzie, and Wagner fit in this puzzle?" asked Lodge.

"It says here that he was arrested in November of 2002. The trial took place in February 2003. Wasn't Wade here then?" asked Maddie.

"I'll look at the personnel records to find out for sure, but I think he was," answered Reed. "Do you know this guy Lizzie?"

"No, I was in college at that time," Lizzie replied. "Drake and I were dating then. We may have crossed his path together. Wasn't he one of the people on Megan's list?"

"You're right!" said Reed.

"What does any of this have to do with the Coleman case?" asked Odom.

"According to the file, this man was dating a woman named Sharla Coleman. He attacked her and a man she was with using a baseball bat," said Reed. "Do we have the background check on this guy yet?"

"Not yet," said Maddie. "His was in the last group. I'll get it started now."

"Dig deep. We need to know everything there is to know about Jameson Monroe," said Reed. "Odom and Lodge find out where he is and bring him in for questioning."

The team went about their assigned tasks. Jameson Monroe was located and brought in for questioning the next day. He admitted to the 2002 charges and explained the circumstances.

"I've tried to be a model citizen since I got out of prison," said Monroe as he sat in the interrogation room. "I haven't done anything. Go ahead and ask your questions."

Reed opened the file with the photos and obituaries inside. Monroe denied knowing any of the people in that file. Reed showed him the file of the victims.

"This guy looks familiar," said Monroe when he saw the photo of Jensen. "I think I remember him. He was a real nice guy for a deputy. I don't remember the other two."

"Do you know these people?" Reed asked, showing him the photos of Lizzie, Drake, and Megan.

"I've seen them around, but I don't know them. I know her, though," he said as he pointed at Megan's photo.

"How do you know Miss Ford?" Reed asked.

"I took her out a few times," replied Monroe. "All she cares about is how much money you're willing to spend on her."

"The relationship didn't end well?"

"Nope."

"Who ended it?"

"I did."

Megan had been watching the interview with the team through the two-way mirror.

"Is that true?" Maddie asked.

"We went out a few times," Megan replied. "He was kind of scary, so I broke it off. It took a while to convince him that I wasn't interested in seeing him anymore."

"Do you recognize anything in these photos?" Reed asked Monroe as he indicated a random group of photos.

"Those tires look like the ones I have on my truck."

"What size shoe do you wear?"

"I wear a ten-and-a-half. Are you going to tell me what this is all about?" Monroe asked.

"Mr. Monroe, there have been two murders, and two attempted murders in the last several weeks," said Reed. "At three of the crime scenes, we found tire tracks and shoe prints. The tire tread on your truck tires matches those tracks. Your shoe size matches the size of the shoe prints at the crime scenes."

"Wait a minute, I didn't kill anybody," Monroe said. "You can't pin this on me! I want to call my lawyer!"

"All of those murders and attempted murders were either by fire or explosion. Someone impersonated a firefighter at one of the fires. The fire department is missing a set of turnout gear. Would we find that missing gear if we searched your home?" asked Reed.

"I'm not saying anything else without my lawyer!"

Reed showed Monroe a list of dates. "Where were you on these days?"

"I was working!" replied Monroe. "Call my boss. He'll tell you I was at work!"

Reed left the interrogation room. Maddie met him in the hallway.

"Megan says she ended the relationship," said Maddie. "His

background check isn't finished yet, but it shouldn't be much longer."

"I'm going to call his boss," replied Reed. "He wants to call his lawyer. If his boss doesn't verify his story, let him make the call."

"Yes, sir."

Reed completed his phone call and returned to the interrogation room.

"Mr. Monroe, your employer confirmed that you were at work during the times in question. You're free to go for the time being."

Megan tapped on Reed's door later that day.

"What can I do for you?" asked Reed.

"I've been thinking about it, and I'd like to go home now," she said. "I can't hide out here forever."

"You might still be in danger," Reed replied.

"You haven't found anything that would prove that. I need to get back to work."

Reed nodded and said, "We'll take you home when you're ready."

Megan smiled sweetly and said, "Thank you, Gordon."

Lizzie drove Megan home and returned to the office. She settled down at her desk to finish some paperwork before the end of the day.

"Reed! You'd better look at this!" said Maddie.

"What is it?"

"The background check on Monroe is finished. You're not going to believe it."

Reed read the report. Monroe was dishonorably discharged from the Marine Corps for multiple counts of fighting with fellow Marines. He had been required to attend anger management classes, but they did little to improve his temper. Before being discharged, he was an explosive ordinance technician.

"Lodge, call the judge," Reed ordered. "We need a search warrant for Monroe's home and place of business. See if he'll issue an arrest warrant, too."

"Yes, sir."

"We had him, and I let him go! Dammit!" Reed shouted as he slammed his hand down on the nearest desk.

"Do you want us to pick him up?"

"Find out where he is so that we can pick him up when the warrant is issued."

"Yes, sir."

"I'll call Miss Ford and tell her to keep an eye out for him," said Reed. "We'll be searching his place in the meantime."

The search of Monroe's home revealed the missing gear from the fire department. The team also found all of the necessary parts and equipment for making explosive devices. Monroe had yet to be located.

An all-points bulletin was issued for Monroe. Every officer in Wilbarger and the surrounding counties was looking for him. He had not been located by the time Lizzie drove home for the evening.

Lizzie showered and decided to have a short nap before dinner. She wanted to be well-rested before going to see Wade. She stretched out on the couch and dozed off. She was in the middle of a pleasant dream when her cell phone rang. She looked at the caller id and saw Gloria's name. With her heart in her throat, she answered the call.

"Hello, Gloria," said Lizzie. "Is something wrong with Wade?"

"Nothing's wrong," laughed Gloria. "Everything is fine. Someone wants to talk to you."

"Hi, baby," said Wade weakly.

Lizzie burst into tears and said, "You're awake! Am I dreaming? Is it really you?"

"It's me, sweetheart. It's so good to hear your voice."

"You can't imagine how good it is to hear yours," said Lizzie laughing and crying at the same time.

"I can't wait to see you," said Wade. "Are you planning to come to the hospital tonight?"

"Yes, I'll be there as soon as I can. I can't wait to see you. I have so much to tell you."

"I'll see you soon. I think I'll nap until you get here," said Wade.

They ended the call, and Lizzie screamed at the top of her lungs with pure joy. Her family ran to the den, terrified that something horrible had happened. Lizzie turned and laughed when she saw them.

"He's awake! Wade's awake!"

Lizzie grabbed her keys and her bag. She ran to her jeep and had to concentrate to keep from speeding. At the edge of town, her cell phone rang. She looked at the caller id and saw a number that she didn't recognize. She pulled to the side of the road and answered the phone, fearing that it was a call regarding Wade.

"Hello?"

"Hi, this is Megan. I'm going to have to cancel our dinner plans for tonight."

"We didn't have dinner plans. Did you mean to call Lizzie?"

"Yes, I know, but we can go another time."

"Is something wrong, Megan?"

Megan laughed, "Yes, that's so true."

"Are you at your house?"

"I know that's right."

"I'll send help right away," said Lizzie.

"I'm looking forward to it. See you soon," said Megan, and the call ended.

Lizzie immediately dialed the sheriff's department and told Lodge about the strange phone call from Megan. Every available officer was immediately en route, but Lizzie got there first. She didn't carry a weapon, and she didn't know what she was going to do until she noticed a small stuffed animal on the floor of the jeep.

Lizzie parked in front of the house, picked up the stuffed animal, and walked to the front door. She knocked and waited, looking around as if she had all day. Megan answered the door and rolled her eyes to her right, indicating that someone was there.

"What are you doing here?" said Megan snidely.

"I found this in the floor of the jeep and thought you might like to have it back."

"Thanks," said Megan. She didn't want Lizzie to leave, but she didn't know what else to say. "Goodbye."

Lizzie winked at her and started down the steps. Suddenly, she fell to the ground holding her ankle. A man rushed out of the house to help her.

"Miss Fletcher, are you hurt?"

Lizzie looked at him and said, "I'm fine. I just turned my ankle."

"Let me help you into the house," he said as he took a step toward her and offered her his hand.

"I'm fine. I'll walk it off."

"Come now, Miss Fletcher. You know that I can't let you leave."

"What are you talking about?" Lizzie asked.

"I'm no fool, Miss Fletcher," the man said with a sneer and took a gun from his pocket. "You'll join us inside."

Lizzie stood and walked without a limp into the house. She knew that he had seen through her pretense. She wondered if he knew that she was the recipient of Megan's phone call.

"It's quite fortunate that you dropped by this evening," he said. "I can prove my love for Megan by disposing of another of her enemies. She'll get to witness my undying affection for her."

"People are expecting me. I was on my way to the hospital. They'll look for me if I'm not there soon."

"Did you tell anyone that you were making a stop first?"

"No, I didn't," admitted Lizzie.

"I'd wager they wouldn't think to look for you here," Graham Shaffer said. "Why did you stop by?"

"I noticed the stuffed animal on the floorboard. I thought Megan would want to have it back. Besides, I didn't want anything of hers in my Jeep. It was bad enough that I had to babysit her at the jail and drive her home," said Lizzie.

Roxanne sat quietly on the couch. She looked from Lizzie to

Megan, then at Graham. She was confused by the exchange but said nothing.

"I failed to dispose of you at the inn, and I failed to dispose of Drake Wagner. I won't fail tonight. You're going to call him and ask him to meet you here."

"No! You can't do that! You can't kill anyone else!" Megan screamed, trying to hold back the tears. "I'll do anything you want. Just don't hurt anyone else."

"I'm doing this for you, my dear," Graham said as he gently wiped a tear from her cheek. "You understand, don't you, that we can't leave Miss Fletcher alive. She knows too much."

"I don't know why you burned my inn," said Lizzie trying to keep him talking.

"Don't be so naïve, Miss Fletcher. You know perfectly well that I burned the inn, hoping that you would die in the fire. I had hoped that Sheriff Adams would be there as well, but I realized he wasn't coming when you went to bed. It had to be done while the Fire Department's B shift was on duty. I knew that the arsonist would be blamed for the fire and your death."

"I don't understand why you would want to kill any of them," said Megan.

Lizzie noticed movement on the lawn and nodded at Megan, hoping she'd understand that she needed to keep Shaffer's attention.

"We've had our differences, but I never wanted any of them to die," Megan said. "Why would you do such a thing?"

"I had to, Megan. When I realized that you're still in love with Drake Wagner, I knew that I'd have to do something to get him out of the way before you would even consider marrying me. I decided to kill the others because they had mistreated you and implicated the arsonist."

"You think that I'm in love with Drake Wagner?" Megan asked in surprise. "Why would you think that?"

"I saw how you looked at him at the restaurant the night of our first date," said Graham.

"Don't you understand?" said Megan. "I'm not in love with Drake Wagner. I was trying to make you jealous. I wanted you to help me clear Daddy's name. I was trying to manipulate you into doing what I wanted."

"If that's the case, then you'll call Mr. Wagner and ask him to join us," Graham said with a sneer.

Megan laughed, "He'd never come here. He hates me! I wouldn't get two words out before he hung up on me."

Lizzie could see someone outside the window with a rifle pointed at Shaffer. She was about to signal to Roxanne and Megan to get on the floor when a voice called from outside the house.

"This is the Wilbarger County Sheriff's Department! The house is surrounded! Come out with your hands where we can see them! We don't want anyone to get hurt!"

"Very clever, Miss Fletcher," said Shaffer as he turned and glared at her. "Somehow, you knew to alert your friends before coming here."

Lizzie's knees shook as she began to move slowly across the room. Shaffer was still holding the gun. She needed to get him away from the Fords so that they would be out of the line of fire. She began taunting him, hoping he would come after her.

"You aren't as smart as you think you are. Those anonymous envelopes turned up at the office after you had been there. We know that you're Monroe's attorney. It was probably pretty easy to set up your own client. He'd be arrested and probably get the death penalty. You'd be free to do whatever you want."

"I underestimated you," said Graham as he moved toward her.

"Come out now with your hands where we can see them!"

"I know this house isn't surrounded!" shouted Graham. "You don't have enough manpower to surround an outhouse!"

Lizzie smiled at him and said, "Are you sure about that? Don't you know anything about law enforcement officers?"

"What are you talking about?"

"They may be in different departments, but each and every one of them considers each and every officer a part of their brotherhood. If someone kills a cop, they all want a piece of the killer. You killed a Texas State Trooper and a Deputy Sheriff. You seriously wounded the Sheriff. You're in deep trouble, Shaffer. You better do as they say if you want to live to see tomorrow."

Lizzie had maneuvered Shaffer where she wanted him. She could see that Megan and her mother had moved behind a heavy piece of furniture.

"Face it, Shaffer. It's over. You're going to jail," said Lizzie with false bravado and a huge grin on her face.

Shaffer roared with anger and pointed the gun at Lizzie's head. In an instant, she quickly dropped to her hands and knees, and the officer at the window took the shot. Shaffer was dead before his body hit the floor.

CHAPTER THIRTY-THREE

LIZZIE TOOK a deep breath to calm her quaking body as she stood. She looked to make sure that Megan and her mother weren't hurt.

"Are you okay?" she asked Megan.

"We're fine, thanks to you," replied Megan.

"We make a pretty good team for two people who've hated each other for years," Lizzie said with a smile.

Megan laughed and said, "We sure do."

"Would someone please explain to me what just happened," said a wide-eyed Roxanne.

"I'd like to hear this, too," said Reed as he came through the front door.

"Mom and I were discussing what we wanted for dinner when Graham knocked on the door," Megan began. "He was acting really weird and kept insisting that I leave with him. I had left my suitcase at the bottom of the stairs. He picked it up and took it to his car. I got really scared when he started talking about how we would leave town and go where no one would be able to find us. I told Graham that I had made plans that I had to cancel if I was going with him. I called Lizzie, hoping that she'd figure out that I was in trouble and send help. I never expected to see her when I opened the door. I thought she'd be visiting Wade."

"I was on my way to see Wade when Megan called. I wanted to let her know that help was on the way. I knocked on the door under the pretense of returning a stuffed animal. I could see how frightened Megan was, so I decided to try to lure who I thought was Monroe out of the house. I pretended to fall off of the porch and hurt my ankle. I almost lost it when Shaffer walked over to me and said the same thing that the fireman at the inn said. When he reached toward me, I had no doubt it was him."

"He must have known that Lizzie figured it out because he forced her into the house," said Megan.

"Then we tried to keep him distracted and talking until you arrived to save our skins," said Lizzie. "Thank you, by the way!"

"I'm glad no one was hurt," said Reed. "Let's move out of here and let the police department get to work. I'm going to need detailed statements from all of you."

"Megan, how did you get my number?" asked Lizzie.

"I didn't know whose number I was dialing," replied Megan. "I updated the department contact information for Maddie. I dialed the first number that popped into my head."

Lizzie's cell phone rang. She looked at the caller id and said, "I was supposed to have been at the hospital by now. This is Wade's mom calling to check on me. Can I give you my statement tomorrow? Wade's awake and asking to see me."

"Wade's awake?" asked Reed. "Why are you just now getting around to telling me?"

"I've been a little busy," Lizzie replied with a laugh.

"Go!" said Reed. "You can give me your statement first thing tomorrow."

Lizzie didn't waste another minute. She called Gloria to let her know that she had been delayed and sped away to see Wade.

The team searched Graham Shaffer's apartment and office. They found a notebook where he had written down every detail as he planned how to hide his part in the fires. He knew when each shift was on duty with the fire department, and he knew that the other fires had been started with an accelerant. His mistake was that he had used gasoline instead of alcohol. He hadn't been aware that the original arsonist was in custody when he burned the inn.

In addition to his car, he owned an SUV. A receipt was found in the glove compartment for four new Michelin Premier LTX tires. Deputies found a pair of Wolverine hiking boots sized ten-and-a-half in his closet. They were a perfect match for the shoe prints found at the crime scenes. The history on his computer revealed that he had researched how to make explosive devices. It was still a mystery how and when he gained access to the fire department's turnout gear.

Shaffer knew that Megan would be implicated when he began to eliminate the people connected to her. To protect Megan from arrest, he needed someone else to take the fall. He decided to frame Jameson Monroe from the moment he read his old case file. Some of the people who had hurt Megan were also involved in his arrest. He decided to point the way to Monroe with the clues he sent in the mail.

Megan was so shaken by the ordeal with Shaffer that she decided to change the way she'd been living. She approached each person on her list of potential enemies and made a sincere apology for her behavior. She thought apologizing to Lizzie and her ex-husband Dan Hayes was difficult. Apologizing to Drake was harder. It took her days to work up the courage to apologize to him and his family.

Finally, she drove to the Wagner farm. She confessed what she had done, apologized, and asked for their forgiveness. To her surprise, they, too, were willing to forgive and forget.

Michael Clark, also known as Cacus, was scheduled for a psychological evaluation in September. The results of that evaluation would be used to determine his sentence.

Tiffany Douglas Pruitt managed to get into Wade's room undetected by the hospital staff and his parents. She sat on the edge of his bed and took his hand, waking Wade from a nap.

"Wade, you're awake," she said happily.

"Tiffany? What are you doing here?" he asked sleepily.

"I came to tell you that I love you. I never should have left you," she said. "Do you think it might be possible that you would take me back? It would be so much better this time. I've grown up since those days. I was so stupid, and I wasted so much time. I want to be with you."

"Tiffany, I've already told you that I love Lizzie."

"Do you love her the way you loved me?" Tiffany said as she caressed his hand.

"No, I don't," said Wade.

Tiffany smiled. She was about to kiss him when he pushed her away and said. "There's no comparison. I love Lizzie more than I've ever loved anyone in my life. What I felt for you was nothing more than a teenager's crush compared to what I feel for Lizzie."

"That's it then? You won't even consider giving us another chance?"

"There is no us, Tiffany. I think I knew that before you left me. I didn't want to admit it."

Tiffany stood up and squared her shoulders, "So I guess this is goodbye."

"Goodbye, Tiffany."

Tiffany stomped out of the room without another word.

It was the second weekend of August. The repairs on the inn were in full swing. The Fletchers were planning to have a grand reopening celebration as soon as the work was finished.

Wade had been out of the hospital for a week and was recovering nicely. He and Lizzie were sitting in lawn chairs on the sidewalk along Wilbarger Street, enjoying cruise night together.

It was the twenty-sixth annual Summer's Last Blast celebration. Every year the Vernon Street Machine and Classics Association hosted the event. Vintage car owners from all over the country came to Vernon to show off their cars and drag Wilbarger Street on cruise night.

Lizzie was always amazed at how many different makes and models of cars there were. Chris Quintero was driving his red 1955 Cadillac El Dorado convertible. His girlfriend rode beside him while Kanden and Jessica Kyzer rode in the back. Alan Nichols drove his 1974 pearl white Chevy Corvette Stingray with Tanya Balderas riding shotgun. A black Ford Model T Coupe owned by the Tucker family was driven by Aaren Green while her Uncle Jason supervised.

Drivers honked and waved at spectators that they knew as they drove by. Others spun their tires and thrilled the crowd.

"How are you feeling, Sheriff," asked Odom as he stood beside the couple.

"I'm feeling pretty good right now," replied Wade. "The doctor says that I can go back to work at the end of the month."

"That's good news," replied Odom.

"Why don't you join us, Clint," said Lizzie.

"Thanks for the offer, but there's something that I need to do," replied Odom. "I wanted to see what this is all about before going home. I saw the two of you and decided to say hello."

"If you change your mind, we'll be right here," said Wade.

Odom left the festivities of cruise night and drove a few blocks away. He parked his car and walked up the steps to the front door of the apartment. He took a deep breath before knocking.

"Hello, Deputy."

"My name is Clint Odom. I'm sorry to bother you. I know that you're probably busy. I was wondering if I could talk to you for a few minutes."

"Of course," replied Roxanne Ford. "Is this about that mess with Graham Shaffer?"

"No, ma'am. I'm here about another matter."

"Hi, Clint," said Megan as she carried an empty box into the living room.

"Hello, Miss Ford," he replied.

"What did you want to talk about?" Roxanne asked with worry.

"I was hoping that you might be able to tell me about this man," said Odom as he handed an old, worn-out photo to Roxanne.

"Yes, I knew him. He was my husband. What do you want to know about him?"

"I don't really know where to start. My mother gave me this before she died. She told me that he was my biological father."

"Oh my God!" said Megan. "Are you my brother?"

Roxanne began to laugh so hard that tears began to roll down her face.

"Mom, what's so funny?" asked Megan with a smile.

"I thought he was here to arrest you for something," Roxanne said as she laughed louder.

The trio laughed together and sat down to have a long talk. Clint had so many questions about his father and his sisters that they talked for hours.

Lizzie drove Wade to his house after cruise night had ended. They sat on the sofa together, watching the evening news. *The Tonight Show* began, but Wade had lost all interest. He only wanted to look at Lizzie.

"Lizzie, I've decided to run for Sheriff again," said Wade. "How do you feel about that?"

"It never occurred to me that you wouldn't run," replied Lizzie.

"You're okay with it even after everything that happened?"

"Why wouldn't I be? It's part of who you are."

"I was worried that it might have made you rethink being in a relationship with a cop."

"Wade, either one of us could be hurt or killed in a freak accident. Anything could happen to either of us at any time. I prefer to live and enjoy our time together rather than worry about 'what ifs.' That time might be years, or it might be minutes. It doesn't matter to me as long as I can spend it all with you."

"I love you, Lizzie Fletcher," said Wade.

"I love you too, Wade Adams."

Wade reached into his pocket and pulled out a gorgeous ring. He placed it on her finger and said, "Will you marry me, Lizzie?"

"There's nothing in this world that I'd rather do," she said with tears of joy in her eyes. "Yes, I'll marry you."

The End

Sign up for Dianne's newsletter at diannesmithwick-braden.com for the latest news and announcements about upcoming books. (use the QR code below for a direct link)

If you've enjoyed *Flames of Wilbarger County*, follow Wade Adams and Lizzie Fletcher in Book Four of the Wilbarger County Series, *Gambling with Murder.* (use the QR code below for a direct link)

PREVIEW OF GAMBLING WITH MURDER

Chapter 1

Grace Stewart was stopped at a red light. She cranked the air conditioning to high when beads of sweat began to form on her forehead. August in Nevada was too much for her old car. It was a struggle to stay cool even at that time of the evening. The Las Vegas traffic didn't help.

The light turned green, and she pressed the accelerator. A movement to the right caught her eye. She stomped on the brakes and swore under her breath. The driver of the SUV waved, mouthed the word sorry, and continued through the intersection.

Damn tourists, she thought.

Tourist traffic was the main reason she preferred to avoid the Las Vegas Strip. She was running late, and it was the most direct route to her destination. She didn't want to keep Todd Anthony waiting.

They'd met four years earlier when her car wouldn't start after a charity function. Todd was kind enough to stay and help. He captivated her with his warm personality, his twinkling blue eyes, and his boyish grin.

Grace moaned in frustration when she caught another red light. Her thoughts drifted back to Todd while she waited.

Todd was an undercover federal agent and was often kept away for long periods. He got in touch with her when he could. They'd have dinner and spend the night together when they had the chance. A different out-of-the-way diner and hotel were chosen each time.

She remembered a conversation they'd had in the early days of their relationship.

"My work can be dangerous," Todd told her. "Not just for me. Everyone around me could be in danger. I don't want to put you at risk. If we continue seeing each other, we can't tell anyone who doesn't need to know. We can't tell our families, friends, or coworkers."

Grace understood the desire for secrecy. She had secrets of her own.

She knew she could trust Todd with anything. Still, she hadn't told him about her past. It never seemed to be the right time.

At last, Grace drove into the parking lot of a little diner and parked near the entrance. She requested a table beside the front window in order to see Todd when he arrived.

A waitress approached Grace's table. "Hi, my name is Dana. What would you like?"

"Hi, Dana," Grace answered. "May I wait to order? I'm expecting a friend."

"That's no problem. Would you like something to drink while you wait?"

"Diet Coke, please."

"I'll have that right out," Dana promised with a smile and walked away.

Grace looked out the window and scanned the lot for Todd. She toyed with the ring she wore on her right hand while she waited. She had no idea what he'd be driving. He wasn't often in the same vehicle twice. She thought about their relationship while she waited.

Most women wouldn't be happy with their arrangement, but it suited Grace. She was able to focus on her career without the constant demands of a normal romantic relationship. It made the times they were able to meet all the more exciting.

She was startled back to the present when a tall man walked past the window and stopped beside her car. He took a small black object from his pocket and knelt beside the front tire. He reached into the wheel well for a moment, then pretended to tie his shoe. She could see that his hands were empty when he stood and strolled away.

Questions tumbled past each other in Grace's mind like slot machine reels. *Who was that? What did he do to my car? Didn't he see me sitting here?*

"Are you okay?" Dana asked and placed a drink on the table. "You look like you've seen a ghost."

Grace almost jumped from her chair. "I...I'm, yes," she answered with a weak smile.

"I didn't mean to scare you," the waitress apologized.

Grace laughed and said, "That's all right. I let my mind wander a little too far."

Dana patted her on the shoulder. "Give me a wave when you're ready to order."

"I will, thanks."

Grace looked out the window again. *Get a grip on yourself and think.* She twisted the ring on her finger and tried to organize her thoughts. *I'd better call the police and warn Todd. He won't want to risk being seen with the police.*

She stood and made her way to the Ladies' room. Once inside, she checked to make sure she was alone and locked the door. She dug her cell phone out of her purse and took a few deep breaths trying to ease the trembling in her hands and knees.

She tapped Todd's name in her contact list and prayed he would pick up. She needed to talk to him.

She swore in frustration when his recorded message began. At the tone, she left a brief explanation of what had happened.

Grace ended the call and tapped the number for the police. She explained what she'd seen to the dispatcher and was assured officers were on their way.

Her knees quaked during the short walk back to her table. She sat down and sipped her drink while she watched for the police. She hoped Todd would get her message and stay away.

Grace had regained most of her composure by the time a Las Vegas PD squad car pulled into the parking lot. She went outside to meet the officers.

She hoped she appeared braver than she felt when she extended her hand and said, "Hello, I'm Grace Stewart. I called about someone tampering with my car."

"I'm Officer Danny Burnett, and this is Officer Greg Hines. Tell us what happened."

Grace explained what she'd seen and described the man. "He was around six feet tall and weighed between one hundred eighty and two hundred pounds. He was wearing jeans and a dark gray T-shirt. His shoes were black or navy Nikes. His hair was brown and short, like a military cut. I didn't see his face."

"Did he have any distinguishing marks or tattoos?" inquired Burnett.

"There was a dime-sized spot on his right wrist. It might have been a mole or a birthmark."

"We'll check your car and meet you inside," said Hines.

"Thank you. I'm sure it's nothing. I thought it best to have someone check," Grace said, more for her benefit than theirs.

She walked back toward the entrance and glanced at the

window where her table was located. The parking lot was reflected in the glass. *The man couldn't see inside. He didn't know anyone was watching.*

Grace went back to her table and watched the officers inspect her car. They took photos of the right front wheel well with a cell phone and made calls on their radios.

Officer Burnett entered the diner and saw Grace. She invited him to sit down.

"It doesn't appear to be dangerous. It looks like a tracking device," Burnett informed her. "We're calling in our tech guys to make sure. Do you know of any reason why someone would want to keep tabs on you?"

"I'm a reporter, but I work the anchor desk," Grace said with apprehension.

"Yes, Ma'am. I recognized you right away. Are you working on a story that might threaten someone?"

"Not at the moment."

"Are you meeting someone for dinner?"

"I was meeting a friend. I got a text saying that she can't make it after all," Grace told him, amazed at her own bluff. "I don't know of a reason anyone would be following her either."

Another police vehicle entered the parking lot. Officer Burnett excused himself and went outside.

Dana had been watching the police activity and looked at Grace. Grace waved her over.

"My friend can't make it after all. Could I order something to go?"

"You bet. Is everything okay?" Dana inquired.

"Someone tampered with my car. The police don't think it's anything to worry about."

"That's good news," Dana said, relieved. "What can I get for you?"

Grace scanned the menu. Her appetite had vanished, but she'd been there so long that she felt it would be rude to leave without ordering.

"I'll have a club sandwich with a bag of chips and another Diet Coke to go."

"Okay, I'll turn it in. It shouldn't take long."

"Thank you," Grace said and turned to watch the officers from the window.

The device was removed and on its way to the police station for analysis when Officers Burnett and Hines approached Grace's table.

"There's no doubt that it was a tracker," Hines told her. "The man you saw may try again when he realizes it isn't working."

"Did the man look at all familiar?" Burnett asked.

Grace pictured the man before answering and shook her head. "Silver Honda Civics are pretty common. Couldn't it have been a mistake?"

"It's possible," Hines said with a doubtful expression. "It would still be a good idea to stay on your toes."

"It could have been an overzealous fan," added Burnett. "We'll be in touch if we learn anything more."

Grace couldn't control the quiver in her voice when she said, "Goodbye, and thank you."

The words overzealous fan triggered a wave of anxiety. She did her best to calm her quaking body while she waited for her food.

Dana brought Grace's meal and the check to the table. Grace thanked her with a smile. She included a generous tip and left cash on the table before going outside.

She couldn't see anyone that seemed interested in her when she got into her car. She left the parking lot and drove home, watching the rearview mirror for any sign that she was being followed.

Why would anyone need to track me? Why follow me to a place I've never been to attach a tracker? I'm at the station and the gym almost every day. It had to have been a mistake.

Grace used the garage door opener and parked in her garage. She waited until the door closed to get out of the car. She opened the connecting door to the kitchen and waited, listening for any unusual sound.

She crept inside, leaving her purse and her food on the counter. She tiptoed through the house, checking every room. She didn't relax until she was satisfied that she was alone.

Grace went to her desk and used her laptop to check her messages. There were no emails of importance and no messages on her answering machine.

She retrieved her purse from the kitchen counter and found her cell phone. No messages there, either.

Grace put her food in the refrigerator before going to the living room and flopping onto the couch.

She was disappointed with the outcome of the evening. She knew that seeing Todd was out of the question now, but was a phone call too much to ask?

She turned on the television and tried to find a movie to watch. She settled on a rerun of an old sitcom. This wasn't how she'd planned to spend her Sunday night.

Grace had spent the previous day preparing for their date. She looked at her fingers. She kicked off her shoes and looked at her toes. The mani-pedi wouldn't be a total waste, but she'd endured a bikini wax for nothing. *Next time, I won't bother with any of it. We'll see how he likes that!*

Anger and frustration had restored her appetite. She paused the TV and stomped into the kitchen. She took the club sandwich from the fridge and a hunk of cheesecake from the freezer. She eyed the to-go cup but reached for a bottle of wine instead.

***

Monday morning brought regret and a mild hangover. She'd

have to spend extra time on the treadmill to pay for last night's choices.

Grace rolled over, looked at the clock, and groaned when she realized she'd overslept. She would have preferred to relax and nurse her hangover. Instead, she put on her workout clothes, laced up her shoes, and drove to the gym.

She thought about her life while she worked out. She'd chosen a career that preferred youth and good looks. At fifty-five years old, she knew her days as a female anchor were numbered. She'd spent a lot of time and money trying to conceal her age. She seldom took time off for fear that she'd have no job when she returned.

She found herself at a crossroads. She was too young to retire and too old to change careers. The thought of doing something else appealed to her, but what could she do?

She shortened her workout, left the gym, and drove to the post office. She went inside to collect her mail and stuffed it into her purse. She hurried back to her car and drove home.

Grace didn't see anything or anyone suspicious. *It was a case of mistaken identity or mistaken car. There's nothing to worry about.*

She showered and got ready for work. She was checking her appearance in the mirror when she felt that she was being watched. She looked at the bedroom window and the door. No one was there. A shiver danced through her body.

"Come on, Grace. You're letting your imagination get away from you," she said to her reflection in the mirror. "It was a mistake. No one is following you. It isn't like before."

The mirror image didn't look convinced.

Grace walked from room to room and checked to make sure all the windows and doors were locked. She went into the garage, set the security alarm, and got into her car. She opened the garage door, backed into the driveway, and waited for the garage door to close before backing into the street.

She drove to work and saw no evidence that anyone followed. She parked in her designated space and went into the station.

She said hello to the receptionist, poured herself some coffee, and went to her office. She took the mail and a bottle of aspirin from her purse before locking it in the bottom drawer of her desk.

She swallowed two aspirin with a sip of coffee. The workout hadn't helped her hangover.

Thumbing through the mail, Grace saw familiar handwriting. She smiled and opened it with the letter opener on her desk.

"Knock, knock," said the station manager.

Oliver Baldwin was an impeccably groomed man of stocky build with a wide toothy grin and shrewd brown eyes.

"Hi, Oliver."

Oliver stepped inside and closed her office door. "Are you working on a story that you've forgotten to mention?"

The suspicion in Baldwin's voice surprised her. "No, why do you ask?"

"I had an unusual phone call about you this morning."

"About me?" asked Grace. "Who was it?"

"He said he was with the FBI. Said his name was Melborn…or Welborn. Something like that."

"Why would the FBI be calling about me?"

"That's what I wondered. He wanted to know who you associated with and if there was anyone who was a special friend. He wanted to know if you were involved with anyone. I told him that if you were, it was news to me."

"That's strange," Grace replied and tried to ignore the feeling in the pit of her stomach.

"I thought so too." Baldwin paused before asking, "You have any idea what it might have been about?"

"I don't have a clue," Grace said. "Unless…"

"What?"

"Someone planted a tracking device on my car last night. I saw him and called the police. Do you think the two incidences are connected?"

"I'd wager they are," Baldwin said. "You're sure that you aren't working on a story?"

Grace looked him in the eye and said, "I swear I'm not."

"I don't like this," Baldwin said, shaking his head. "I could understand the harassment and stalking if you were working on something. It could be intended to discourage you."

The color drained from Grace's face. She gripped the back of her chair, trying to maintain her self-control. Those were the last words she wanted to hear.

"I'm sorry, Grace. I shouldn't have said that," Baldwin said and patted her on the back. "I didn't mean to bring up old memories. Why don't you sit down?"

Oliver was one of the few people who knew about her past.

Grace stood stock-still. She heard herself say, "I'd almost convinced myself that the tracking device was a mistake. Now, I'm not so sure."

"Did you know the man?"

Grace shook her head.

Their conversation was interrupted when the makeup artist opened the door. "It's time to get you ready."

"I'm sorry, Rhonda. It's my fault she's late."

"I'll be right there," Grace said with a nod and a forced smile.

Rhonda tapped on an imaginary wristwatch on her arm and left.

"Oliver, does anyone else know about that phone call?"

"No, I wanted to talk to you about it first."

"I'd appreciate it if you wouldn't mention either incident to anyone else. I don't think I'm up to whispers about it around the station."

"No one will hear it from me," Baldwin promised. "You'd better go before Rhonda invents something to add to the daily gossip."

Grace smiled, rushed to makeup, and braced herself for questioning.

Rhonda took pride in being the ultimate authority when it came to everyone else's business. She would have made an excellent reporter.

"I'm sorry I'm late," Grace began. "How was your weekend?"

"I heard some interesting news," Rhonda answered. "There are about to be some big changes made around here."

"You don't say," Grace said and relaxed.

Imaginary shakeups at the station were Rhonda's favorite topic of discussion.

Grace listened to Rhonda and nodded on cue. She'd heard this line of gossip so many times that she could quote it without a teleprompter.

"They're talking about replacing reporters. I heard it could even be one of the anchors," Rhonda said and waited for Grace's reaction.

Grace knew that Rhonda would use any response to support her speculations. She did her best to appear unconcerned and show no emotion. No surprise, no fear, no anger.

Disappointed, Rhonda tried another approach.

"You and Mr. Baldwin seemed to be in a serious discussion."

"We were talking about a story idea," Grace told her.

"I see," Rhonda said, unconvinced.

They both knew that news anchors at this station seldom investigated a story. Those jobs went to the younger reporters trying to work their way up. Grace hadn't done an investigative report in years.

She left makeup minutes before the first evening newscast. She settled herself at the anchor desk, pushed everything else to the back of her mind, and smiled at the camera.

"Welcome to the news at five," Grace began. "In today's headlines..."

"I suppose you've heard the latest from Rhonda," Barry said when the newscast ended. "Do you think there's anything to it?"

Barry Townson was Grace's co-anchor, and they made a good team. There were times when she wondered how much longer he'd have an anchor spot. He was a month older than Grace and was already an anchor at the station when she arrived.

"I doubt it. It's the same rumor we've heard from time to time. I wouldn't worry about it until you hear something from Oliver," she reassured him.

"That's true," Barry said with doubt in his voice. "There's no need to get worked up over a rumor."

"How was your vacation?" Grace inquired, changing the subject.

The pair spent the time between newscasts discussing Barry's recent trip to the Bahamas. Rhonda came by to do a few touch-ups, and the news anchors were smiling at the camera when the six o'clock news began.

Grace went to her office when the news ended. She'd have a few hours to relax and have dinner before the last newscast of the night.

She sat at her desk and looked at the letter she'd opened earlier. She took it from the envelope and smiled while she read. *August 20, 2016. That's this coming weekend. I wish I could be there.* She was lost in the handwritten pages when her cell phone rang.

Maybe that's Todd. She unlocked her desk, opened the desk drawer, and took her phone from her purse. She rejected the spam call and stared at the screen.

Why haven't I heard from Todd? Is something wrong? Is he angry with me?

Her thoughts were interrupted by a tap on her door. It was her dinner. She put her phone back in her purse, found her wallet, paid for the food, and tipped the delivery boy.

She picked at her salad and replayed the recent events like a movie in her mind trying to make sense of it all.

Barry tapped on Grace's door. "It's about that time."

Grace pushed her chair back and stood. The letter she'd been reading and the envelope fell to the floor. She picked up the letter and put it in her purse. She relocked the desk drawer before joining Barry in the hall.

"Was that a love letter? Barry teased.

"No, it was a letter from home," she replied with a wistful smile.

To read more of *Gambling with Murder,* use the QR code below to purchase a paperback book.

ABOUT THE AUTHOR

Dianne Smithwick-Braden is an avid reader of fiction but mysteries are by far her favorite genre. It seemed only natural that her own novels would be mysteries.

The Wilbarger County Series is set near Dianne's home town of Vernon, Texas. She was raised on the family farm in the western part of Wilbarger County. She graduated from Vernon High School in 1979.

Dianne currently lives in Amarillo, Texas with her husband, Richard.

Please, take a few moments to rate and/or review this book. Dianne would love to know what you think.

Subscribe to Dianne's monthly newsletter at www.diannesmith-wick-braden.com.